THE SCARS THAT BIND US

JASON L ALLEN

For the ones who matter most...
...you know who you are.

PART ONE

SIGNS

CHAPTER 1

NOVEMBER 1981

SANTI LOOKS at himself in the mirror and like any sixteen-year-old, he sees what he hates, so he hates what he sees. Unlike other sixteen-year-olds, the things he hates aren't zits or blackheads, nor are they chipped teeth or a crooked smile. Santi hates the scars. Or, more specifically, the lack of scars.

In this neighborhood, everyone has scars. On their faces, their arms, their necks, their backs. Where there's skin, there are scars because in Medellín, scars aren't just scars. They're battle wounds. Marks of manhood. Rights of passage. Proof you've done things, seen things. Lived a life that others would either be proud or terrified of.

In Medellín, scars are what make you normal.

Santi has none.

That's not to say he's never been hurt. In fact, you could argue the opposite. Santi has been hurting since the day he was born. The problem is that none of his pain has been the physical kind, but the other, deeper type. The type that's invisible except to the one looking in the mirror. The type that makes you different.

"Santiago!" Abuela shouts from the other room. "Let's go; we're going to be late!"

He hears her but chooses not to respond, a dangerous game to play with any grandmother but especially risky with Abuela. He scoops a handful of water out of the plastic bowl inside the sink and vigorously scrubs his face as if doing so might toughen up his rostro.

Abuela has been looking forward to attending one of Pablo Escobar's speeches ever since he announced his run for political office. When they missed his first event three weeks ago due to a conflicting event at school, he knew his days on earth were numbered until he made things right. Which is why he promised to take her to the next one, even though it killed him inside.

Pablo Escobar is a criminal. Everybody knows it. Most are just too scared to say it out loud. He might paint himself as nothing other than a successful businessman, but anyone with a single scrap of functioning brain tissue knows nobody gets that rich by owning a fleet of taxis. Especially not in Colombia.

He walks out of the bathroom and into the small bedroom he shares with his older brother, Coco. He desperately wants to call back to Abuela to go on without him. To tell her he can't support an evil man no matter how good the cause. But he doesn't. Not because he doesn't want to, but because no good grandson ever disappoints his grandmother on purpose.

He walks across the uneven concrete floor and takes his coat off the nail sticking out from the exposed red brick wall. He glances to the other side of the room and is reminded of why he put that nail in the wall years ago.

Coco's side of the room looks like it recently played host to a boxing match between a tornado and a back-alley dumpster that ended in a draw after going the distance. Clothes strewn across the floor, bedsheets, no longer deserving of their name, crumpled in a heap at the foot of his mattress, with an assortment of rolling papers and empty bottles peacefully occupying any remaining space.

Santi loves his brother, but he hates the mess. He always has. While Coco's clothes gather dirt on the floor, his sit in organized piles inside their secondhand dresser, and while Coco hasn't once made his bed since the day he was born, he never leaves the house without smoothing every wrinkle out of his bedsheet. That's why, when he was eight years old, he found a nail in the gutter outside and used a rock to hammer it into the wall. It was his silent way of asking his brother to kindly keep his mess to himself. And because Coco is a good brother, he listened. The day that nail went up was the last day Coco's mess crossed to Santi's side of the room.

"IF YOU'RE NOT OUT HERE IN FIVE SECONDS I'M GONNA PAINT THE MOON RED!" Abuela shouts again, this time loud enough that Santi can't feign deaf.

He doesn't need to see her to know she has already bent down and taken off her left chancla, the weapon of choice for every Latina grandmother.

He hurries and buttons his jacket, leaving the top button unfastened so he can reach his wallet. He pulls it out, opens it, and kisses the photograph of his mother tucked safely inside the single plastic photo divider. He never got to meet his mother, but he still never goes anywhere without her.

"Ready?" he asks, emerging from the hallway and into the front room where she is standing, sandal in hand.

"If we miss Don Pablo's speech because of you again, the back of your head will never forgive you," she answers, giving him a taste of what she means as he walks past her to open the door to the stairwell.

"I would be more worried about Coco if I were you," he says, rubbing the emerging goose egg on his head. "I'm not entirely convinced he ever learned to count to ten, let alone read a clock."

He stops on the landing outside the door and waits for her to join him, his hand outstretched.

"I don't need help," she says, taking his arm. "And I worry about your brother for plenty of reasons, but him letting me down is not one of them. You boys are too good to me to do that."

"Too good or too scared?"

Abuela ignores him.

They get outside, and she immediately puts her head down and begins marching up the hill. Santi, however, turns around and glances up at the open window to their second-story apartment, the one Abuela never remembers to close, with a sideways expression.

Abuela has lived in the same house for over forty years. A second-story apartment with a thin layer of yellow paint covering the facade like a silk nightgown, doing little to hide the growing cracks in the decades-old stucco. If she hadn't lived here for so long, he might at some point have suggested they move somewhere else. A first-floor place in a quiet neighborhood. One with less violence and fewer drugs, where kids stay kids longer and grandmothers don't take their left sandals off as often.

But she has lived in the same house for forty years, and anyone who knows her knows that telling Abuela she ought to change her ways is about as smart as lying down in the middle of the woods with a salmon-scented candle burning on your bare chest.

Santi peels his eyes off the window and shifts them to the tiendita on the first floor below their house. Outside the shop, like always, hangs an old chalkboard with a short phrase scribbled on it. Javier, the store's owner, has written a different expression on that board every morning for four decades without a single repeat. Today it reads, "If it will make someone you love smile, do it."

"Quit scratching your ass; let's go!" Abuela barks without looking back.

"Speaking of ass," a voice calls from the far side of the street, making Abuela screech to a halt. Andrés Merlano, Coco's best friend, steps off the curb outside his house and crosses the street towards them. "I have two very important questions for you, Abuela: One, where are you off to looking that good? And two, why the hell wasn't I invited?"

From a distance and between his thin frame, charred chin stubble, and ill-fitting clothes, Andrés would have a hard time intimidating a six-year-old. Up close, however, even grown men take a step back. Unlike others his age whose bodies carry tally marks of a childhood spent surviving, Andrés has just one scar. A single stripe of darkened skin stretching from the tip of his left eyebrow down to the corner of his lip that's been there since his dad decided to break a beer bottle across his face on the day his mom slammed the door for the last time. He was ten years old, and hasn't lost a fight since.

"You keep spouting stupid shit like that and the only place I'll be taking you is to see the worst possible surgeon I can find who specializes in larynx removal," Abuela quips back, causing Andrés to howl with laughter.

"God, I love you," he says, wiping the corner of one eye. "Hey, have you guys seen the old man?" he asks, slapping Santi on the back as he steps inside the convenience store.

"Haven't seen him, but I'm sure he's back there somewhere," Santi answers. "I've never actually seen him go anywhere, now that I think of it."

"Good point, good point. JAVI!" Andrés shouts towards the backdoor of the store that leads to the adjacent apartment.

"C'mon, Santi, let's go," Abuela says.

Before Santi can respond, the door opens and an old man with patchy silver hair and a broom in his hands steps out. "Andrés, mijo, come in, come in, come in. How are you, my boy, how are you?"

He leans the broom against an inside wall to give Andrés a hug, but stops when he sees Abuela.

"Doña Rosa," he says to her with a slight bow. "Just getting home? Would you like some coffee? I insist, really, I insist. Come in, come in, come in."

"That's very kind, Javier, but Santi and I are just leaving," Abuela says. "Santi, let's go."

Santi nods a nonvocal apology to Javier and jogs to catch up with Abuela. He takes her hand and marches with her up the hill to watch a criminal disguise himself as a hero using pretty words and wads of cash. Not because he wants to, but because it will make her smile.

———

Coco inhales and opens his eyes as the smoke kisses every inch of his throat on its way to his lungs.

"Beautiful," he exhales.

If you aren't from Medellín, you might wonder why anyone would think to build a city at the bottom of such a narrow valley with the only possible option for expansion being to build houses one on top of another and to pave streets on hills so steep even the cars have to stop halfway up to catch their breath. Spend any time here, however, and the explanation becomes simple. The steeper the hills, the better the view.

The block wall he is leaning against sits about a half-mile above downtown Medellín. Around him, homes, apartment buildings, and parks unfold into the valley below and climb the opposite hills. He has smoked in this same spot for years, ever since he was a kid, yet somehow the view feels new every day. It's just a city, but as far as Coco is concerned, he can see the whole world from here.

He's eighteen, but the number of scars scattered across his face, neck, and arms makes it evident that he has been around more blocks than most people three times his age and has stories that will make you want to sleep with the lights on clinging to a pistol under your pillow until your hands are sweaty and the anxiety makes you pass out. The smoking, of course, doesn't help.

Behind him, a group of kids is playing soccer on an asphalt court with faint lines and two chain-link nets. Years ago, Coco played on that same court four or five times a week with his two best friends, Cristian and Andrés. They would play for hours until they'd rubbed holes in their taped-up shoes and more of their skin was left on the court than on their knees. Afterward, they would walk home together, laughing and recreating moments from the game by kicking rocks between each other's legs.

That happened every day until one evening instead of going home, they hopped the wall that surrounds the court and Coco and Cristian watched Andrés grind up buds of marijuana and roll a cigarette for each of them. They laughed differently that day, and every day since.

Coco looks down at the three sets of initials scratched onto the sidewalk at his feet. They carved those letters the same day they smoked those first joints together. The day they stopped being kids. They've faded through the years, as all things do, and even though the three boys still smoke here every day, not one of them has ever suggested they re-carve them before they disappear entirely.

The sun inches closer to the mountain tops, and he knows it's time to leave. He takes one last pull, then drops the cigarette butt and stubs it out with his toe. He's late but takes his time anyway, kicking rocks along the way, reminiscing on a childhood cut short.

———

When a powerful man makes a promise, it can be assumed it's accompanied by an asterisk. "I'll change your life" is actually "I'll change your life but..." and "I'll take care of it" really means "I'll take care of it if...." The greater the promise, the larger the asterisk, which is why if a powerful man promises you everything you've ever wanted, what he won't mention is that the price of everything you want is everything you love.

———

"I can't see a damned thing. I'm moving to the front," Abuela says.

More than one hundred anxious Colombians stand between

her and the makeshift stage. Still, sixteen years of experience has taught Santi that when it comes to forging a path, Abuela could give even the strongest river a run for its money. She pushes her way through the crowd, stopping only to insult, poke, or curse at those who take too long to realize they have become obstructions on a newly paved road.

Santi follows close behind, doing his best to keep from laughing as he apologizes to those on the receiving end of Abuela's favorite expletives.

When they reach the front, her shoulders relax, her eyes brighten, and the scowl on her face is replaced by the smile of a bumblebee on the first day of spring.

"Isn't it amazing? Finally, one of *us* will be in charge. I only hope my boys can be half the man Pablo is. And his smile! Mmm, such a handsome smile," she buzzes back and forth, talking at the people around her.

"Hola, Abuelita," Coco says, straightening his shirt after pushing his way through the crowd to join them.

"Coco!" she grins, kissing him on the left cheek before locking him in an embrace. "How did you find us?"

"Pretty easily, actually. I just asked if anyone had recently been yelled at by a pissed-off old lady being followed by an *almost* human-looking baboon," he laughs as Abuela smacks his left shoulder and Santi punches his right.

"Be nice to your brother," she says, her eyes making it clear that even in a crowd of this size, she would have no problem reaching for her chancla.

"Sorry, Abuela."

"Don't apologize to me."

"Right," Coco says, facing Santi." Sorry, hermanito."

"Santi," says Abuela, tapping her foot and crossing her arms.

Santi's cheeks are warm as he holds a hand out towards Coco. "Pase lo que pase," he says.

"Pase lo que pase," Coco repeats back, slapping his hand.

When the boys were young, they fought over everything. If

Coco stole a toy from Santi, he retaliated by pushing him down the stairs. If Santi ate the last empanada, Coco took his brother's clothes out of the dresser and dropped them out the window.

As soon as they were old enough to talk, Abuela tried teaching them to say "I love you" after each disagreement as a way of making amends. She quickly learned that even at such a young age, her boys didn't like saying "I love you" any more than she did, so instead, they settled on a phrase that meant essentially the same thing without requiring such an open expression of emotion.

Pase lo que pase. Through whatever may happen.

"Good," she says. "Now shut up, here he comes."

A dusty, blue Toyota SUV pulls to a stop beside the stage, and Pablo Escobar steps out of the passenger's seat to a deafening chant of "PABLO! PABLO! PABLO!" from the impatient horde of followers. He raises both hands when he steps on stage, and the crowd lets out a final roar before falling silent.

Two men in dark sunglasses stand on either side of him with pistols tucked into the waist of their jeans and arms folded in front of them, their eyes jumping around the crowd. Thin with patchy beards and crooked teeth, they look more like little brothers than bodyguards, but their body language shows that if there's one thing they've learned from their boss, it's that it isn't the man with the bigger gun who wins, it's the one who's not afraid to pull the trigger.

Pablo steps to the microphone and smiles, then begins his speech by spouting a string of inactionable half-truths about corruption, poverty, and patriotism, only a fraction of which Santi actually hears. His own thoughts are too loud, his opinions too stubborn.

He casts a glance at Abuela and sees her eyes aglow and her hands clasped in front of her chest as if she were standing at the feet of God himself. Beside her, Coco has a similar look on his face. Santi looks at the the crowd, hoping to find anyone as disgusted by the heavy dose of irony being served to them as he is, but sees no one. Every eye is fixed on Pablo.

Unbelievable, he thinks.

The second Pablo's speech ends, the crowd goes back to chanting his name. Abuela's eyes drip with admiration, and her hands are red from clapping when Coco grabs her arm and leads her to the corner of the stage, face-to-face with Pablo and the two men next to him, who are now holding open duffle bags full of cash.

"Señora, thank you for your support," Pablo says to Abuela, shaking her hand with both of his own. "Are these your boys?" He nods at Santi and Coco.

"My grandsons," she replies, "although, to me, they are sons. Their mother passed when they were young, so I've raised them as my own."

"That's very brave of you. I'm sure you're quite proud," he says with a smile. "It's an honor to meet you...."

"Rosa."

"An honor to meet you, Doña Rosa," says Pablo. "I trust you'll put this to good use."

He whistles at one of his men and holds up two fingers, and the man reaches into a bag and tosses back two small stacks of cash bound together with rubber bands. Pablo catches them and passes them on to Abuela.

"Chicos," he says, directing his eyes to the boys, "take care of your grandmother. And remember, la familia va primero."

"Yes, sir," Coco responds, like a child being told to *"Be good"* by a shopping mall Santa Claus.

Santi says nothing.

Together, they maneuver their way out of the crowd and begin down the hill towards home.

"Mijos," Abuela says, "remember this day. We just met the man who will save Colombia. The man who will save all our lives."

———

Swish, swish, swish

Javier sweeps the sidewalk outside his store without looking at the ground. He isn't accomplishing much, mostly moving dirt from one side to the other and back again, but he's okay with that. He's too old to care about such unimportant things as whether the walk is clean or dirty. He just knows he'll go crazy if he sits inside all day. And so, he sweeps. Once when he gets up in the morning, once again after lunch, and once more just before closing time.

He also sweeps anytime his upstairs neighbor, Rosa, leaves the house, because it's impossible not to have a conversation with someone when they're sweeping the sidewalk outside your front door.

Swish, swish, swish

The broom moves back and forth, hardly skimming the concrete, and Javier watches Rosa work her way down the hill, flanked on either side by her two boys. He blinks slowly and transports himself to a place inside his head. A place in which he tells her he loves her every time he sees her, and she tells him the same thing back.

Swish, swish, swish

"Doña Rosa," he says, half-nodding, half-bowing in her direction as she approaches.

"Javier."

"H-have you noticed today's quote? It's a beautiful one. I'm quite proud of it," he says, motioning towards the chalkboard on the wall with the broom.

"Mm," she responds, turning to look at it as Coco and Santi silently excuse themselves to go upstairs. "Well said, I'll give you that."

"Thank you, thank you, thank you," he smiles, pushing a few strands of silver hair behind his ears. "Would you like to join me for a cup of coffee?" he asks. "I insist, really, I insist."

"Has anybody ever told you that you talk too much?" she asks back, ignoring his invitation.

"Only you, Doña Rosa, only you."

"Well, you do," she says, opening the door to the stairs. "Maybe you should write that on your board tomorrow. 'Don't talk so much.' Would be a good reminder."

"Of course, of course, of course," he smiles. "Have a lovely evening, Doña Rosa."

"I always do."

She closes the door sharply behind him, and Javier clutches his chest. His heart is in his cheeks, but the rest of him is on the floor. He closes his eyes and momentarily escapes inside what should be their perfect love story.

But perfect love stories don't exist.

Everybody knows that.

———

Santiago has never been the type to have a lot of friends. He could go through the process of arguing with himself over whether or not that is by choice, but it wouldn't change the fact that he's at home on a Saturday night with no intentions of being anywhere else.

He lies on his bed and throws a green and white soccer ball as clean as the day he bought it at the ceiling. He's thinking about Javier. They've grown close in recent years. Santi often drops in the store on his way home from school and listens to him tell stories. The first twenty-five years of his life could fill volumes, and the more he gets to know him, the more Santi wishes Abuela would give him a chance. She would never admit it, but he can tell she gets lonely. He sees it in her eyes every morning when he kisses her on the cheek on his way out the door. She tells him to go on and have fun, but her eyes beg him to stay. Abuela's eyes have always been her most reliable form of communication.

"Hey, have you seen my good jacket?" Coco asks, walking into the bedroom.

"I'd guess it's wherever you left your half of the floor," Santi responds, throwing the soccer ball at the ceiling, "I haven't seen either one in months."

He's been a little brother long enough to know what happens next, and he rolls to the edge of his mattress half a second before Coco swings his arms in an attempt to get him in a headlock.

"Might be time to learn a new move or two," he mocks, swinging his leg around and digging a knee into Coco's back, pinning him to the mattress.

"I'll learn new moves when you get strong enough to pin me for real," Coco laughs, throwing him off him as if he were flicking a dead fly from the windowsill before locking him in a full-nelson and shoving his face into his pillow, leaving Santi no choice but to tap out.

"Your jacket is in the corner under your jeans," Santi says, sitting up.

"Thanks," Coco says, pulling it from the bottom of a wrinkled pile of clothes on the floor. "Tell Abuela I'll be home late."

"Where are you going?"

"Not sure I can answer that," says Coco, ruffling Santi's hair with his hand. "You're too young."

"Just try not to get anyone pregnant, alright? Abuela and I struggle enough to keep one baby alive," Santi says, making Coco howl with laughter.

"Pase lo que pase, hermanito."

"Pase lo que pase."

The two brothers slap hands and embrace, and Coco leaves. Santi watches him go, then stands up to smooth the wrinkles out of his bedsheet before crossing the hall to Abuela's bedroom.

"Coco says he'll be home late," he says, sitting at the end of her bed, its wooden frame digging through the thin mattress and into his legs like an amateur masseuse.

"Sounds about right," Abuela replies. "I stopped waiting up for him years ago. You two have already knocked enough years off my life; you're not taking my sleep too."

"Fair enough," he laughs.

He stands to leave but sits back down.

"Abuela," he says, "can I ask you something?"

"You just did," she answers, "but sure, ask away."

"Do you ever get lonely?"

As the words leave his lips, her eyes lose focus and her witty smirk straightens just long enough for Santi to notice.

"Never," she says with a gentle smile. "Grandmothers with grandsons like you never get lonely because grandsons like you never leave us alone. Not even to take a shit."

Santi laughs.

"Do *you* ever get lonely?"

"Me?" he asks, his eyes smiling wide. "Never. Grandsons with grandmothers like you never get lonely because grandmothers like you always insist we be there holding your hand. Even while you're taking a shit."

This time it's her turn to laugh.

"This is true," she says. She moves her hand to his cheek. "Te amo, mijito."

"I love you too. And jokes aside, you know I'll always be here for you."

"Like hell, you will," she says, smacking the back of his hand.

"Ouch! What was that for?!"

"How are you supposed to live your life if you never leave mine?" she asks, ignoring his stammering. "Huh? I might be old, but I'm not completely helpless. And I'll be damned if my grandson fails to make a life for himself because he's too busy making sure I have enough to eat or that I don't fall down the stairs anytime I leave to buy a bag of rice."

He doesn't respond, his eyes scanning the floor for answers that aren't there.

"Not to mention I'm terrified of your mother coming back and dragging me to the other side with her if I so much as *hint* at the idea of you skipping college just so you can give me sponge baths and wipe my ass," Abuela continues. "Coco? Fine. School was never his thing anyway. But you? HA! She'd have my head faster than I could say, 'Oh shit.'"

He laughs, only this time not out loud. The kind of laugh where you exhale hard out of your nose and half-smile, all while lowering your gaze to your feet. The thoughtful kind.

"I miss her," he whispers.

"I miss her too."

They say the same words but miss her in different ways, one missing a piece of his heart he never got to have, the other missing the whole thing. It's hard to hurt with somebody when you feel such different pain.

He kisses her once on the cheek and says goodnight, then shuffles back to his room. He takes his wallet from his coat pocket and pulls out the photograph of his mother and older brother holding hands. There isn't anything he wouldn't do to hold her hand. To see her smile.

It's fascinating the difference between a picture *of* someone and a picture *with* someone. That's something you can never understand if you've never lost anyone without ever getting to have them in the first place.

————

Back in her room, Abuela kisses her fingers and touches them to the photograph she keeps framed beside her bed. She's younger and stronger in that photo, laughter and heartache having yet to carve their names so deeply into her cheeks and the corners of her eyes. In her arms sits her baby girl. The most perfect little girl there ever was—the only person to change her life twice.

Beside that photo sits another, this one of a man, clipped from the local paper's front page. A man she sees today as a savior, but who she will one day, many years from now, see for the devil he really is. The man who will be responsible for taking away everything she holds dear. Everyone she loves. A man with four names but who only needs one. Pablo.

CHAPTER 2

DECEMBER 1981

IT'S 6:24 A.M., and Abuela has been awake for over an hour. She enjoys these early hours. It's the only time she gets to enjoy the world before so many people start to wake up and overcomplicate it.

She hasn't always thought that way of people. For many years she chose to give everyone she met the benefit of the doubt. After all, they were all just trying their best and doing what they considered necessary to stay on top of their lives instead of the other way around. Of course, that was back before she became Abuela. Back even before she was Mamá. Back when every day of her life went exactly according to plan, if only because their was no plan.

Everything changed on the day she learned she was pregnant with María. For the first time in her life she was responsible for taking care of someone besides herself. She knew she couldn't continue living the way she had before, so she changed. Leaving that life behind was a simple choice, but not an easy one. It made her more irritable. Less patient. More cautious. It also made her a better mother.

She moved to Medellín before María arrived, choosing to call home a second-story apartment with uneven concrete stairs situated above a convenience store with impeccably clean floors and a chalkboard hanging outside that read, "When you think it's over, turn the page. The best books never limit themselves to a single chapter."

Now every morning is the same.

The clock flips to 6:25 A.M. and she pulls herself to a sitting position and takes a deep breath before standing up and stretching both arms high above her head. She tiptoes across the hall and pulls back the curtain acting as a door to the second bedroom where Santiago and Coco are fast asleep. She stands there a moment and listens to the rhythmic sounds of their breathing and remembers doing the same thing when María was young, and she would watch her tiny chest rise and fall like the ocean kissing the shore. Wave after wave, second after second.

She slides the curtain closed and walks into the kitchen, where she scrambles an egg, warms an arepa, and pours a cup of coffee. She turns on the radio and sits at the kitchen table to listen to another day of the same news with different names. News that has become all too common in Colombia. A shooting here, a bombing there, with an assassination attempt or two sprinkled in between.

She listens until exactly 7:04 A.M. when the newscaster starts talking about the weather, at which point she shuts it off, takes her basket from a hook beside the door, and walks downstairs.

———

Every day begins the same way for Javier. Wake up, make coffee, write the day's quote on the chalkboard, hang it outside, open the store, sweep. Every day, like clockwork, for forty years and counting.

It wasn't always that way. Earlier in life, there was a time when he woke up smiling with a string tied around his heart with the other end attached to the finger of his first love, Luz. Wherever she pulled, he went. With Luz, every day was an adventure because the only thing that scared her was standing still. For five years, they wandered through all of Colombia. Fueled by an insatiable aching for something unknown, they woke up someplace new each morning, finding odd jobs to pay their way, and hoping truck drivers would pretend not to notice them laying atop bags of coffee beans and finding animals in the clouds between cities.

Together they ran, chasing what made them the happiest. For Luz, that was sitting on a park bench in the middle of a city she'd never seen, a hot cup of tinto in her hand, wishing people she'd never met a good morning. For Javier, it was her. And everything she brought with her.

Their bucket list was both the shortest and longest in the world. It had just one word: Everything.

They gave it their all for five years until, as instant as rain in the desert, it was over. She was gone. Her heart beat faster with each adventure until it could no longer keep up and had to stop. When she left, she took a piece of him with her. Wherever she pulled, he went.

A week after his twenty-fifth birthday, he woke up alone, unsure which side of the bed was colder. Within a week, he packed up the small room they had been renting and moved to Medellín, where he opened a small convenience store on the ground floor of a two-story apartment building.

Now every morning is the same.

Wake up, make coffee, write on the chalkboard. "When you think you've lost it all, keep looking," it reads today. Then, at precisely 7:04 A.M., he opens his doors and picks up the broom. That's the part of his morning he looks forward to the most because it's the part that reminds him that the string tied around his heart is still there, only now it's attached to a different finger.

———

Santi knows what time it is as soon as he hears the bedroom curtain slide back. He also knows Abuela is watching them sleep, so he stays rolled onto one side with his eyes closed and the sheet tucked tight under his chin until the curtain slides shut, at which point rolls to his back and stares at the ceiling.

He stays there for several minutes, memorizing and re-memorizing every crack and imperfection above him until his clock beeps once, signaling 7:00 A.M. He jumps up from his mattress, smooths the wrinkles out of his sheets, and strips down, folding his worn underwear and adding them to the neat stack of dirty laundry at the foot of his bed.

He enters the kitchen exactly as Abuela shuts the door to the stairwell behind her, and takes two plates off the shelf, loading each with an arepa topped with scrambled eggs. Then he pours a coffee, grabs a book, and sits down at the table.

Today is his last day of school. He doesn't have a test or a due date coming up. Most students in his position would set the book down and flip on the radio. Coast to the finish line. That's where Santi differs the most from the others in his class. To him, there is no finish line.

For him, the race will never end because there will always be a life out there that is better than the one he's got now. A life with a bit more money or a bit nicer home. A life that is a bit more normal.

That's why even today, he picks up the book. Because something about the weight of it in his hands and the roughness of its pages beneath his fingertips feels like making progress.

Coco walks in from the hall like a zombie with a hangover and throws himself onto a chair. He pulls the plate of food in front of him to the edge of the table and shovels mouthful after mouthful into his mouth as if hoping a man in a referee jersey might grab his arm and raise it into the air when he's finished.

"You know today's your last day of school, right?" he asks, his mouth overflowing with half-chewed scrambled eggs.

"It's my last day of *high* school, not my last day of school," Santi corrects.

"Santi, I'm going to say something, and when I do, I want you to know that I mean it in the kindest way possible," Coco says.

"I can't wait to hear it," Santi responds, picking up his fork and taking a bite from his plate.

"You gotta stop sniffing pages all day and get your nose in something else, if you know what I mean." He pushes his empty plate to the center of the table and leans back in his chair, folding his arms across his chest. "Enjoy life for once."

"You'll have to excuse me if smoking and partying every night like some deadbeat bum doesn't scream 'fun' to me like it does to you," Santi says without lifting his eyes off the page.

"What'd you say?"

"What?" Santi asks, looking up at Coco and seeing a flash of red in his eyes. "Nothing. I didn't mean it like tha–"

"I think you did mean it like that," says Coco. He snags the textbook from Santi's hands and throws it across the room. "Say it again, go ahead."

"Coco, seriously, I didn't mean anythi–"

"No, please. Tell me again exactly how shitty you think my life is. I'm all ears," he says, leaning forward and resting his chin atop clasped hands.

"Whatever, man, let's just forget about it."

"We'll see who forgets about who when I've got money spilling out of my pockets, and you've still got your nose stuck in that damned book," Coco says, pointing with his chin at the book lying face down on the floor.

"I think you're forgetting that to have money you need to get a job first. And who do you think would ever hire a drug-addicted, lazy piece-of-shit like you?" he asks, raising his voice.

Before the words have even left his lips, he wishes he could somehow reach into the air in front of him and grab them all back, but he can't.

Coco's eyes widen, then narrow. He stands up to leave, and at the same time, the front door opens, and Abuela walks inside.

"What's going on?" she asks.

Coco walks out without answering, slamming the door behind him.

"Santi?" Abuela says, shifting her gaze to Santi, his cheeks and eyes red for different reasons.

What he said to Coco still hangs heavy in the air, and he struggles to stand up from his chair. He walks to the middle of the room and picks up his textbook, carefully straightening the pages that folded over when it landed.

"Pase lo que pase," he says to himself. "Pase lo que pase."

———

Cristian stares between his feet at the initials on the sidewalk. It was Andrés's idea to carve them there five years ago, but this was his and Coco's spot long before that. The two of them spent hours here together every day, talking about everything and nothing and making jokes until they couldn't stand up straight and their cheeks were wet with laughter.

Before Andrés, he and Coco were inseparable. But since? They've been more like tree branches, growing further and further apart while standing in the same place.

Which is why while Coco and Andrés talk about girls or money or living life *hasta morir* in Medellín, Cristian listens without chiming in. Because the things he wants are the exact opposite. Things they would never understand. They want to stand in the same place forever, fantasizing about a life they'll never live. He wants to shut up and leave without telling anyone where he's off to, leaving nothing behind but memories, cigarette butts, and a pair of faded initials scratched into the sidewalk.

He exhales and watches the smoke from his lips rise and mingle with the clouds. He sees Coco approaching him out of the corner of his eye, a lit cigarette perched between his lips.

"You're late," he says, looking straight ahead.

"Hard to be late when the world revolves around you," Coco responds with a grin.

"Q'hubo maricas," Andrés says, walking across the fútbol court and hopping the wall to join them. He smacks Cristian on the back of one shoulder and slaps hands with Coco before taking a seat on the wall. "You would not believe the night I had last night," he says, wasting no time launching into an obscene narrative involving multiple pairs of legs and enough drugs to restock a pharmacy.

Cristian lights a fresh cigarette and peers through the smoke with glazed-over eyes at the ground around his feet, noticing the positioning of the three sets of initials for the millionth time. His on the left, Coco's in the middle, Andrés's on the right. The order doesn't matter. What bothers him is the distance between his initials and Coco's, and the fact that it's just greater enough than the space between Coco's and Andrés's for him to have to question whether that was by choice or coincidence every time he sees it.

He exhales, absentmindedly nodding along to Andrés's story while his mind loses itself in a daydream. A finca in the hills. Two rocking chairs on the porch. The type of place where the only sounds you hear are the whistling of the breeze and the pounding of your own heart.

"Oye, Cris," Andrés says, snapping his fingers in Cristian's face, "are you even listening?"

"Cómo?" Cristian replies, tumbling through the wormhole in his brain and crashing back to earth. "Yeah, of course—crazy night. I've never been so jealous in my life. Next time throw out an invite."

"As if you could handle that kind of action," Andrés grins.

Coco laughs. Cristian slips the cigarette back between his lips. He looks at the sidewalk and drags a toe across four out of the six initials on the ground, pretending not to notice the space between them growing larger.

CHAPTER 3

JANUARY 1982

DEATH IS FAIR. It comes for all of us. At different times and in different ways, sure, but it can't be escaped. Not forever. Because death is fair.

It is also entirely unfair.

Never is death more unfair than when it takes a mother away from her children, leaving them an anchorless ship in an unpredictable sea. From that point on, whether that sea is kind or cruel is decided by life. All death does is take the anchor, leaving in its place a feeling of helplessness impossible to ignore, even in the calmest of waters.

———

Santi stands in front of a cold stone wall. In seventeen years, it's just the second time he has come to visit his mom. The first came seven years ago after he read an article about cremation in the newspaper and asked Abuela where his mother's ashes were scattered. She told him that she hadn't been cremated but laid in a coffin and pushed into a hole in a wall.

The next day she brought him here to the cemetery, and stood him in front of the stone with his mother's name on it. He took one look and walked away. Something about it made her death feel too concrete. Too permanent. Too cold. Since then, anytime he needs to talk to his mom, he talks to her photograph. At least there she is happy. Warm, even.

There's something about leaving home for the first time, however, that makes even the places you don't like feel nostalgic. Which is why today, instead of talking to a photograph, Santi is talking to a stone wall, because this is one conversation he felt ought to be had in person.

"Hola Mamá," he says, passing his fingertips back and forth across her name. "I leave next week for college in Bogotá. I'm going to be an accountant," he continues with a forced smile. "My teachers all tell me I'll make an excellent one. Although, between you and me, I don't care too much if I'm excellent at it or complete shit. So long as I can put a roof over my head and food on the table.

"Abuela said last night that if it were Coco who was going, she would sit by the phone all day long praying the police called before the morgue," he laughs. "With me, the only thing she's worried about is that I'll fall in love with the freedom of being away from home and never come back to visit." He pauses, twisting the yellow carnation he's brought with him in both hands.

"Both her and Coco keep asking me if I'm more excited or nervous. I never know how to answer that, because as excited as I am to keep studying and to experience college, I'm absolutely terrified at the same time. Not for me, but for them" he clarifies, shaking his head. "I don't think they see it, but they're far too alike for their own good. With me out of the house, they'll either become best friends, or find themselves in a fight over something completely inconsequential and each dig their heels in so hard that the rope between them finally snaps. That's what scares me."

He twists the flower in his hands again.

"Abuela always says how proud you must be of me," he sniffs, wiping his nose with his coat sleeve. "I hope that's true."

He stands there quietly for a moment waiting for her to say something. Anything. Make a single hair on his neck stand straight so he knows she's listening.

"I miss you," he finally whispers.

He slides the flower in between the cracks in the wall and runs his fingers over her name one last time. Then he floats away, an anchorless ship still learning to navigate its way through life.

Death is fair. But to Santi, it will always be entirely unfair.

———

"You know what I don't understand?" Cristian says, struggling to carry eight bottles of Águila in each hand, his legs burning as they scale the stadium steps. "How is it that I bought the tickets and still ended up paying for the beer?"

"Believe me when I say I am just as confused as you are," Coco says, shrugging his shoulders. "You know sometimes I lie in bed at night and wonder how I got so lucky."

"Shut up," Cristian says, wishing he had a third hand he could use to punch the grin off his face.

By the time they reach their seats, the oxygen has thinned significantly, and the players on the field look less like people and more like ants whose trail has been wiped away by the boot of an ill-willed fifth-grader holding a magnifying glass.

Cristian sets six bottles down in front of him, handing a seventh to Coco and using the seat in front of him to pop the cap off the eighth.

"You gave Andrés his ticket yesterday, right?" Coco says, tapping Cristian on the arm and causing him to spill an embarrassing amount of beer on his pants.

"Last night, yeah," Cristian says, attempting to dab his pants dry with the inside of his shirt. "I'm sure he'll be here any min–"

"Q'hubo maricas," Andrés says, walking down the stairs behind them and smacking Cristian on the back. "Forget your diaper, Cris?"

He slides past him, snaking two bottles of beer as he goes, and settles into the seat on the other side of Coco.

"What were you doing up there?" Coco asks him.

"I like to come early and scope things out," he answers. "And when I say things, I obviously mean...."

"...girls," Coco finishes.

"Putas, exactly," he says. "See those two right there?" he asks, pointing and waving at a pair of women a few rows behind them who smile back. "We have a bet going. Medellín wins; they come home with us."

"And if we lose?" Coco asks.

"We go home with them, duh," he smiles. "Sorry, Cris, there's only two of them. You're more than welcome to come watch, though."

Coco laughs and sprays the row of chairs in front of them with a mouthful of beer. Cristian rolls his eyes and goes back to drinking and watching the players run through a series of warm-up drills.

"Ladies and gentlemen," the team commentator says over the loudspeaker, "we welcome you to today's match between Los Millonarios de Bogotá and your Deportivo Independiente Medellín!"

The crowd roars its approval, red and white jerseys jumping and waving matching red and white flags throughout the stadium.

"We also want to give a special welcome to today's guest of honor," the announcer continues, "Congressman Pablo Emilio Escobar Gaviria!"

Pablo Escobar stands up from a seat in the front row and spins in a slow circle, waving at each section of fans in turn, all of whom respond by chanting his name.

"Holy shit," Coco says, smacking Cristian on the shoulder and adding more beer to his pants. "Pablo's here?"

"El Patrón himself," Andrés says. "What a badass. Look how many guys he brought with him too." He points at the entourage of people surrounding him at centerfield. "The things I would do to be inside that circle, I tell you what."

"You gotta be out of your mind to want to get involved with Pablo Escobar," Cristian chimes in, dabbing his pants.

"Out of your mind to wake up drowning in tits and cash every morning?" Andrés asks. "Call me crazy then because I'm in," he says, causing Coco to throw his head back in laughter. "The guy gets anything he wants like that." He snaps his fingers to illustrate his point. "Sure, you might have to get your hands a little dirty, but I imagine life as one of Pablo's right-hand guys would be alright."

Coco laughs again, his eyes narrowing in on Pablo and the group around him, all tossing back shots of aguardiente and hurling insults at the opposing team's players.

Who would ever hire a drug-addicted, lazy piece-of-shit like you? asks a voice inside his head.

Pablo, he thinks, *that's who.*

CHAPTER 4

JANUARY 1982

JAVIER HAS NEVER BEEN the type to have a lot of friends. He could go through the process of arguing with himself over whether or not that's by choice, but it wouldn't change the fact that despite seeing the same faces enter his store day after day, year after year, the "How are you"'s and "Nice to see you"'s remain almost entirely one-sided.

Despite that, he's still enjoyed watching the neighborhood grow up around him. Especially the two boys who lived upstairs. He saw himself in them in many ways, albeit a much younger version. From time to time Rosa would pester him about getting to know them, even going so far as to send them down to the store when they misbehaved or when she needed a nap.

"You want to annoy somebody so bad why not go do it to someone who might enjoy it!" she would yell through the open upstairs window. "And you," she added, turning her attention to Javier, "put that damn broom down and say something to these two. God knows they could use a strong male presence in their lives."

In those moments, he always found himself at a complete loss for words. If what they needed was a strong presence, who better than Rosa?

The first time Santi stopped in the store of his own free will, he was a curious teenager wanting to know the story behind the words on Javier's chalkboard.

"You may not see them now, but family is forever," it read that day.

He had written hundreds of phrases on that board throughout Santi's life, thousands maybe, but this was the first to capture his attention. When he asked what had inspired it, Javier assumed he was looking for a simple answer, a smile, and a Coke on the house, so that's what he gave him. But Santi persisted, and the simple answer ballooned into five unabridged years of Javier's life packed into two years of daily afternoon conversations.

Before Santi, he had never talked about Luz with anyone. Not because he didn't want to, but because nobody had ever asked. Telling their stories out loud was like lighting candles in a blackout. With each small flame, his life got a little warmer, a little brighter, but no number of candles could ever replace the electricity.

Those afternoon conversations ended a few weeks ago when Santi graduated high school and no longer had any reason to walk past the store. Today, he is packing for college while Javier sits at his kitchen table with a custom-made leather wallet in one hand and a sheet of baby-blue wrapping paper in the other, wondering if he might be in over his head. After all, he hasn't given anyone a gift since Luz, and even then, he never learned to wrap because they never left each other alone long enough for him to try.

He looks at the wallet again, noticing the light scuff marks along each of its edges, and finds himself second-guessing whether Santiago will even want it. He opens it up and unfolds the four plastic photo dividers, the first three of which he has already filled with pictures of Abuela, Coco, and himself. Into the fourth, he slips a photograph of Santiago's mother. The one thing Javier knows he never goes anywhere without.

Of course he'll like it, says a voice inside his head.

He closes it again and reads the phrase stamped on the outside.

"You may not see them now, but family is forever," it says, something Javier believes with his whole heart.

He runs his thumb over each word, somewhat annoyed with himself that the first half of the sentence is imprinted deeper and significantly more crooked than the second half, but pleased overall with the job he's done.

"Here goes nothing," he breathes, then he sets the wallet in the center of the sheet of wrapping paper and proceeds to use an entire roll of tape to wrap a gift for his best friend.

———

Today is different, but that's no reason for Abuela to act differently.

The couch she's lying on is as uncomfortable as the day she bought it, the same metal bar prodding her in the back as if it were holding her at gunpoint. Her eyes are closed, and she's doing her best to keep from cursing at it for long enough to take a nap when somebody knocks on her door.

She stands up and walks to the door, ripping it open with a loud, "WHAT?" A not-so-subtle effort to discourage whoever happens to be on the other side from making future visits.

"Forgive me, Doña Rosa, forgive me. I didn't mean to bother," Javier says, smoothing the untamed silver strands of hair around his ears and wishing he had brought his broom with him, so he knew what to do with his hands.

"Oh," she says, "it's you."

The corners of her mouth twitch when she sees him but stand their ground.

"What do you need, Javier?" she asks.

"Is Santi around?"

"He's back in his room packing up his things. I'll go and get him for you," she says, then leans her head over her shoulder and shouts, "SANTIA—"

"No no no, it's fine, it's fine, it's fine," he cuts her off. "I only came up to give him this." He holds out the baby blue ball covered in tape now holding the wallet hostage. "Forgive the wrapping," he says, scratching the back of his neck. "I've never been much of a gift-giver, if I'm being honest."

"No kidding," she replies, accepting the gift from him and examining it from all angles. "Poor tape never stood a chance. Next time you might try taking the blindfold off, and using your hands instead of your elbows."

"Of course, of course, of course," he says, attempting once more to smooth the hair around his ears.

"Are you sure you don't want to give it to him yourself?"

"No no no, it's fine, it's fine, it's fine," he answers. "I wouldn't know what to say or how to react or..."

Abuela holds up her hand to stop his derailed train of thought before it hurts someone. "I'll get it to him," she says.

"Gracias, Doña Rosa, mil gracias."

He gives her a curt bow, turns, and works his way down the stairs. Abuela watches him until the top of his head disappears from view.

At least Javier is never more than a flight of stairs away, she thinks.

Most days, that thought would inspire mixed feelings. Today is different. Today it makes her smile.

———

Santi zips his suitcase and breathes a sigh of relief. Seventeen years shouldn't fit inside a single bag, but it does, and he's okay with that. He closes the dresser drawers, triple-checking he hasn't left anything behind and crosses the room to smooth the wrinkles out of his sheets.

He decided weeks ago to use what little money he had saved up to get a new set of sheets when he arrived in Bogotá. That way, he figures, Abuela won't have to buy any the first time he comes to visit. It makes leaving easier, knowing he has a proper bed to come back to anytime he wants.

He steps back and lets out a sigh of uncertainty. If any single moment could make a person want to go back and live their whole life over again, it would be in the minutes standing in the middle of an empty bedroom full of memories, holding your entire life in a suitcase and staring at the walls that kept you safe for years without asking anything in return. The moment before your home becomes your parents' house and your bedroom becomes the room you sleep in on the rare occasions you decide to visit.

There's no good way to describe that moment, but standing here, looking at his side of the bedroom, now empty except for a nail in the wall and a mattress on the floor, reality closes a fist tight around Santi's chest and forces a smile to his lips and a tear to his eye.

"Q'hubo, hermanito," says Coco, walking into the room.

"Hey," he replies, wiping his eye with the knuckle of his middle finger.

"Wow," Coco says, taking in the emptiness of the far side of the room for the first time, "I guess you're really leaving then, huh?"

"I guess so."

"Have you worked out how you'll get from Bogotá to Medellín every morning to make me breakfast yet?" he asks. "You can't just let me starve here, you know. That wouldn't be very brotherly."

"I'm sure you'll figure something out," Santi grins. "That reminds me, I got you something."

"Oh, you did? Damn, I didn't know we were doing presents or anything, or I would have..."

"Here," Santi says. He pulls a balled fist from his pocket and opens it to reveal a copper, two-inch nail. "I can show you how to put it up."

Coco swings an arm around his little brother's shoulders and tousles his hair, and they both laugh. Not just at a nail, but at seventeen years of insults and inside jokes. Seventeen years of fighting over everything because they were always too proud to admit how much they have in common. Seventeen years of brotherhood.

"C'mon," Coco says, taking the nail from Santi and slipping it into his pocket, "let's go before Abuela gets pissed at us over how slow we're moving. Unless you're trying to get the chancla one last time before you go?"

"I'm good," Santi grins.

He picks up his suitcase and takes a last look at the mattress on the floor, the fist in his chest again inspiring mixed feelings, then he turns and leaves, pulling the curtain closed behind him on his way out.

Outside, Coco is standing around the corner from the living room with a finger pressed to his lips. He signals to Santi to peek around the corner at Abuela asleep on the couch, her arms folded tight across her chest, her eyebrows pulled down into a 'V' between her eyes. He tiptoes across the room towards her but doesn't get within ten feet before she senses him.

"Try anything funny, and I'll put my foot so far up your ass you'll feel my big toe tickling your nose," she warns.

"Dammit," Coco says.

Behind him, Santi walks out of the hall, laughing and shaking his head at both of them.

"We're going to be late," says Abuela, opening her eyes without moving her eyebrows and popping up off the couch. "Why the two of you are incapable of telling time is beyond my comprehension."

"Hey, you raised us," Coco shrugs. Then he turns to Santi and says, "I told you she was going to be pissed."

"If you want to see pissed, keep running that mouth of

yours," she says, pointing a finger of warning at him and he raises his hands in surrender.

He lowers them an inch at a time until one hand closes around the handle of Santi's suitcase, and he picks it up and makes a break for the door.

"I got this; you get her!" he yells on his way out.

Abuela watches him go, and the corners of her mouth dance as she struggles to remain in character.

"You ready?" she asks.

"No," Santi shakes his head.

"You will be," she reassures him, stepping out to the landing outside the door. "Here, before I forget," she says. "From Javier." She hands him the ball of tape and wrapping paper and starts walking down the stairs

He puts it in his pocket and takes her hand.

"I don't need help," she says, gripping his hand tighter than ever.

"I know," he says, tightening his own grip. "I know."

By the time they get downstairs, Coco has hailed a cab, loaded the luggage, and made himself comfortable in the front seat, chewing the fat with the taxista as if they were old drinking buddies seeing each other for the first time after briefly experimenting with sobriety.

"Airport," Abuela says before Santi is even in the car.

The cab driver nods at her in the rearview mirror and turns and looks at Coco. "You were right," he says, "she is pissed."

Abuela's eyes dart towards Coco. She sees him smiling and quickly slips off her sandal and proceeds to give him the best beating she can in such close quarters.

"Worth every penny," he laughs, pulling from his pocket a wrinkled bill and handing it to the driver.

"Idiot," Abuela says, the corners of her mouth dancing again. "You," she says, looking the taxista in the eye through the mirror. "Airport. Drive."

The trip to the airport is different for each of them. Coco and the cab driver argue about fútbol in the front seat, Abuela stares silently at the seat in front of her, suffocating Santi's left hand with both of her own, and he passes the time counting street signs and motorcycles and anything else he sees, all to keep his mind away from his upcoming flight.

Truth be told, he would have preferred to take the bus to Bogotá. He's never been on a plane before, and, to put it mildly, they scare the shit out of him. He loves math, but no number of hours studying physics could convince him that being stuck inside a giant metal tube miles above the ground is a good idea. When he tried expressing those thoughts to Abuela, she insisted he fly.

"Anything to have some extra time with my boy," she said, patting him on the cheek. "Plus, I already paid for the ticket, so you're going."

That was that.

By the time the taxi pulls into the airport parking lot, Santi's stomach is in knots. The three of them step out onto the curb, and Abuela takes his hand and leads them into the terminal, leaving Coco to pay the cab fare and get the luggage. They find the departure door where a line is already forming for Santi's flight, and Abuela squeezes any remaining life from his hand.

"Now or never, I guess," he says, masking his anxiety with a smile. "Te quiero, Abuelita."

She wraps him in her arms so tightly the blood from his chest threatens to escape through the tip of his nose. Instead of responding, she lets her eyes do the talking. He sees the pain inside them, but they're smiling through it, telling him to be safe. To be strong. To stop holding her hand so he can start living his own life.

"Here you go, hermanito," Coco says, catching up to them and handing over the suitcase. "From what I hear, the girls over there aren't as sexy as the paisas, so that bodes well for you."

"Shut up," Santi says.

Coco laughs and slaps him on the back. "Pase lo que pase," he says.

"Pase lo que pase."

The two brothers clap hands and embrace, and with that, their childhood is over.

———

Santi's fumbling fingers struggle to clasp the seatbelt and cinch it tight around his waist. The padless armrests on either side of him offer little in terms of moral support, but any comfort is better than none, so he holds each one tighter than a toddler does an ice cream cone.

"First time?" asks the man sitting beside him. He's wearing a black suit and tie and has a black fedora resting on his left knee.

Funeral attire, he thinks. *Fitting.*

"Relax," the man says, recognizing Santi's nerve-induced inability to speak. "We're a hell of a lot safer in the air than we are on the ground, what with the cartel monitoring every interstate in the country."

He takes the cap off his knee and puts it on his head, pulling it down over his eyes. Then he leans back and kicks his legs out beneath the seat in front of him. Santi takes deep breaths as the plane sprints down the runway and keeps his eyes pinched shut for several minutes until he works up the courage to look out the window, by which point the plane has leveled off, and the ground below has transformed into a sea of jagged green mountains extending into the horizon in every direction.

He pulls the gift from Javier out of his pocket and admires the wrap job with a smile before tearing it open. The wallet falls from the paper into his lap, and he turns it back and forth, over and over in his hands. He flips through the plastic photo dividers inside and feels a pang of homesickness slip between his ribs, prompting him to close it again and instead run his fingers over the words stamped on the outside cover.

"You may not see them now, but family is forever."

Now more than ever, he hopes that's true.

The plane shakes violently without warning and Santi abandons the wallet and clings to the armrests.

"Relax," the man next to him repeats, unbothered. "Just a little turbulence. Nothing to worry about."

PART TWO

DECISIONS

Chapter 5

January 1986

CHOP!

The machete comes down in a single motion, sending a pineapple stem tumbling into the the trash bag below.

Five, Sofia says to herself, silently counting the number of pineapples she has left to cut before her blade needs resharpening.

She sells every kind of fruit imaginable, but pineapples are her favorite. If you asked her why, she would tell you it's because they make the best juice, but somewhere not-so-deep-down, she knows that isn't true. Pineapples are her favorite because they're beautiful and fierce at the same time. Sweet enough to make you want more but sour enough to keep you guessing. They're formidable, hard to handle, and only open up to someone who really knows them, and even then, it takes a fair bit of effort. More than anything, pineapples are her favorite because even if a pineapple has a few bruises on the inside, you would never know it just by looking at her.

CHOP!

Four.

Around her, the busiest street in Bogotá rouses itself from its extended weekend slumber. The first taxi horns sound at regularly shortened intervals, and everywhere you look, coins and cups of

coffee exchange hands, the suits and ties of Calle 72 doing whatever it takes to purge the last few drops of New Year gatherings
from their bodies. A baggy-eyed, single-file line lumbers along in
front of her, stepping forward one at a time to drop change into
the basket on the counter before taking cups of fruit from the
table beside her.

Sofia isn't from Bogotá, but from the day she arrived here she
knew she was home. The constant flood of people, cars, and buses
was like a warm blanket wrapping itself around her shivering soul
and slowing her speeding heart. She didn't know one person in
the entire city when she came, yet she felt less lonely than ever.

She grew up in a town much different than this. The type of
place that's too big to know everyone by name but too small to go
completely unnoticed. Her father was a drunk, her mother an
empty head. They were both bad people, her dad for a list of
reasons too long to count and her mom perhaps for no reason
other than that she never did anything to stop him, making it
impossible to know which of them was more responsible for her
broken childhood.

CHOP!

Three.

Looking back in time, all she sees is black. She hears the
shouting and crying coming from the next room, the crash of a
bottle thrown against the concrete floor, and the *pound, drag,
pound, drag* of her father's drunken footsteps stumbling towards
her. She smells the alcohol in his words, telling her he would never
do anything to hurt her. She shivers beneath the chill of his hand
on her back and feels the muscles around her spine contract and
tighten, her jaw clamp shut, and her fingernails draw blood from
her palms.

All she sees is black. But that doesn't mean she's forgotten.

CHOP!

Two.

On her seventeenth birthday, she decided she'd had enough.
She brought home two stolen bottles of aguardiente and watched

her parents get weekend drunk and pass out on the couch. Then she packed a backpack with a change of clothes, a pack of arepa, and what little money her mother had stashed inside a cigarette box hidden under the kitchen sink and took the midnight bus to Bogotá, figuring it would be the most challenging place for them to find her. Not that they would come looking.

CHOP!

One.

For two weeks, she spent her nights on park benches and her days behind busy cafes where her sarcasm and good looks could be exchanged for free loaves of bread and half-drunk bottles of Aguila. Then, on day fifteen, she somehow convinced an elderly bodega owner to let her take over the day-to-day of his sliced fruit business in exchange for a kiss on the cheek and an 80/20 profit split. As luck would have it, her kiss proved too much for his aging heart, and he died six days later, making Sofia the sole owner of a decades-old fruit stand on the corner of one of the busiest streets in downtown Bogotá.

She looks down at her palms and sees the eight familiar half-moon scars looking back at her. They've faded with time, as all things do, but are still visible enough to remind her of both how far she's come and how far she has to go. She looks up briefly at the line of people extending out from her door, ticking forward with the efficiency of an assembly line and without the burden of small talk. Only one person in the entire line manages to screw that up. A baby-faced man wearing an ill-fitted black suit, a brown leather belt, and a pair of over-shined black shoes.

"Hola," he says, "I'm Santi."

CHOP!

———

With how much stress Santi experienced throughout college, you would think he had a difficult time in school. In reality, the schoolwork had been about as difficult for him as Maradona taking a penalty kick on an empty net. He took the maximum number of credits allowed, adding advanced courses wherever they were offered. He turned in assignments early, stayed late after lectures to chat with professors about additional learning opportunities, and read every textbook from cover to cover and back again. He was every professor's favorite student, and every student's best friend come exam day.

The only times he wasn't focused on schoolwork was at nights bussing tables at the café below his studio apartment, or on Saturday evenings at 5 o'clock. That's when he took an hour-long study break to call Abuela and listen to her recount stories of cursing out a group of teenagers for making too much noise outside her window or using a self-constructed twelve-foot pole to knock the neighbor's clean clothes off the line behind their house after overhearing her complain to her husband over Abuela's insistence on hanging her underwear out to dry on the front balcony. To most college students, their grandmother's life is a silent movie compared to their own action-comedy. Most college students aren't Santi, and none of their grandmothers are Abuela.

The students Santi met in his classes were friendly enough but never seemed to remember him when it came time to invite people to a party or a night of drinks and dancing. Not that that bothered him much. He was used to being the type of person who slipped through the cracks.

His alarm clock beeps, signaling 6:30 A.M., but he lets it ring. He's been awake for hours already, counting every bump, crack, and chip in the ceiling to distract from the nervous energy firing in his chest.

Finally, he peels himself from his mattress with an appropriate sluggishness given the two hours of sleep he managed last night. His eyes beg for rest as he smooths the wrinkles out of his sheets and folds his dirty clothes, adding them to the stack at the foot of his bed. The same clenched fist around his stomach that kept him up most of the night tightens its grip, making eating breakfast sound as appealing as swallowing a hand grenade.

With everything else he has to worry about on his first day of work, he's grateful only to have one suit and tie to choose from, both of which are neatly laid out over the chair in the corner of his room. He pulls on his shirt and buttons it, then picks up his coat and slides it on, hoping nobody in his department notices the unfilled fabric around the shoulders or the coin-sized bleach spot below the right flap pocket.

He ties his tie, unties it, and ties it again before fastening his belt and sitting down to put on his freshly shined shoes. He hears the *swish, swish, swish* of a neighbor's broom and wishes Javier were there to see him off. He always had the words Santi needed to hear. The ones Abuela's eyes tried to communicate, but that never quite made it to her lips.

"Here goes nothing," he says under his breath, standing up and walking to the door. He takes his wallet from his jacket pocket and kisses it four times. "Wish me luck."

He steps outside, and the Bogotá winter greets him by throwing invisible icicles at his cheeks, and Santi subconsciously adds "warmer weather" to his mental list of things he misses about home.

"The usual, mijo?" his former boss asks him from his post behind the counter of the café.

"Not today, Rodrigo," Santi says, bending his will to that of the angry fist in his stomach. "No time."

He gets to the bus stop late but still manages to catch it thanks to an elderly man who had dropped a fistful of coins on the sidewalk and insisted on picking up each one before boarding.

The bus ride itself is short and uneventful. Some passengers keep their faces buried in the morning newspaper. The rest busy themselves attempting to get a few more winks of sleep; a task made impossible by the driver who rounds corners at twice the suggested speed limit and treats the brake pedal like an uninvited spider crawling across his kitchen floor. Santi, meanwhile, passes the time introducing himself to the back of the seat in front of him, practicing for the moment he meets his new boss.

"Hola, Señor Gómez, my name is Santiago... Señor Gómez, such a pleasure. I'm Santi... Hi, I'm Santiago. You must be Señor Gómez..."

"Calle setenta y dos!" the driver shouts, punching the brakes with both feet.

The wind chases the nerve ending in Santi's face into hiding as he steps off the bus. He shoves his hands into his pockets, his fists balled, and starts across the street, stopping halfway when he sees her. On the opposite corner of the road, wearing a green apron and lopping the stems off a stack of pineapples, stands the most beautiful woman Santi has ever seen. From fifty feet away and without even knowing her name, she puts a pound in his heart and a weak in his knees that blindsides him.

After being offered his job at a prestigious accounting firm downtown, Santi asked the hiring manager what advice he had that might help him get ahead.

"Unless you want to be the kind of employee that goes invisible for forty years and retires, you had better start making a better first impression," he said, without hesitation. "You're a bright kid. That got you the job, but it won't get you much else. From here, it's about doing whatever it takes to get noticed by the right people."

Santi hears a horn honk and realizes he's still standing in the middle of the street. He waves at the driver, who waves back with one finger, and crosses to the sidewalk where a steady stream of customers drops coins in a basket and takes cups of fruit from a table beside the woman in the green apron. He checks his watch. Five minutes early. Plenty of time.

"Whatever it takes to get noticed by the right people," he says to himself and gets in line.

When he reaches the front of the line, he realizes he doesn't have a plan, so he smiles, even though the woman isn't looking at him, and says, "Hola. I'm Santi."

"What do you want?" she asks, taking a sharpening stone

from under the table and scraping it across the blade of her machete without making eye contact.

"Oh, uh... how much for a cup of mango verde?"

"Thirty-five pesos," she answers, slapping the machete and the sharpening stone on the tabletop and looking at him with the impatience of a parent of four halfway into a cross-country road trip. "Is that what you want?"

He knows he ought to say something, anything, but he can't. He's just seen her eyes for the first time, and like thick, golden honey, they overflow onto the sidewalk and glue his feet to the ground and his words to his throat.

"Hello? Is that what you want?"

"I, uh, I don't think I have enough money," he sputters. "Sorry."

She stares at him for a few seconds, then picks up the machete and grabs another pineapple from the stack next to her. "Next," she says calmly.

Santi steps aside to allow the next customer in line to step up to the counter. His brain is still processing what just happened, reliving every detail: her voice, her eyes, her seriedad.

Her.

Sometimes a single decision changes your life without even bothering to let you know, like getting in line at a fruit stand without any money when you're late for your first day of work.

"Shit," he says, looking at his watch, and takes off running.

———

"Shit!" Coco exclaims, ducking his head to avoid the bag of rice flying through the air. "Are you trying to kill me?"

"Is that my coffee you're drinking?" Abuela answers, shaking off her coat and hanging it on the hook by the door.

Coco looks at the mug in his hand and shrugs. "I thought you were finished with it."

"I was," she says, "but that doesn't mean I can't use you drinking it as an excuse to practice my aim."

"You're unbelievable sometimes, you know that?" he smiles, taking another sip. "How's Javier?"

"Same as always," she responds.

She walks past him into the kitchen and sets her basket of groceries on the counter.

"He likes you, you know," Coco says.

"Everybody likes me, Coco."

"Yeah, but Javier *like* likes you."

"He *like* likes me? What am I, eleven years old?" she scoffs, taking three eggs from her basket and adding them to the over-flowing bowl beside the fridge.

"C'mon, Abuela," he responds, taking another sip of coffee. "Even a couple of bone bags like you two have needs that need fulfilling from time to time," he continues, making a thrusting motion with his hips from his chair.

"The more stupid shit that comes out of your mouth, the more I miss your brother," she says with a shake of her head. "Goes to school for four years and then has the audacity to take a job in the capital?"

"Quit trying to change the subject," he keeps on. "I know you've dreamt about it. You talk in your sleep." He closes his eyes and wraps his arms around his back, puckering his lips and swaying back and forth. "Oh, Javier. Dámelo. Dámelo todo. Mmmm, Javier, no pares. No pares."

"Don't you have deliveries to make," she asks, ignoring him.

"Nah," he responds, leaning back in his chair. "Got fired. Apparently, you show up high three times in two weeks, and suddenly you're 'irresponsible' and 'a liability we can no longer justify.'"

"What?"

"That's what I said! I tried telling him it helps me focus on the road, which it does, by the way, so really it's safer when you stop and think about it," Coco shakes his head. "He let me keep the motorcycle, though, which was cool of him. Even if it is a piece of shit."

He goes to take another drink, but she smacks the back of his hand before the cup reaches his lips.

"What the hell?!" he exclaims, ducking to avoid a follow-up blow to the head.

"Oh, I'll tell you what the hell. What the hell is you drinking my coffee at my table in my house when you don't have a job. That's what the hell."

"Relax, I'll find another one," he replies. "Just give me a couple of weeks."

He tries again to sip his coffee, but again she smacks him, this time harder, and knocks the cup to the floor, where it breaks into a dozen pieces.

"Sebastián González Navarro," she says, pointing a finger at him.

He scowls at her without saying anything, his eyes a combination of disbelief and anger. Abuela stares back, looking as though her only regret is that he hadn't been holding two mugs instead of the one so she could do it again.

If only he were more like his brother, then she wouldn't have to be so hard on him. Wouldn't have to push him so hard to live up to the version of himself she knows he's capable of. Maybe she is still bitter at Santi for taking a job in Bogotá instead of looking for work closer to home, but at least he *has* a job, instead of sitting at her table drinking half a mug of cold coffee because he was too lazy to get his own. At least Santi is *trying* to create a better life for himself than the one he had before. The one Abuela gave him.

"You find a job," she says, "or you don't come back."

Coco opens his mouth but closes it again. Then he stands up, crosses the room, and walks out.

The door slams shut, and Abuela collapses into Coco's still-warm chair, her head falling into her hands. She's mad. But more than that, she's tired. Tired of not being enough.

Tired of knowing she never will be.

———

Coco's anger has peaked and settled when he pulls his motorcycle behind the taxi parked against the curb outside the fútbol court. He's been on the receiving end of too many of Abuela's outbursts to let them bother him for long. He knows she misses Santi. He does too. He also knows how much she wishes it had been him who moved out instead of Santi. That way she could spend less time disciplining her screwup son and more time idolizing her perfect baby boy. The one with the college degree and the fancy new job who wears a tie and shines his shoes and would never, *ever* get fired for going to work high. That's nothing new though. It's been that way since the day Santi was born.

He sees Cristian drop a cigarette butt to the ground and feels a breeze in his chest. For more than a decade, this place was a sanctuary for him and his two best friends. The conversation: medicine. The smoke: a daily ritual they couldn't live without.

That's over now.

Andrés left and took the conversation with him. Coco came daily for a while afterward, but time passed, and his priorities changed, and now he mostly shows up anytime he needs someone to spot him a few bucks or give him a lift somewhere.

"You're late," Cristian says when he sees him.

"Hard to be late when the world revolves around you," Coco responds, stepping off his bike and walking to where Cristian is standing. He fishes a cigarette from his pocket, lights it, and faces the city, his eyes glazing over as if the smoke floating off the ends of his lips were sticking to them. He sees him dragging a toe across the sidewalk in his peripherals and wishes he could hold any of the million thoughts flying free inside his head for long enough to strike a conversation.

What the hell happened to us? he thinks instead.

The day Coco met Cristian, he punched him in the face. It happened right behind where they're standing when they were both eight years old. Cristian was new to the neighborhood, and it was clear he only joined their game because somebody somewhere needed him out of the house and didn't know where else to send him. He was short and fat, couldn't tell his foot from his ass, and spent most of the game sitting on the ground or standing on the sideline, covering his face with both arms. That is, until fate decided to roll the ball directly to Cristian's right foot five steps away from an empty net at the end of a tie game.

He took a deep breath and kicked the ball straight out of bounds, and Coco walked up and punched him in the mouth.

He felt horrible as soon as he did it, as if he'd punched himself in the gut at the same time. Cristian started crying, and Coco led him by the arm and sat him down on the short wall around the court, then told him to wait there while he ran to get a bag of ice from Javier's tienda. He thought he'd be gone by the time he got back. He was wrong. Cristian's eyes were red and his lip was swollen, but he hadn't moved.

"Here," Coco said, handing him the bag of ice.

"Thanks," Cristian replied. "I'm sorry I suck at fútbol."

"Don't worry about it," he said, waving his hand. "I'm sorry I punched you. My abuela tells me I have a hard time controlling my temper."

"Don't worry about it," Cristian smiled. "I'm Cristian."

"Sebastián, but everybody calls me Coco."

"Cool."

"Cool."

It wasn't much of a conversation, but at that age, it doesn't take much conversation to become best friends. In the days that followed, he taught Cristian how to score a goal on an empty net, and Cristian taught him how to not punch people in the face. They spent hours sitting by the court, talking about anything and everything and doing whatever they could think of to avoid going home.

Back then, they were the type of best friends who had no choice but to be open books because they were writing their pages together.

Now, they're the type who only ever miss each other when they're together.

"Q'hubo, maricas."

No two words could have pulled him back to reality faster. So much so that he thinks he must have imagined it for a second. If it weren't for the scar on Andrés's face, Coco might not have immediately recognized him. It's been that long. His shoulders are filled out, and his legs no longer look lost inside his jeans. A new scar, a perfect pink circle hardly noticeable behind his left ear, has joined the one on his cheek. He smiles as he approaches, walking with a bounce in his step.

"I knew I'd find you idiots here," he says. He slides a faded red backpack off his shoulder and carefully sets it on the wall next to them. "You guys miss me or what?"

Cristian says nothing, just slides his fists into his pockets and sits down.

Coco knows he should act happy to see him, but instead, he feels the anger from earlier that morning bubble up from his chest and settle in his cheeks.

"Where've you been?" he asks. "You leave for three years without saying a word to anybody, and now you're back asking if we missed you? Like you just left town for the weekend or some shit?"

He looks at Cristian, who keeps his mouth shut, dragging his toe back and forth across the concrete.

"What'd you expect, a postcard? A love note?" Andrés laughs. "Or have you been waiting up for me at night, hoping I would sneak in through your window and spoon you to sleep?"

"You could have at least told me where you were going. We're your best friends," Coco responds.

"Damn, Coco. It's a good thing I came back when I did. Cris has got you acting soft on me."

"Shut up," Cristian says, his eyes not straying from the ground in front of him.

"If you only came back to talk shit, you can turn around and take it with you," Coco says.

"Look," Andrés says, his hands raised, "I left because I had to, alright? Because I woke up one morning to my dad giving me this," he points to the scar behind his ear, "and telling me I could expect the same wake-up call every morning until I started buying my own food and paying half the rent. So I packed my shit and took off. You know how he is. One day it's a cigarette to the neck; the next, it might be a cuchillo to the throat." He pauses long enough to take a breath and scratch the side of his neck. "I didn't tell you guys because I didn't want you knowing where I was if he came looking for me."

"Shit, man," Coco says, embarrassed. "Sorry, I had no idea."

"Doesn't matter now," Andrés responds, shrugging his shoulders. "Anyway, I slept around for a few days then got in touch with a guy I used to buy weed off of to see if he needed a runner, seeing as I was flat out of cash. Next thing you know, I'm sitting on his couch while he tells me how he got out of the lightweight game and started running errands for Pablo. Now he's making shit-tons of money and drowning in mujeres. And when I say mujeres, I mean mujeres," he says, cupping his hands in front of his chest. "He told me he could use a guy like me if I was up for it. I signed the dotted line on the spot."

"You're working for Pablo?" Coco asks.

"Kind of," says Andrés, "but not really. More like working for the guys that work for the guys that work for Pablo. Still pays good, though." He cups his hands in front of his chest again.

"Unbelievable," Coco says.

He looks at Cristian again to see if he's thinking the same thing but Cristian doesn't look up from the ground.

"Enough storytime, maricas. Here." He unzips the backpack on the wall and reaches in, pulling out two nine-millimeter handguns. "Word is Pablo's looking for more hands," he says with an excited grin, extending the guns towards them. "My guy asked if I knew anyone who might be interested, and I thought of you two."

"How generous," Cristian scoffs, shaking his head.

Coco, however, takes a gun from Andrés and feels the weight of it in his hand. It's heavier than he would have thought. Colder too. He turns it over and sees a dark spot forming on his knuckles where Abuela smacked him.

She wants me to get a job so she can pretend I'm more like Santi? Coco thinks. *Fine. I'll get a job. And a higher paying one than he'll ever have at that.*

"Cris," Andrés says, waving the other gun in front of Cristian's face, "you in or what, maricón?"

Cristian looks at him, then at the gun, then at Coco.

"Cris?"

"I'm good," he says, looking Andrés in the eye.

Andrés looks back at him, stoneface, then he smiles.

"I told you," he says, smacking Coco on the arm. "Soft."

Coco laughs and tucks the gun into the waistband of his pants.

"Whoa, hey, whoa," Andrés jumps, grabbing him by the wrist. "Never in the front, parce, these things aren't made of plastic." He slides the barrel of the second pistol beneath his belt on his back, and Coco follows suit. "Better to live with half an ass than half a dick."

Coco nods. Cristian snorts and shakes his head.

"Ciao, Cris. Call if you ever decide to nut up," Andrés mocks, slapping him on the back before walking off towards the street. "Vamos."

"Coco," Cristian says, grabbing his arm, "don't do this. Andrés might be selling this as a dream but there's no way it can actually be that glamorous."

"Eh, probably not," he admits, "but to be honest, I got nothing else going for me right now. So I'll take my chances."

Cristian's grip on his arm tightens. "Pablo is dangerous. And so is everyone around him."

"Probably good to be on the inside then, don't you think?"

"I'm serious," Cristian pleads. "Don't."

Coco smiles. "You worry too much, Cris. I'll be fine."

With that, he turns and follows Andrés to the street. When he gets to his motorcycle, he swings a leg over and looks back at Cristian sitting on the wall with his hands in his pockets.

"Vamos, marica," shouts Andrés, kicking his bike into gear and taking off down the street.

He takes a last look at Cristian and kickstarts his bike.

Sometimes a single decision changes your life without even bothering to let you know, like putting a gun on your back and riding away from the one place that has always felt like home, without even saying goodbye.

"Vamos."

————

Cristian balls his hands into fists inside his pockets. Instead of watching his two friends walk away, he keeps his eyes pointed in front of him. A thousand questions run through his mind as he listens to the noise from their motorcycles fade into nothing, but only one stays there long enough for him to process it.

What the hell happened to us?

As a kid, you think that everything will last forever. Growing up is realizing one loss at a time that nothing ever does. It's opening your eyes one day and seeing that while you've been holding onto a friendship with all the strength you have, the person on the other side has already let go, and is just waiting for your grip to give out and set them free.

Cristian looks at Coco's initials on the sidewalk, just far enough away from his own that if you didn't know any better, you might question whether they were even meant to go together at all. He pulls another cigarette from his pocket, lights it, and lets it dangle between his fingers at his side. He rubs the toe of his shoe back and forth across the letters on the ground. God, he hates those letters.

Two of them, anyway.

In front of him, the city of Medellín paints itself from horizon to horizon, homes and skyscrapers erupting from the hills and cascading like spring water into the valley below. His whole world is down there, but as far as he is concerned, it's just a city. A city he doesn't belong in. He never has.

And yet, here he is. Sitting in the same place and smoking what feels like the same cigarette, wondering which will fade away first: his initials or him.

CHAPTER 6

JANUARY 1986

"YOU READY?" Andrés asks.

Coco nods, afraid if he opens his mouth, he might vomit.

Ready? How could he be when he doesn't even know where they are or what they're doing here? All Andrés said when he had asked where they were going was, "It'll be worth your time, I promise." Then he rode away, expecting him to follow. Which he did, because what else was he supposed to do?

Andrés slides off his bike and walks towards the house nearest them, leaving Coco alone on the street.

"Are you coming or what, marica?" Andrés turns and asks.

Coco nods again. He steps onto the curb and follows him through an open gate that leads to the front door, careful to stay two paces behind him to eliminate the possibility of Andrés hearing his heartbeat through his shirt.

"You want to do this one?" Andrés asks with a crooked grin as he loads his gun.

Do what one? Coco thinks.

"I'm just messing around," Andrés laughs, "relax. You look more nervous than a puta at the pearly gates." He slaps him lightly on the cheek and then pulls a shiny, silver key from his pocket. "Ready or not," he says, twisting the key in the lock and pushing the door open.

Andrés walks inside and flicks on the light, a single, dust-coated bulb hanging from a blackened cord in the center of the one-room apartment. On one side of the room sits a dresser with a small television set perched on top, filling the room with static. In the opposite corner, a man is lying on a plaid, burgundy-colored wool couch. The man's pants are at his knees, and the buttons on his shirt have either been ignored or gone missing, exposing a mess of scars and wiry chest hair beneath. In one hand, he clutches a near-empty bottle against his chest. The other hangs limply over the edge of the sofa, inches away from a handgun that appears to have fallen from his grip the moment he lost consciousness. The entire room reeks of alcohol and bodily fluids, and Coco covers his nose with his jacket sleeve to keep himself from adding to the stench.

"Jorge," Andrés says, nudging the man with his foot, "get up."

The man doesn't move.

"Despiertate, pues," he repeats.

Coco watches his eyes as he kicks the man called Jorge again with his boot. They aren't the least bit nervous or angry or bothered. No, they're smiling.

He's enjoying this.

Andrés gives Jorge another firm nudge, rolling him onto his side facing the wall. Jorge responds with a grunt and a wave of his hand, telling them to go away. Andrés laughs and taps him with the barrel of his gun, first on the temple, then the forehead, then the crotch.

"Get out of here, maricón, hijueputa," Jorge grunts, rolling to his stomach and spilling the contents of the bottle in his hand onto Andrés's leg.

Andrés sniffs twice and kicks the bottle from his grip, sending it spinning to the opposite corner of the room. At the same time, Coco sees blackness flood Andrés's eyes. He raises his gun over his head and brings it down sharply behind Jorge's ear, drawing blood.

"Get up," he instructs. "Now." He grabs him by the hair and drags him off the couch and onto his knees on the floor, where he hits him again, this time across the cheek. "I have a message for you."

Jorge looks up at him with one hand cupped over the gash on the back of his head, more awake than he has likely been in days, and opens his mouth to respond. But before he can get a word out, Andrés raises his pistol and fires once, twice, three times, drawing a triangle between the man's nipples and genitals.

"Next time, keep your mouth shut," he says.

Blood sprays across the concrete floor and onto the couch behind where Jorge is kneeling. His eyes flicker in shock until life abandons them entirely, and he falls face-first at his feet.

Coco covers his nose again and clamps his mouth shut to swallow the scream erupting from his lungs. He tries to move, but his feet won't listen, and for a second, he thinks his shoes must be glued to the floor by the blood pouring out of Jorge's chest.

"Time to leave," Andrés says, sliding his gun onto his back. He grabs Coco by the arm and drags him out the door. "You feel that, parce?" he laughs, grabbing his crotch and shaking it tauntingly as they walk towards the street. "Right there, you feel that? That's called adrenaline." He laughs again and swings a leg over his bike. "Plenty more where that came from."

Coco swallows, his eyes wide.

"Hey," Andrés says, "that dude in there? He was a bad guy. The type of guy who would shit all over people like you and me if he had the chance. I don't know about you, but I'm tired of getting shit on. For once, I want to be the one in charge. And this," he pulls his gun and waves it at him, "this is how we do that."

Coco nods and climbs onto his bike. He grips the handlebars until all ten knuckles go white to match his cheeks. Across the street, he sees a light turn on and wonders how long they have before the police arrive and find Jorge's body.

Andrés is halfway up the street by the time Coco's trembling legs can work up enough strength to kickstart his bike. Finally, it roars to life, and he shifts into gear and rides away from the house, his feet still glued to the man called Jorge's floor.

―――――

Santiago's feet are glued to the floor outside the large, oak double doors.

"Come in," the voice behind them calls again, a bit more impatiently than the first time.

He takes a deep breath and looks over both shoulders before reaching for the knob. The entire office is dark now, save for the lamp inside his cubicle and the light illuminating the edges of his boss's door, where he stands now. He exhales and twists the knob, opening the door and taking a single step inside.

"What is it, Sergio?" his boss asks, glancing up from the paperwork in front of him just long enough to recognize Santi, even if he doesn't quite remember his name.

Santi pushes a hand through his hair and clears his throat.

"Spit it out then, we don't have all night," his boss says. Ironic considering that obviously neither one of them has anything they're at all anxious to be getting home to.

"Right, right, right," Santi says, stepping closer to his desk. "I just... I was looking over the Martinez file one last time before tomorrow, and I found something I thought you should take a look at."

His boss cocks his head, then waves him over. Santi approaches and places the folder on his desk, opens it, and points at a single digit amongst the sea of numbers printed on the page.

His boss looks at where his finger is pointed, then leans in and looks closer. He picks up the folder and begins thumbing through the pages. "You said this is the Martinez file?" he asks.

"Sí, Señor."

"Did Diego ask you to review this again? I thought this was all closed and ready to go?"

"It was, but I had some extra time on my hands tonight and wanted to be sure everything was correct before the meeting tomorrow."

His boss nods.

"I guess I like to be thorough," Santi says with a half attempt at a laugh.

Another nod.

"How would you like a promotion, Sergio?"

Santi pinches his leg through the pocket of his slacks and stands up a bit straighter. "I want whatever is best for the company, Señor."

His boss smiles, then holds up one finger and picks up the phone, dialing a number.

"Hola. Diego, por favor. Sí," he says to whoever is on the other end. Then, "Buenas noches, Diego. You're fired."

He places the phone back on the receiver, stands up, and holds out his hand.

Santi takes it.

"Good work," his boss says. "You can have Diego's old office."

"Gracias, Señor."

He turns and leaves, closing the door behind him. Instead of walking back to his cubicle or toward the elevator, he walks down the hall and into another office.

Good work. Simple words, and yet somehow, they were all it took for all the late nights and missed parties and hours upon hours of studying to feel worth it.

He opens the door to his new office and steps inside, his feet planted firmly on the floor.

CHAPTER 7

JANUARY 1986

SWISH, swish, swish

Javier's broom passes back and forth across the sidewalk like a metronome. His eyes bounce back and forth, looking anywhere but down as if he were searching a crowd for a lost friend. The sun has only just taken hold of the tops of the houses on the other side of the street, and the hairs on his arms reach longingly for its warmth.

It's on mornings like this one that he wonders if the day will ever come when he gets bored of the life he's chosen. If he'll ever wake up and decide there's nothing left for him, here or anywhere else, and begin to wish for nothing more than to leave it all behind, or if he'll be here, sweeping, until the day he dies.

In the days that followed Luz's accident, every decision he made he made to forget the life he was leaving behind. He came to Medellín because it was big enough to feel lost but not so big to feel lonely. He settled on a street overflowing with families and children hoping it might replace some of the feelings of adventure he and Luz had grown so accustomed to over the previous half a decade. He opened the store instead of finding a safer, more traditional job for the same reason–because the constant flow of people filtering in and out, day after day, hour after hour, meant he was never on his own long enough to do anything he might regret.

Before he knew it, his entire life was one long list of habits. "The h-word," she used to call it.

"Habits are for people afraid of living," she would say before grabbing his hand and pulling him out of his comfort zone.

And he would agree with her because he could see she meant it. What would she say to him now?

He stops sweeping, rests his chin atop his locked hands on the broomstick, and looks at the phrase scribbled on the chalkboard on the wall.

"Life only happens when you stop watching it so closely," it reads.

It hasn't been fifteen minutes since he wrote those words, but already he's forgotten what they mean.

Abuela's door opens without warning, stopping only when it finds Javier's pinky toe. The broomstick topples to the floor, and Javier is dangerously close to following it when she grabs his arm to steady him.

"How many times have I told you not to sweep so close to the door?" Abuela mutters.

"Not enough, I suppose, not enough," he responds, one hand on his chest. "It won't happen again, Doña Rosa, never again." Between her arrival and her hand on his arm, he's struggling to coerce his heart back down to a healthy rhythm.

"I must've scared you pretty good; you're hardly breathing," she says. "I can watch the store for you for a minute if you need to run inside and fetch a fresh pair of underwear. No shame."

She chuckles and releases his arm, stepping around the broom on the sidewalk and into the store.

"Of course, of course, of course," he says, touching the place on his arm her fingerprints left warm. "I mean, it's fine, really, it's fine. I'm fine."

"If you say so," she calls from inside.

She gathers the things she came for and carries her basket to the front of the store, and Javier goes to meet her.

"Just one egg today?" he asks, examining the basket's contents.

"Coco didn't come home again last night," she answers.

He pauses, taking a moment to gather his thoughts, and says, "Forgive me if I'm overstepping, Doña Rosa, but this is hardly the first time young Sebastián has spent the night in a bed that wasn't his own."

"I know that," she sighs, looking anywhere but his eyes. "This time is different, though. This time, I'm not sure he'll come home."

He sees a flicker of pain in her eyes. "Did something happen?" he asks.

"Oh, we got in this stupid fight," she says.

Javier pauses. "He'll come back," he says, after a few moments. "Do you know why? Because you love him, and that boy needs love. More than he'll ever admit."

She lays her hand on top of his, and every muscle in his body tenses in unison.

"Thank you, Javier."

He takes a moment to regain his composure, then asks, "And what's the latest from Santiago? How is he faring in Bogotá?"

She removes her hand from his and he sees a hint of a smile skip to her face. "Santi? He's wonderful," she answers. "Calls like clockwork, and he told me he's already received a promotion at that fancy job of his."

She pauses.

"María would be so proud," she continues, looking him in the eye.

"Yes, she would be," he responds. "And you must be too?"

"Of course. All Santiago has ever done is make me proud. Now what do I owe you?" she asks.

"On the house today, Doña Rosa," he bows, "I insist, really, I insist."

"Of course you do," she responds. She pulls a pair of wrinkled bills from her pocket and sets them on the counter. "That should cover it. Have a good day, Javier."

"You as well, Doña Rosa."

He watches her leave and feels a tug in his chest when he hears the door to the stairs close behind her.

Perhaps not all habits are bad, he thinks.

"Perhaps not," he whispers to himself. "Perhaps not."

———

Coco's eyelids weigh one-thousand pounds each but won't shut. He's lying on his side on a mattress that would look out of place anywhere but behind a dumpster or on the side of the highway. His eyes drill holes in the concrete wall in front of him. The handgun Andrés gave him sits fully loaded on the ground between the mattress and the wall, and he tries his hardest to block it from his peripherals.

He hadn't pulled the trigger the other night. He hadn't even touched his gun. So why does he feel responsible? Why does 'murderer by association' inspire the same feelings of guilt and nausea as 'murderer'? And why, *why* can he not close his eyes for one single second without being back in that rathole of a house watching the emptiness chase life from a dying man's face?

The events from the other night play on a loop inside his head, each moment tattooing itself deeper into his memory, disrupting his thoughts. Motorcycle, door, man, shots, blood, laughter. Motorcycle, door, man, shots, blood, laughter.

Laughter.

Laughter.

How many triggers do you have to pull for taking a life to be comical? he wonders, not wanting to know the answer.

The door opens behind him, and he pulls the sheet tighter underneath his chin. He had hoped Andrés would be gone all day, leaving him alone to stare at the wall and coerce his eyelids to rest, even if just for a few minutes, but it seems his luck would be no better today than yesterday.

"Q'hubo, marica," says Andrés. He drops his keys on the counter and walks through the kitchen to the corner of the small room where Coco's mattress sits on the floor. "Despiertate pues," he directs, nudging the mattress with his toe.

Coco rolls over and props himself up on one elbow to look at him.

"Damn. You look terrible," Andrés says, noticing the deep bags under Coco's red-rimmed eyes. "Here," he says, "this should help." He drops a roll of bills onto his lap. "For last night."

He grabs the money and thumbs through it. 10,000 pesos. More money than he had made in over three months at his last job.

"I told you it'd be worth it, huevón," says Andrés. "And for what it's worth, my guy tells me that dude Jorge was just a warm-up. Target practice." He cracks his knuckles and breaks a smile, turning away from Coco and looking out the window. "Big plans, hermano, big plans."

Coco swallows the puke crawling into the back of his throat, and forces a smile. He tries to think of something to say, some way to change the subject but finds his brain only knows six words: motorcycle, door, man, shots, blood, laughter. Motorcycle, door, man, shots, blood, laughter.

"Hey," Andrés says, kicking Coco's arm, his eyes pointed out the window at a woman walking by on the sidewalk, "you hungry?"

Coco rubs his eyes and shrugs. Hungry? He isn't sure he'll ever be hungry again.

"Nah, I think I'm going to go home, maybe eat something there."

"Home?" Andrés laughs. "I hate to be the bearer of bad news, parce, but this is your home now. See that cash in your hand?"

Coco looks down.

"That isn't just a thank-you card. That right there just bought your soul. Just be grateful this devil has deep pockets. C'mon, I'm starving. We can go find you a new mattress too," Andrés says, lifting the corner of the bed with his toe and making the face of a new father changing a diaper for the first time. "There is no way you're getting any action sleeping on this STD trap."

He doesn't wait for him to respond. Just turns and walks out the door.

Coco peels himself from the mattress, pulls on a t-shirt and jeans, and follows him out. He pulls the door closed behind him and stops to look at the yellow and green bruise on the back of his hand, his thoughts drifting back to last week.

Is Andrés serious? Or, more importantly, is he right? Can he really not go home? He saw one guy get shot, who is he going to tell?

Abuela, that's who, he thinks.

She'll see in his eyes the second he steps through the door that something's not right, then she'll beat it out of him with her chancla, and beat him again once he's told her.

He looks back at the bruise on his hand and hears her voice ringing in his ear.

"You find a job, or you don't come back." That was what she said, but what she meant was, "You'll never be good enough. You'll never be your brother."

Maybe Andrés is right. Maybe this is his home now. Not because it has to be, but because at this point, the only other option he has feels even less like home than a disgusting mattress he may never fall asleep on.

CHAPTER 8

FEBRUARY 1986

FOUR WEEKS HAVE PASSED since Santi first saw her. Four weeks of leaving his apartment fifteen minutes early with thirty-five pesos in exact change tucked safely in his inside pocket. Four weeks of unreciprocated smiles and cups of mango verde. Four weeks of listening to the voice inside his head tell him that perhaps this love was doomed from the start to be as one-sided as a cheap casino and that the only way to salvage any remaining pieces of his heart would be to simply give up.

He might have listened to it too, had it not been for another voice making its own argument. Where the first voice was pushy and loud, the second was subtle but convincing, and anytime the first made an argument for giving up, the second offered its rebuttal.

"No."

He flips off the lamp in his cubicle, pulls his wallet out of his coat pocket, and kisses it three times before grabbing his briefcase and heading for the elevator. He locks his office door and takes a second to admire his name written in gold letters stamped on the plaque that hangs outside. He's worked late every night since his sudden promotion a month ago, making it easy to navigate the sea of cubicles without having to turn on a light.

It's been an interesting month to say the least. He expected his coworkers to be resentful at the fact that one of the most junior employees in the firm was now their senior. As it turned out, however, there wasn't a soul in the entire building who hadn't hated Diego, which meant that even though he was the new guy turned boss, he was also the person who managed to get Diego fired at 9:00 p.m. on a Tuesday by pointing at a single number in a file the size of a double-wide. That alone, he learned, was worthy of respect.

He exits the last row of cubicles and gives a quick knock on his boss's door, then opens it, not waiting for a reply.

"Buenas noches, Jefe," he says with a wave.

"Buenas noches, Santiago," his boss replies, setting his pen down and looking up from the notepad he had been scribbling on. "Why don't you take a break one of these days? You've earned it."

"Tell you what," he answers, "I'll take a night off the day after you do."

His boss grins. Santi waves goodbye, shuts the door, and walks to the elevator. He checks his watch when he steps outside the building. 7:27 p.m. Early. He's been sitting for nearly twelve hours, but somehow his feet still ache as if he'd spent the day doing jumping jacks.

He looks up from his watch, already imagining how nice it will feel to kick his shoes off when he gets home. Then he sees her. A block away, packing fruit into crates and covering them with damp towels.

Suddenly, his feet don't hurt so bad.

He jogs towards the bodega, weaving through a steady stream of late-night office workers, and slows to a walk a few paces away to catch his breath and straighten his tie before he steps inside.

"Hola," he says.

"We're closed," Sofia responds with her back to him as she continues packing crates and sliding them under a table towards the back of the store.

"Oh. Right, alright," he says, looking back at his watch. "Well, could I... I mean, do you want any help with closing up or anything?"

She stops what she's doing and looks him up and down three times before responding.

"Hasn't anyone ever told you not to wear a brown belt with black shoes?" she asks.

"What?" he asks, looking down at his feet and awkwardly tapping them together. "No, I guess not. Although you kind of just did, right? So if you count yourself, then I suppose yes." He laughs uncomfortably and runs a hand through his hair. "It is my only belt, though, so I'm kind of stuck without any other opt-..."

"If you're going to hang around, do me a favor and grab those crates from behind the door," she interjects, "and maybe don't talk so much."

"Right, you're right, sorry. I was rambling. Sorry."

"The crates," she says, nodding towards the door and looking as though she'd very much like to snap her fingers in his face but is refraining, not to be polite, but because she's afraid that might somehow make him talk more.

"Right, sorry," he stutters. He picks up the two plastic crates from beside the door and sets them on top of the table with the machete, and begins packing pineapples inside each one. "I'm Santi, by the way," he says, extending his hand towards her.

"Sofia," she replies with her back to him.

"I actually work just down the street, so I stop here every morning on my way in. You probably don't recognize me though. I don't know how you could remember anyone with how long your line is every day," he says, lowering his hand. He packs the remaining pineapples into the second of the two crates and covers it with a damp towel, waiting for a response from her that never comes. "Right, well, I'll leave you alone then. Unless there's anything else I can do to help?" Santi says, wiping his hands on his pant legs.

Again, she doesn't reply, and he bends down to pick up his

briefcase from the floor just inside the door. He turns to walk away, but before he gets out the door, she grabs him by the arm and spins him around.

"Thanks for the help, Santi," she says and puts in his hand a plastic cup of sliced mango verde with a purple toothpick poked into the topmost piece.

He looks at her and tries to respond. To say something, anything. But he can't. Instead, he gives her a disjointed nod and allows his feet to subconsciously carry him out of the shop and towards the bus stop. After a few paces, he hears the bodega door slide shut behind him, and a smile spreads across his lips.

For the first time in four weeks, only one voice is present inside his head. The other is silent, knowing that any attempt at salvaging his heart would at this point be hopeless. It belongs entirely to somebody else now.

———

When people talk about love, they talk about it like it's this immense thing that's impossible to ignore. As if the only kind of love to exist were the kind that fills you to the brim until it explodes out of your chest and fills the room around you with fireworks and candy hearts and little red arrows.

Nobody talks about the other kind of love. The love you don't even call love at first. The kind you only feel along the edges, hardly poking its nose in to see if you'll invite it in or load the double-barrel shotgun and send a warning round through the ceiling.

Sofia slides the bodega door shut two minutes earlier than she ever has. She tries to tell herself that that's the only thing about tonight that's any different, but she knows it isn't true. Something else is off—something in her chest.

Only the naive and the lonely believe in love at first sight, and she's neither of those things, so she won't call it that. Not yet, anyway. For now, it's more like a nuisance. A nuisance she hopes comes back tomorrow.

She watches the boy in the brown belt, black shoes, and too-big suit walk slowly down the street and realizes she's doing something she hasn't done in years.

She's smiling.

———

"Ha!" Andrés throws his head back in laughter and slaps his hand against his thigh.

Coco, meanwhile, grins and motions to the server in the bubblegum pink lingerie standing diligently in the corner to bring him another drink. She nods and lifts the thick, velvet rope barring access to the VIP lounge, replacing it back to its hook after stepping out.

He sets his empty glass on the table in front of him and looks down at the horde of sweaty bodies on the floor below. There must be two-hundred of them down there, bumping and rubbing against each other. All after the same thing but looking for it in bad ways and worse places. Places like this.

Up until a month ago, he would have killed to even get into a place like this. Now he's done just that and all he can think about is how trivially people use that phrase. As if killing were as simple and ephemeral as shaking someone's hand or taking a piss.

The waitress returns with his drink and he takes it, takes a sip, and tips her with a bill in her waistband and a slap on the ass.

"Coco!" Andrés shouts at him from two feet away. "Coco, you gotta hear this one. Tell it again, Juancho."

The man on the sofa opposite Andrés smiles and leans forward, raising his hands. "OK, so sixteen priests, a pitbull, and a couple of middle-schoolers walk into a butcher shop," he starts.

Coco listens to him tell the rest of the joke, shaking his head and grinning like an idiot until he reaches the punchline. At which point he and Andrés both throw their heads back in child-like laughter.

"Isn't this guy hilarious? I told you he was hilarious," Andrés cracks. "And what about this place?" He holds up his arms, splashing the drinks he's holding in each hand onto the two girls under his arms. "Sure beats smoking a cheap cigarette at la cancha or risking a broken arm nicking a beer from Abuela's fridge, eh?"

That's true, he won't deny it. Whether it was worth what it took to get here is an entirely different question.

"To a damn fine life," Andrés chants, raising his drink.

Coco swirls the last swig of deep brown liquor in his cup until he finds his reflection. Then he raises his glass. "To a damn fine life," he echoes.

———

There comes the point in every child's life when they replace their parents with something else. Something new. Part of being a parent is knowing that day is coming. Another part of being a parent is hoping you're wrong.

It's five o'clock on a Saturday evening, and Abuela sits in the same spot on the couch as every week at this same time, the same glass of tepid water in her hand. If she were the type who obsessed over details, she might be counting down the seconds until the phone rings and she gets to hear her boy's voice on the other end, but she isn't, so she won't.

The phone rings from the table beside the couch, and she lets it ring three times before picking it up.

"Alo," she says calmly.

"Hola Abuelita," Santi smiles back.

"Hola, mijito. How are you?" she asks. "How was—"

"You're never going to believe what happened this week," he cuts her off.

And then he tells her a story.

It's a story about a woman. One with perfectly golden eyes

75

who slices fruit for a living. A story about late nights in the office and pineapples packed into crates beneath damp towels. A story about thirty-five pesos in exact change and cups of mango verde, and a face that knocks you dead without even cracking a smile.

It's a story about love. It's also a story about being replaced.

He finishes speaking, and Abuela's grip on the receiver slips a little as she forces a smile at him through the phone.

"I'm so happy for you, mijo," she whispers, her eyes reflecting the colors of the setting sun through the open window to her left. "She sounds lovely."

"She is, she really is," he replies. "Someday, you'll meet her, I'm sure of it."

"I believe you."

"Hey, how's Coco doing? I haven't heard from him in a while."

She takes a breath and twists the phone cord around her ring finger.

"Hello?" he says. "Did I lose you?"

"No, I..." she starts, then clears her throat. "Coco left, Santi. A while ago, actually. I'm sorry. I should have told you sooner."

"He left? What does that mean, he left? Where did he go?"

"I don't know," she shakes her head.

"How can you not know? He lived with you didn't he? I'm assuming he didn't just up and disappear for no reason?"

"I said I don't know," she repeats, her voice harsher this time. "We got in a fight over God knows what and he walked out. That's all I remember. He hasn't been back since."

There's a brief pause on the other end, and she hears a shuffling of papers and the faint sounds of a fútbol game being played in the background.

"I gotta run, Abuela; I'll talk to you next week. Te quiero."

"Y yo a ti," she says.

He hangs up without saying goodbye, leaving her with a silent phone pressed tightly against her ear.

As a parent, you know the time you'll be replaced is coming.

It's inevitable. But what you never expect is for it to come so quickly or hurt so profoundly.

Perhaps the reason it hurts so profoundly in this case is that instead of being replaced by one child, she is being replaced by two. One she expected, even if she didn't see it coming. Santi was bound for love from the day he was born. The soul always searches the hardest for that which it lacks the most; or in his case, that which had been unjustly taken away.

Coco is a different story. She always assumed he would come back to her no matter what. Why else would she be so hard on him? Only this time he didn't. He replaced her too, and with God knows what.

Outside, she hears the familiar swish of a broom on the sidewalk. She looks across the room at her coat hanging beside the door, and a thought crosses her mind. She quickly chases it away before it can take root and instead curls up on the couch and closes her eyes. The same protruding metal bar digs into her back, but she doesn't move, grateful to have something to distract her from the pain inside she's feeling.

PART THREE

BEGINNINGS

CHAPTER 9

APRIL 1936 - APRIL 1986

JAVIER WAS BORN in a middle of nowhere town on a middle of nowhere day to two parents who loved each other, and who loved him too from the moment they saw him. To one of them, he was a farmer's boy; to the other, an angel.

In their house, the angel boy's mother made the rules, and the farmer boy's father made the money. His mamá taught him to read and write and wipe the corners of his mouth clean after supper, and his papá taught him how to plow a straight line with a crooked donkey and sell the same coffee beans that the farmer on the other side of the fence was selling but at a higher price. Every day his hands got a little more calloused, his skin a little more leathered, but he never complained. Not because he had nothing to complain about, but because anytime he got that look in his eye, his father would put both hands on his shoulders and say, "Son, every time life gets hard, you have a choice to make. You can say something negative, or you can do something positive."

Javier took that to heart.

For twenty years, his entire world was either just over an acre large or just under, depending on who you asked to show you the property line. And for twenty years, that was enough.

Then, in one single second, it wasn't.

It was a quarter-past seven o'clock on a Sunday evening the first time he saw her. He was sitting on an oil-stained chair with three good legs outside of the only bar in town when she walked straight to the center of the park in front of him and sat down on a bench.

She had brown hair and wore a dress so yellow it would have been the brightest thing he had ever seen, had it not been for the smile on her lips. The string of pearls around her neck suggested she came from money, but the way she watched the world around her, as if everything and everyone she saw brought her complete and absolute joy, told him that she cared nothing for wealth and everything for authenticity.

At the table next to him, he saw a group of men a half-hour deeper into drinking the night away than he was grinning and pointing at her and knew he had to intervene before any of them did something they might not remember enough to regret. So he dropped a pair of coins onto the table, walked across the street, and sat down beside her, bound and determined to stay there forever before he even knew her name.

"Hola," he said, "I'm Javier."

"Luz," she replied, her auburn eyes encircling him and pulling him closer to her. "How long have you lived here, Javier?"

"How long have I lived here?" he repeated, confused.

"That's right."

"My whole life, I suppose."

"Perfect," she said, "show me everything."

He tilted his head to one side, and she mirrored him, raising her eyebrows.

"Ok," he shrugged. Then he held out his arm, and she smiled. "Vamos."

She never told him why she decided to take his arm that evening in the park. Why she chose to trust a farm boy she had never met who was covered in dirt from head to boots and couldn't have smelled much better than the bottom of a feeding trough. Maybe she saw the other group of men looking her way and assumed he was her best option. Maybe she was bored and figured at the very least they might have a little fun together. Or maybe...

...maybe it was love.

"Show me everything."

Three words. One second. All it took for Luz to change his life forever.

————

Santi stands up and flicks off the lamp in his cubicle, wishing more than ever he had opted for flowers, if for no other reason than to mask the scent of perspirated nervousness beneath his arms and on his lower back.

His heart beats through his ribcage as he steps outside his office building and onto the still-crowded downtown sidewalk. He's never asked a girl on a date before. Before meeting Sofia, he could count on one hand the number of complete sentences he'd spoken to a woman who wasn't Abuela or his school professors. Those types of conversations have always been just far enough outside his comfort zone for him to want to spend the emotional energy on. Until now.

That's the thing about girls like Sofia. They don't just make you want to step outside your comfort zone, they make you want to live there.

Down the street, he sees her bend down to slide a pair of crates inside the bodega door and notices a strand of hair fall across her cheek. He inhales deep, holds it for three seconds, and exhales slowly. Then he starts running.

"Hola," he pants as he approaches her, flapping his arms like an optimistic ostrich to keep his anticipation from staining his only good white shirt. "Need any help closing up?"

"Santi, how many times are you going to ask me that?" she asks as he sets his briefcase on the floor and pushes his sleeves up past his elbows. "We both know you're going to stay no matter how I answer, so you might as well just shut up and get to work."

"Right right right, you're right," he says, smiling. He grabs a pair of crates from the corner and gets to work. After a couple of minutes, he stops what he's doing and steps toward her. "Can I ask you something?"

"Ha!" she snorts, her way of saying, *"Here we go again."*

"Right," he nods. "So, I was thinking the other day, or today actually, and the other day too, I guess, so I probably should say I've *been* thinking, not I *was* thinking, but I already started so..."

"Santi," she says, raising her eyebrows at him and lowering her chin.

"Sorry, right, sorry. I've *been* thinking, you can only get to know somebody so well when you see each other for just a few minutes a day. Don't get me wrong, I love helping you close up every night, but I thought, if you're up for it, maybe we could get to know each other better, or something, sometime. Do you know what I mean?"

He takes a deep breath and sees her trying to suppress the smile tugging hard at the corners of her mouth. When she doesn't respond, Santi shakes his head, making him look like a bobble-head in a mild earthquake, and says, "I'm sorry, I don't even know what I'm trying to say. I was going to bring you flowers. I should have brought flowers. That would've made what I meant more obvious, but I guess what I'm trying to say is, do you want to go out together sometime? Like to dinner or something? If you don't or can't or whatever, that's fine; I get it. But I just thought..."

Sofia's face is caught somewhere between pity and amusement, and she grins and interrupts him.

"I hate flowers," she says.

"You...you hate flowers?" he exhales.

"Absolutely. You don't?" she asks. "They're completely over-rated. Pretty for a few days, sure, but then what? The petals wilt, and they fall apart and leave you with a mess to clean up that you never asked for. Useless." She covers the crate that sits in front of her with a towel and slides it towards the back of the shop along-side the others. "I'll never say no to free food though."

"Free food?"

"You said dinner, didn't you? I'm assuming you're paying for it since this whole thing was your idea?" she says. She picks his briefcase up from the floor and unbuckles the clasps, flipping through the stacks of paperwork inside and pulling out a sheet covered in graphs and grids. "Is this important?" she asks, holding it up to him.

"That?"

"Yeah, is this important?"

"I mean, sort of," he shrugs. "It's for a client of ours who asked us if..."

"Here's my address. Pick me up at 8 o'clock tonight," she says, ignoring him. She pulls a short pencil from the pocket of her apron and scribbles her address above one of the graphs on the paper. "Don't be late."

"Right, okay, right. 8 o'clock. Don't be late," he nods like an obedient parrot. He takes the paper from her outstretched hand and slides it into his pocket. "I'll be there."

"Good," she smiles.

"Good," he smiles back.

"Ciao, Santiago."

He waves and stumbles backward out of the bodega. He walks to the curb and puts a hand over his breast pocket to ensure the paper with her address on it hasn't grown wings and flown off. He feels the thick edge of the folded paper through his shirt and allows himself to exhale.

"Taxi!" he shouts, waving his arm.

Usually, he takes the bus home, but not tonight. Tonight, he doesn't have time. Tonight, he has a date.

CHAPTER 10

APRIL 1986

"I'M BORED," Andrés says, laying on his back on Coco's mattress, tossing his gun from hand to hand. "You bored?"

Coco doesn't answer, but Andrés knows he's listening. He's always listening. And he always goes along with whatever Andrés's boredom-stricken imagination comes up with because that's what good friends do. Like the time they tied all of Abuela's underwear in knots and tossed them out the window at strangers shouting "Grenada!" Or when they got expelled from school when they were sixteen after they spray-painted a certain, recognizable piece of the male anatomy on the ground outside the administration building.

So even though Coco looks asleep on the couch with his eyes closed and his arms folded across his chest, Andrés knows he's awake, listening to every word he says. Waiting to be told what to do.

He stands up, tucking his gun into his waistband, walks across the room to the couch, and flicks him in the crotch.

"C'mon," he says, "let's go do something."

"It's almost 8 o'clock," Coco responds without opening his eyes, "if you're bored, go to sleep."

"You think I'm capable of falling asleep at 8 o'clock at night?" Andrés shakes his head, "Plus, I'm running short on cash."

"Maybe it's time to cut the nightly hookers from the budget," Coco says with a smile, his eyes still closed.

He ignores him and walks to the front door, taking Coco's jacket from a nail in the wall and throwing it onto his lap.

"Come on. I have an idea," he says. He pulls on his coat and opens the front door, welcoming in the calm Medellín night. "You're driving," he says over his shoulder and walks out.

Coco surrenders and puts on his jacket before digging his pistol out from under a pile of dirty clothes. He walks outside and sees Andrés waiting for him on the back of his motorcycle, his face illuminated by the flickering orange glow of the cigarette dangling from his lips.

"Manrique," he directs as soon as Coco sits down in front of him.

Coco nods and drives away.

———

Santi opens the small gate that leads to Sofia's front porch and simultaneously wipes away the beads of sweat gathering along his hairline.

"Right on time," he whispers, looking down at his wristwatch. "That's a first."

Knock, knock, knock

His fist crashes against the metal face of her front door three times as the second hand on his watch ticks to precisely 8 o'clock.

"Be right there," a voice calls from inside the house.

"Take your time!" he yells back, making a mental note to buy his voicebox a thank you gift for not cracking as it has a habit of in high-pressure situations.

His legs are shaking inside his jeans, and he feels a drip of sweat crawl down his back. Maybe he should leave, save them both the trouble of an awkward situation and just go home. But then what would he do every morning when he sees her on his way to work? He could take an alternate route. Work an hour later each night to avoid seeing her. He shrugs at the idea and nods his head, then turns to walk away when something in his head says something, just one word, that stops him from taking a step.

"No."

The door opens, and she steps out onto the patio wearing a blood orange dress and carrying a small purse that's a deep shade of yellow in the crook of her left arm. The most beautiful sunset he has ever seen.

"Ready?" she asks.

How could I be? he thinks, stepping out of her way and signaling for her to go ahead.

He holds open the gate as she walks past, then follows her out onto the quiet street where they walk side by side with just enough space between them to eliminate the chance of an incidental brush of hand against hand or arm against arm.

They walk like that for several minutes making forced small talk about things like the weather, cobblestones, and aguacate salesmen, until finally Santi kicks a rock with his toe, takes a deep breath, and says, "Can I be honest with you? I have no idea what I'm doing."

She stops and looks at him with her head cocked to the side, her eyes reflecting the glow from a nearby streetlight and brightening the sidewalk around her. He stops too, wondering how much time he has before she turns around and walks home. He clenches a fist in his pocket and with the other rubs the back of his neck, avoiding her eyes by looking down at his shoelaces.

"I've never gone out with anyone before, and I feel like I'm already screwing it up. I mean, we've been walking for what, ten minutes? And I haven't said one thing to you that you would find even remotely interesting, and..."

"Hold on," she says, cutting him off. "So when you pointed

out that that guy selling aguacates was missing a shoelace, you don't think I found that interesting?"

"What?" he responds, looking up at her.

She doesn't answer. Just looks at him as though he were a piece of art she had stumbled upon in the backmost room of a dimly lit gallery that instantly and uniquely spoke directly to her soul. Then she laughs.

"Oh boy," he sighs, taking a step sideways and plopping himself down on top of a low brick wall lining the front patio of an adjacent house, deep shades of red spilling across his face.

"I'm sorry," she giggles, attempting to contain herself. "I promise I'm not laughing at you, I'm just...this whole situation is just so..." She exhales and shakes her head, then, with one hand, lifts his chin and holds it until he looks at her. "Did you think I knew what *I* was doing? Because I've never gone out with anyone before either."

"Really?" he asks.

She sits down on the wall next to him and rubs both palms on her thighs. "I like you, Santi," she says coolly, "and I don't say that to many people. Nobody, in fact."

He laughs.

"You're different," she goes on, "and you make me different. Happier, more confident. If you knew me better, you'd know those are two things that have never made a habit of sticking around in my life for very long."

He smiles and realizes that he has been holding his breath the entire time she's been talking.

"I like you too," he exhales. He stands up and nods over one shoulder, reaching out to her with one hand. "Now, how about that free food I promised you?"

"Yes, please," she smiles, taking his hand for him to help her up, "I'm starving.

From there, the night is different. They walk and laugh and talk and eat and spend several hours getting to know each other better than anybody else in their lives ever cared to. The crowd around them in the open-air market where they came for dinner clears out, and the music playing through the oversized, static-tinted speakers stops. The food runs out, and the conversation between them slows, leaving them smiling silently, their noses inches from one another's.

He hesitates, then scoots to the edge of his seat and wraps an arm around her back, where his fingertips find a home resting gently in the crook of her spine. He leans in slowly, closing his eyes a moment before his lips meet hers, and for one single second, all is as it should be.

One second later, everything falls apart.

She pulls away from him and jumps up from her chair. "I don't... I can't... I..." she stutters, shaking her head and looking anywhere but at Santi's face. "I need to leave."

She turns around and takes off down the sidewalk towards her house, leaving Santi to watch her go, his eyes wide, his palms damp with nerves. He watches her until she turns a corner and disappears from view, then stands up and does the only thing he can think of. The same thing he has done every evening for the past forty-two days.

He runs.

———

"Turn left here," Andrés says, pointing down a broad road in the middle of the neighborhood.

Coco obeys and rounds the corner. Andrés smiles behind him, watching the final pieces of the puzzle dropping into place inside Coco's head. Halfway up the street in front of them are two police officers, one leaning against a wooden barricade, smoke rising from his fingertips and an assault rifle slung across his back, the other standing beside him holding a gun of his own, his head on a swivel. Their presence alone doesn't mean much, but between them, Andrés's thinning wallet, and a hefty reward paid by Pablo for any dead uniform, all the elements needed for a deadly collision are in place and speeding towards each other.

"Don't slow down yet; they'll get suspicious," he warns as he pulls Coco's gun off his back with his left hand, his own pistol occupying his right.

Coco keeps the accelerator steady as commanded until they reach the barricade blocking access to the heart of the neighborhood.

"Where are you going?" the second officer asks. Behind him, his partner stands up straight and drops his cigarette, scraping it into the pavement with his boot.

"Buenas noches, Señores," Andrés responds with a polite smile.

"Where are you going?" the officer repeats, louder this time over the high-pitched rumble of Coco's bike.

"Whoa, whoa, whoa," Andrés says, raising his hands, "there's no need to raise your voice."

The officers react to seeing the two pistols in his hands but not quickly enough to compete with his more conditioned trigger finger. By the time they raise their rifles, he has already pulled both triggers, sending their bodies to the pavement in a crumpled heap. The sound of the shots hangs heavy in the silence of the night around them, and Andrés decides it's time to go. He prods Coco in the back, who turns the motorcycle back in the direction they came and rides away without asking questions.

Andrés smiles. His wallet just got significantly heavier. Any other night that would have been cause for celebration, and he would have had Coco drive them to his favorite whore house to pick out some company for each of them, his treat. But not tonight. Tonight is different.

The first time he took a life, it took two days for his hands to stop shaking and a week before he could look anyone in the eye. With a little practice, the shaking and the guilt turned into a puffed-up chest and a deep feeling of satisfaction. Tonight, it changed again. The nerves are gone, but now so is the euphoria. Tonight he feels nothing.

Do bad things long enough, and the day will come when anonymity stops moving the needle. What you need is recognition, notoriety, fame. You need to be seen.

For Andrés, that day comes on the same night that two police officers lose their lives without a single witness. Their bodies will soon be collected and the street cleaned by sunrise. Their families will mourn their loss and curse the name of the man who did this to them. The only problem with that is that not one will know whose name they ought to be cursing.

Andrés Felipe Merlano Gutiérrez.

He's done being unknown. He wants to hear it.

CHAPTER 11

APRIL 1986

SOFIA SPRINTS the dozen or so blocks back to her front porch and collapses to the ground outside her door. It's several seconds before she realizes she isn't breathing, and she gasps for air, swallowing oxygen in sporadic mouthfuls in between emotion-induced heaves of her chest. At the same time, tears bubble to her eyes and drop onto her cheeks like a geyser reawakening from years of dormancy, forcing her to admit once more what she's known her whole life.

She is broken.

When Santi offered to help her at the bodega all those nights ago, she said yes. Because she wanted him to. Earlier today, he asked her out, and she said yes again. Because she wanted him to. Just minutes ago, he had put his hand on her back to kiss her. She wanted that too, but when she closed her eyes to kiss him back, all she saw was black.

That's when she heard him. Smelled him. Felt him.

Her father clung to her like the smell of smoke after a fire, and as far as she could tell there was nothing in existence that could purge her of that. No one who could stitch together the thousands of pieces he broke her into.

Not herself.

Not Santi.

No one.

———

Human beings have a tendency of making everything about themselves. It's something the humblest of humans go their entire lives working to overcome and that the rest of us turn a blind eye to.

It is because people want to make everything about themselves that so many of us ask all the wrong questions and say all the wrong things anytime we hurt someone we care about. We ask what we did, not what they felt. We tell them it isn't a big deal instead of telling them to take all the time and space they need. We say things like "In my defense," or "I didn't mean it like that," or "I couldn't help myself," instead of simply saying "I'm sorry." We call ourselves empathetic, but the truth is, most people get empathy wrong far more often than they get it right.

Santi isn't most people.

He arrives at Sofia's house with a cramp in each leg and one in his gut and sees her sitting with her back against the door and her head on her knees. Tears roll down her nose and fall to the ground one after another like the tick of a metronome. He doesn't quite know what to say, so he says nothing, just sits beside her. He takes his hand and gently rests it on her knee. When he does, he feels her take a breath of relief.

Years from now, he won't remember any of the stupid little things that cross his mind during the time that they sit there, like the way the street light above them flickers exactly four times a minute or that each breath she takes last exactly three seconds. All he'll remember are the six words she whispers when she finally chooses to break the silence.

"I come from a dark place," she says.

Then she tells him everything.

She tells him about a house that never felt like home, about a mother who was never more absent than when her daughter needed her the most, and about a father whose grip on her arm only ever got tighter.

By the time she's finished, Santi's blood runs hot through his veins. There are so many things he wants to say to convey just how angry he is that she had to live through that and that he wasn't there to protect her, to keep all of it from happening in the first place, but he says none of them. Instead, he pulls her head to his chest and wraps his arm around her, holding her while her sputtered breaths find a steadier rhythm.

"I'm sorry," he says. "I'm so sorry."

He feels her chest rising and falling in longer and longer sequences and doesn't let her go until he knows she's fallen asleep. He reaches around her and picks up her small yellow purse, filtering through it until he finds what he assumes is her house key. He reaches over his shoulder and twists it inside the lock to open the door, then lifts her and carries her inside. He lays her on the sofa and covers her with a thick, wool blanket he finds on the floor beside a lopsided oak coffee table. He pushes a strand of fallen hair behind her ear with his ring finger and walks away.

Before he leaves, he fumbles around in the dark, looking for something to write with until he finds a miniature purple pencil in the inside pocket of her apron hanging on a hook by the door. He pulls a scrap of paper from his pocket, the same one she wrote her address on earlier that day, and writes six words of his own on it. Then he slides it underneath the pillow on the couch where her head rests, careful not to wake her.

If theirs were a perfect love story, tonight would be the night they would look back on decades from now as the moment they decided to be together forever. The moment they knew that for better or for worse, in sickness and in health, it was them or it was nothing. If theirs were a perfect love story, tonight would be just one chapter in a book that never ended.

But perfect love stories don't exist.

Everybody knows that.

———

Coco follows Andrés inside their apartment, shutting the door sharply behind him.

"All I'm saying is you could have at least told me where we were going," he says while Andrés snakes a pair of beers from the fridge, setting one on the counter and popping the top off the other.

"You know what I don't understand?" Andrés replies. "I don't understand how any single word could be coming out of your mouth that isn't 'Thank you, Andrés for making me significantly richer tonight without asking me to do a single fucking thing.'"

Coco shakes his head. "You've got a problem," he says. "This," he points him up and down. "This is a problem. Have you looked at yourself in the mirror at all recently?"

"Stop with the self-righteous bullshit," Andrés says. "You and I both know that as soon as you get your greedy little fingers on the cash I just made us, you'll be smiling like a fat kid in a bakery dumpster."

"I don't know, man. Killing someone who deserves it is one thing, but those guys? They didn't do anything wrong. If anything, they were doing the opposite."

Andrés shrugs. "At the end of the day, it's all killing for cash. Not much room for moral high ground, my friend."

Coco doesn't reply.

Andrés stands up. "I'll get you your money tomorrow," he says, walking away.

"And if I don't want it?"

"Then I'll slip it under your pillow," he calls from his room down the hall, "but next time I make you rich, it better come with an attitude change."

He slams his bedroom door. Coco exhales and grabs the beer Andrés got for him from off the counter, spinning it around in his hand.

"To a damn fine life," he says to himself, and takes a sip. "To a damned, broken, caked-in-shit, good-for-nothing, silver-lined, fine life."

———

Every person who has ever entered Sofia's life has seen her for what she is: broken. Most of those people left immediately after realizing it. A few more stubborn ones stuck around long enough to see the absoluteness of the darkness inside of her and shake her and shout at her to "TURN ON THE LIGHTS" before branding her a lost cause and following the rest out the door.

When Santi came around, she expected the same treatment. She expected him to run, just like the others.

She never expected that he would see her pieces, broken and scattered across the ground, and choose to leave them there instead of attempting to force them back together. Or that he would willingly walk along the jagged edges of the darkest rooms inside what she always considered an inhospitable heart and sit beside her on the floor, holding her until the darkness lost its bite. That he, of all people, could convince her that just because she isn't put together doesn't mean she can't be whole.

She wakes up just before three o'clock in the morning, hoping for and expecting two different things.

Santi is gone. She knew he would be, but that doesn't stop disappointment from flooding over her when she reaches out and finds nothing but a cold couch cushion where she wishes his chest would be. She rolls to one side and slides her hand under the pillow. Her fingertips brush against the torn edge of a folded scrap of paper, and she pulls it out and opens it, holding it out in front of her where a sliver of moonlight shines through a narrow gap in the window curtains.

Years from now, she won't remember any of the stupid little thoughts that cross her mind before and after she reads that note, like where in the world he had found a pencil or whether or not he had noticed the pile of dirty clothes outside her bedroom door. All she'll remember are six words scribbled on a perfectly folded piece of paper.

We won't let the darkness win.

She holds that note tighter than she's held anything else her entire life. She closes her eyes to go back to sleep and when she does, all she sees is black, but for the first time, the darkness doesn't scare her.

CHAPTER 12

APRIL 1986

ABUELA WAKES up cursing at the couch for treating her back like an archaeological dig site and at herself for leaving the window open again and letting the cold in. Her bones are too stubborn to move, so she stays where she is, craning her neck to look at the clock. Almost midnight. Beside her, the phone sits as silently as it has all day.

The old Santi could have been in the hospital having a leg amputated and he still would've found his way to a phone at five o'clock on a Saturday evening to call her.

The old Santi.

She hates that she calls him that now anytime she talks about him inside her head. He's always been one-track minded, Santi. The type of boy you couldn't tell to tie his shoelaces while he put on his belt, otherwise he would leave the house with his shoes on tight but his pants around his ankles. That hasn't changed. What has changed is Abuela's place in the queue.

"Damn old bones," she mutters to herself, massaging her sternum and fighting the urge to drop her head back onto her pillow and stare at the ceiling until she falls asleep.

If only Coco were here, she would yell at him to come and carry her to bed, and he would yell back at her to go to hell, but

99

do it anyway. For as much as he pretends not to be, he's a good kid. A good son. God, she wishes he were here.

She peels herself off the couch, shuffles to her bedroom, and gently lies down, cursing at the kink in her neck one last time for good measure before closing her eyes.

———

Javier is asleep on the stoop outside Rosa's door, his jacket on and his shoes tied, a broom in his hands.

Every Saturday evening, he picks up the broom at a quarter to five and sweeps for fifteen minutes, waiting until he hears the phone ring through the open window upstairs. Then when it does, he leans the broom against the wall and goes inside to give her and Santi their privacy.

He doesn't know why he does it. Maybe it's because hearing the phone ring tells him that Santi is okay, wherever he is. Maybe it's because he knows how badly she needs the phone to ring to be okay herself. Or maybe it's because he thinks that if she hears the sound of the broom in the minutes before he calls, she'll remember to tell him that he is okay too.

Tonight, five o'clock came, but the phone didn't ring. By 5:01, he knew it wasn't going to. So he did the only thing he could think of. He kept sweeping. He wishes he was the type to set the broom down, knock on her door, and tell her to her face that even though her boy didn't call tonight, she's still okay, she isn't alone, and she never will be.

But he's not that type.

He's the type who sweeps for hours beneath an open window without ever looking at the ground until eventually his arms give out and he falls asleep on her doorstep. He's the type she needs, even if they're both too stubborn to admit it.

———

"Shit," Santi says, slapping his forehead with his palm after checking his watch.

"Wow," his coworker, Antonio, says. "Golden boy with the potty mouth. Must be serious."

"Sorry," he says. "I just realized I forgot to call my Abuela earlier, that's all."

Antonio looks at him, visibly chewing on his words, while running his index finger around the rim of the now lukewarm glass of beer in front of him. "Let me see if I'm following," he says, grabbing a handful of nuts from a bowl on the bar. "It's Saturday night, we're in a bar with drinks, music, food, women, and you're thinking about your Abuela? You really are one of a kind, aren't you?"

Antonio is a good friend. Or at least, a good work friend. The type of friend it's nice to grab drinks with but who you can't quite trust to get you home in one piece if you have one too many. Not that Santi is in the business of making those kinds of distinctions. He just calls him a friend.

"If you knew my Abuela, you'd understand," he replies.

"Is yours a sandals-wearer or a slippers-wearer?"

He cocks his head.

"I have two Abuelas of my own," Antonio grins.

Santi laughs. "Sandals. Yours?"

"Oof," Antonio says. "I have one of each. Sandals don't have nearly as much cushion."

"I wouldn't know."

"Right," he nods.

Santi shifts his weight on his stool and signals the bartender to bring him another round. The bartender sets a fresh bottle beside the three empty ones in front of him and he takes two long swigs and pushes it to the side. He's never been a heavy drinker, so he really has no idea how well he can hold his liquor, but he's come to learn that three and a quarter beers seem to go down with ease and pull most of the stress out of his shoulders without affecting his balance. So far, he hasn't been willing to push that envelope any further.

"So you call her every Saturday?" Antonio asks.

"Every Saturday."

"I'm sure this place has a phone back there somewhere they'd let you use."

"Nah," Santi shakes his head. "It's almost midnight. I'm sure she's asleep by now."

"More likely she's on a bus headed our way to kick your ass," responds Antonio.

Santi laughs.

Antonio tosses the remnants of his glass into his throat and winces. "Probably going to kick mine too while she's at it seeing as I'm the reason you even came out tonight," he says, wiping his mouth dry. "Which I appreciate, by the way."

"Of course," says Santi, because *"You're welcome, but between you and me, we've worked together long enough now for me to confidently say that whatever your so-called shit-crazy wife called you yelling about was probably justified and I really think you should have gone straight home and apologized for it instead of dragging me to this depressing bar and ordering drinks on my tab,"* isn't something that friends are supposed to say to each other. He thinks.

"Hey, you want to get something to eat that isn't bar food?" Antonio asks. "I'm starving."

"Shiiiiiiiiit," he groans.

"What now?"

He grabs his coat off the back of the stool. "I was supposed to get dinner with Sofia an hour ago," he says, pulling his coat on. He pulls enough money out of his wallet to cover the bill, then kisses it four quick times before replacing it to his chest pocket. "I gotta run. You get it, right?"

"I guess," Antonio replies. "You know, I'm starting to see why the boss gives you all the high profile clients, but only lets you work on them one at a time."

"What do you mean?"

"When you're focused, you're focused," he answers, "but you only got room up there for one thing at a time."

Santi pauses, his bottom lip curled, his chin furrowed. "Never thought about it that way," he nods.

"Really?"

"Had my mind on something else, I guess."

Antonio laughs.

"I'll see you Monday," says Santi, making for the door.

"If you're still alive."

"If I'm still alive."

PART FOUR

FALLING

CHAPTER 13

NOVEMBER 1986

THE FRONT DOOR crashes open against the wall, and Coco jumps up from his chair and reaches for his gun on the table.

"You gonna shoot me?" Andrés laughs, walking inside and dropping his backpack onto Coco's recently vacated chair.

"Maybe," he says, tossing the pistol back onto the table and grabbing a beer from the countertop.

"Ha," Andrés mocks, "you wouldn't shoot the devil if he punched you in the polla."

He shakes his head in response and sits on the couch across the room.

"We need to talk," Andrés says.

"What about?" asks Coco, popping the cap off the bottle in his hand and flicking it behind his head.

"About this," he answers, digging through the pockets of his jacket. "While you've been sitting at home touching yourself all day, I've been out changing our lives."

"Is that right?" Coco rolls his eyes, swallowing a mouthful of beer and wiping his mouth with the back of his hand. "How so?"

"I'll show you as soon as I find this hijoepu...ah! There you are," he pulls a tightly crumpled newspaper clipping from his pocket and tosses it towards him. "I got us a job, parce. A real job, no more of that little kid shit we've been doing."

He picks up the wadded scrap of newspaper and slowly unravels it.

"Only bad news is it's in Bogotá, so pack a bag because we leave in an hour."

He flattens out the paper, using the edge of the coffee table to smooth the wrinkles, and lays it down. On the front is a picture of a man whose face he recognizes from the news. His hair is combed, and his uniform is neatly pressed with a row of shining pins and medals decorating his chest.

"What is this?" he asks.

"I just told you, it's a job," Andrés says. "Hey, how do I look?"

He looks up at Andrés leaning against the countertop with a cigar in his teeth and a mini uzi in each hand pointed towards the ceiling.

"Not bad, eh?" he mumbles, careful not to let the cigar slip. "Consider it a promotion, here," he says, handing one to Coco, "this one's yours."

Coco takes it from him and feels the palpable weight of death in his palms. It's been just over eleven months since the last time Andrés handed him a gun and promised him the world. Most of which hasn't been half bad. Of course, he could do without the senseless murdering of cops and other seemingly insignificant men, but at least the pay had been good. Really good. So good that lately it had all started to feel worth it. Until now.

His eyes shift back towards the wrinkled photograph on the coffee table, and he feels a shifting tide in his stomach. He doesn't need to ask any more questions to understand what he's looking at.

This isn't just another senseless kill to fatten their wallets.

This is an execution order.

Santi stands in line, watching dozens of people in front of him drop exact change into a wicker basket on one table and pick up plastic cups of sliced fruit from another. Behind the first table, the most gorgeous woman in a million-mile radius is chopping the heads off a pile of pineapples one at a time. He takes one look at her, and his heart begins banging angry fists against his ribs, trying desperately to break free of its prison cell and run to her.

Every morning when he drops his change in the basket, Sofia shakes her head and tells him he can skip the line. Every morning he tells her no. She thinks it's because he's too good a person to walk to the front when others have to wait their turn, but really it's because he likes the way she stops whatever she's doing the moment she sees his shoes approach the table so she can look him in the eye and smile. Because no matter how long the line, her smile is worth the wait.

He steps up to the table and tosses a trio of coins inside the basket, and she sets down her machete and looks at him.

"Hola," she says with a smile.

"Hola," he grins back.

She hands him the cup of mango verde she set aside for him earlier that morning, and he promptly pops a slice into his mouth and walks away before she has time to fish his money from the basket and give it back to him.

Seven months of the same two words, the same matching smiles, and the same cup of mango. One might think Santi would eventually tire of it, but no. Instead, the countdown to tomorrow starts the moment he walks away.

CHAPTER 14

NOVEMBER 1986

SANTI STEPS into his office and shakes off his coat. He turns to hang it on the coat rack behind the door and almost jumps out of his skin when he sees Coco leaned against the window grinning, and Andrés in his chair with his feet kicked up and one of Santi's ballpoint pens behind his ear.

"Nice place you got here, little bro," Andrés says, pulling his feet off the desk.

"What are you two doing here? You scared the hell out of me," he replies.

"Not the most cordial of greetings, but I'll take what I can get," Andrés nods.

Coco steps away from the window and walks over to his brother, slapping him once on the back before pulling him into a brief embrace. "Hey, hermanito," he says. "Long time."

"Was it?" Santi smirks.

"Too long," Coco corrects himself.

"Yeah, I guess you're right," he says. He sits down in the chair opposite Andrés and Coco takes a seat on the corner of his desk. "So, seriously, what are you guys doing in Bogotá?"

"If you think we came to talk shit about you to your coworkers, you can relax," says Coco.

"Why do you think we got here so early?" Andrés adds.

Coco points at him and nods. "Jokes aside, we're here for work. We have a job to do tomorrow morning outside the city. We were hoping you'd let us crash at your place tonight?"

"Do I want to ask what kind of job it is you're doing?"

"Probably not," Coco answers.

Santi nods. "So how'd you find out where I work?" he asks.

"Would have been a lot easier if you invited me to town once in a while."

"I might have, if you hadn't disappeared for two years without so much as a phone call."

The words come out hotter than anticipated and Santi sees them strike a nerve between his brother's eyes, pulling his eyebrows down into a "V" shape. Instead of waiting for Coco to respond, he shakes his head and waves one hand in front of him.

"Sorry, low blow. I'm sure you had your reasons for staying away," he apologizes.

Coco's face relaxes. "All good, hermanito," he says. "Oh, and since you asked, we found your office after we called your old school and one of your professors told us you'd taken a job down here after you graduated."

"And that lovely young lady there," Andrés chimes in, pointing over Santi's shoulder and out the door to a blushing receptionist, "was kind enough to point us to your office." He gives her a wink and a wave, causing her to turn an even deeper shade of red..

Santi stands and closes the door.

Coco laughs.

"So you need a place to crash tonight?" he asks.

"If it's not too much to ask," Coco answers.

"Dibs on the bed," Andrés adds.

Santi reaches into his pocket and pulls out his keys. Then he stops. "One condition," he says.

"Name it."

"After this job of yours, which I will never ask about by the way," he says, "you need to go home."

Coco chews on the inside of his cheek.

"And I don't mean home to wherever the two of you are living now, although I'm sure that's a lovely, well-maintained, squeaky-clean place. I mean home to Abuela. Make sure she's okay. Show her that you're okay. Promise you'll do that, and my door is wide open."

Coco clears his throat and shakes his head. "Nope. Can't," he says.

Santi looks into his eyes and feels his own face start to grow warm. He squeezes the keys in his palm, the tiny steel teeth biting at his skin. How could he be so selfish to just abandon her like that? To leave without saying a word and never go back? Doesn't he know her at all? Doesn't he know how badly she needs someone? How badly she needs him?

He asks the questions inside his head and realizes he isn't just asking them of Coco, but of both of them.

Don't they know her?

How could they be so selfish?

Or could it be that it isn't quite that simple?

He stands up and extends his hand out, letting the keys drop from his palm while still holding them between his thumb and index finger.

Andrés plucks them from him, says thank you, and slips out the door towards the reception desk.

Coco nods without a word and turns to follow him out.

"Coco," Santi says, grabbing his shoulder.

"We'll be out of your hair first thing tomorrow morning."

He shakes his head. "Stay as long as you need, that's not a problem," he says, then holds out his hand. "Pase lo que pase?"

Coco nods again. He slaps his brother's hand and embraces him. "Siempre, hermanito. Pase lo que pase."

———

Before a few months ago, Sofia assumed she was destined for a life of solitude. Whether that was by fate or by choice, she wasn't sure, but either way, she never did anything to try and change it. She never waved hello to strangers, rarely smiled, and refused to wander into crowded downtown clubs on the weekends looking for someone to buy her a drink or ask her to keep them company for the night. Instead, she spent her time avoiding eye contact and refusing to return anyone's smile as she was always afraid of doing it wrong.

That's why the fruit stand suits her so well. She gets to keep to herself while at the same time being engulfed in a constant flow of bodies and voices. It's the only job she knows of that lets her be alone without feeling alone, and she wouldn't change it for anything.

She's served thousands of people over the years, each a different shape and size with yet another unnecessarily long job title and hopeless personality. To them, she's the fruit girl who doesn't make change and who pretends not to hear you anytime you say "Good morning." To her, they are transactions. It's a perfect relationship.

Of course, there have been those customers who felt it necessary to tell her how beautiful she looks as they drop their coins in the basket. As if she'd asked their opinion. She never entertains them though, and they never come back for seconds. When Santi stumbled into her life at the beginning of this year, wearing dangerously over-shined shoes and looking lost in the loose fabric of his suit coat, she figured he would be the same. He wasn't.

He came back.

She counts the minutes until 7:27 P.M. She empties her basket of coins and bills into her purse and wipes the top of her slicing table with a wet towel, shaking any seeds or loose pieces of rine onto the floor.

"Closed," she says to a woman in a beige pantsuit who approaches the bodega, erasing the smile on her face.

The clock in her head strikes zero, and she glances up the

street and sees him emerge from his office building, straighten his tie, and begin jogging towards her. When he reaches the bodega, he pauses to catch his breath, then kisses her forehead and sets his briefcase on the ground inside the door.

"Sorry I'm late," he says, grabbing a stack of empty crates from beneath the table. He takes the one on top and begins pulling bundles of platanos off the table and piling them inside.

"That's alright. Everything okay at work?" she asks, removing the platanos from the crate Santi is filling and pointing at the handwritten card taped to the side that reads *Maracuyá*. "You seem a little distracted."

"What?" he responds. "Oh, work, yeah. Work's fine. Great."

She doesn't believe him, but doesn't pry. They've reached that point in their relationship, where they each know when the other is holding something back, but they also know that if they just give it some time, whatever it is will come out, because there's not a person on earth either of them trusts more to take the weight off their mind. It's a beautiful thing, trust. Dangerous too.

They pack the rest of the crates in silence, each with their minds on other things. When they're finished, she slides the bodega door shut and clamps a padlock on the outside, double checking her pocket for the key.

"You don't have to walk me home every night, you know," she says, taking his awaiting outstretched hand.

"I know," he replies, pulling her under his arm.

After walking a pair of blocks, she stops.

"Something wrong?" he asks.

"No," she answers. "I was just thinking, what if tomorrow, instead of you walking me home, we walked each other home?"

"How would that work?" he asks, raising an eyebrow.

"Well," she answers, her heart and lungs playing double dutch with her ribs, "we would have to live a lot closer to each other."

"I mean, I guess I could break my lease and look for a place in the same direction as–"

"Like in the same place. The same house. We would have to live in the same house. Together."

He squints at her.

She sighs and rolls her eyes. "Santi. Move in with me?"

"Oh!" he laughs, slapping his forehead. "Boy, am I dumb."

"Not dumb," she smiles, "just distracted. I'm getting used to it though, this whole 'can't focus on more than one thing at a time even if it kills you' thing you have going on. It's cute."

"I'm sorry," he says.

"Don't be," she shakes her head. She looks him in the eye and can see that they are someplace else. "Really. It was stupid of me to even ask, honestly."

"No. No it wasn't, of course it wasn't," he says, and takes her hand. "Of course I'll move in with you. Quite literally nothing would make me happier. You were right, I had my mind on other things. Coco showed up at my office earlier with Andrés."

"Coco? Why? What did he want?"

"Nothing," he shrugs. "Just came to say hi and to see if they could crash at my place tonight. Said they had a job outside the city tomorrow morning they have to take care of."

"A job they have to take care of? That sounds–"

"I didn't ask," he answers, "but I've never seen the two of them together not getting into trouble, so I can imagine it isn't the type of job that requires you to wear a suit or be clean shaven."

"Right," she nods. "Are you okay?"

He looks her in the eye and she can tell she won't be getting an honest answer to that question.

"Yeah," he says. "Yeah, I am."

She gives his hand a tug to get them walking again towards home. "Good," she says. "Now that's out of the way, when are you moving in?"

"Oh, so now it's when not will?"

"That's right."

"Okay then. How about tonight?"

"You can't be serious."

"What?"

"Didn't you just get done telling me that Coco and Andrés are staying at your place tonight?"

"Shit, yeah," he smacks his forehead again. "Tomorrow?"

They reach her front gate and she opens it and shakes her head at him. "Goodnight, Santi," she says, kissing him and walking inside. "Don't forget to pack."

CHAPTER 15

NOVEMBER 1986

Coco's left leg bounces up and down while his right hovers above the brake pedal. He rests one hand on the gear shift knob and uses the the other to keep the sweat running down his forehead from reaching his eyes.

"You feel that? Right here, you feel that?" Andrés asks, holding his crotch. "There's nothing that gets your blood going quite like this, parce, I tell you what."

Coco ignores him, gripping the steering wheel tighter until his knuckles are the same color as his face.

"This is it, marica. You know that, right?" Andrés rants. "One job and we're in. We're *in*. You thought the money was good before. Ha! Did I tell you what the purse is if we pull this shit off? One million..."

"One million pesos," Coco finishes. "You mentioned it, yeah. A couple of times." His left leg bounces faster, and he twists his grip on the steering wheel.

"You sure you don't want me to drive?" Andrés asks. "You're sweating like crazy, look at this." He reaches across the center console and wipes his forehead with his shirt sleeve, and shows it to him. "Wetter than a puta on a cucumber farm."

Coco laughs. "No, I'm cool," he says. He's talking more to

himself than Andrés, who has stopped paying attention to him and is now singing along to the radio and tapping his gun on the dash to the beat.

They're sitting in the front seats of a red Renault sedan on the shoulder of a highway ninety minutes outside of downtown Bogotá, swallowed up on all sides by jagged green mountains and low-hanging clouds. Ahead of them, a bridge stretches across a muddy river with traffic inching along its back at a snail's pace in either direction.

He looks away from the bridge towards the city. He cringes at the thought of Santi finding the cash Andrés left for him on the counter and assuming it had been him that left it. As if they weren't even brothers, but a hotel guest and a chambermaid.

He wonders what Santi would say to him if he were here right now. His head has always been on too straight to get too angry or judge too harshly, so chances are he would look him dead in the eye and say something poetically poignant like, "You're too smart to be doing stupid things," or "The future looks a lot brighter when you pull your head out of your ass," then he would slap his hand with a quick "Pase lo que pase" and walk away, leaving him alone to make his own decisions.

"Here he comes," Andrés says, pointing towards oncoming traffic. "Be ready; we're only gonna get one shot at this."

Coco presses his foot on the brake and starts the engine. As he does, a dusty white minivan rolls past the red Renault and he recognizes the man in the driver's seat as the same man from the newspaper clipping, only now his uniform and stern facial expression are replaced by an unbuttoned canary yellow polo shirt and a side-to-side smile aimed at the woman next to him who is using her hands as much as her words to pull his attention off the road and onto her as she tells him what appears to be a wildly intoxicating story. Their two teenage sons ride in the backseat, one leaning forward, latched onto his mother's every word, the other with his head in his palm looking out the window.

He ignores the incessant pain in his chest and slides the car into gear, inching the Renault forward into the steady stream of traffic three cars back from the van, where he follows them until they pull onto the bridge.

"Now," Andrés instructs when the minivan reaches the halfway point over the river, his voice calm.

Coco shifts gears obediently and maneuvers into the center lane, accelerating until their car pulls even with the van, and Andrés raises his weapon and hangs it out the window. In the half-second it takes to pull the trigger, Coco sees the man's face change as he understands what's taking place and notices the stoic confidence and intimidation from the photograph missing in his eyes, leaving behind them nothing but fear. The fear of a man realizing in real-time that the people he has always promised to keep safe are now at the complete mercy of somebody else.

Andrés squeezes the trigger, and bullets splatter across the side of the van, painting it the way raindrops do a sidewalk during a thunderstorm's opening act. The boys in the backseat cover their heads with their arms and duck between their legs, saving them from having to watch as a bullet explodes through the front window and tears through their father's throat. His head slumps forward onto the steering wheel, sending the van swerving into the curb at the side of the bridge, where it slams to a stop.

Coco pulls the Renault to the side of the road behind it, and Andrés throws his door open.

"You want in?" he asks before he jumps out onto the street, looking at Coco, who glances down at the gun sitting on his lap but makes no moves to pick it up. "Marica. Give me that."

Andrés grabs the gun from him and hops out of the sedan. He approaches the door to the van just as the man's wife limps around the hood of the car. She stops when she sees Andrés and he kicks her to the ground with his boot before spitting at her.

"Move again, and you're coming home with us," he says, raising his voice above the sound of the car horn erupting from beneath the weight of the woman's husband slumped over the steering wheel.

He pulls the driver side door open and lifts the man off the wheel, then pushes him back into a seated position and unloads half a clip into his chest from a foot away.

Coco watches the whole scene unfold as if he were taking it all in from the front row of a crowded theater. Andrés fires a pair of rounds into the roof of the car above the backseats, a warning to the two boys, then walks back to the Renault and climbs in next to him.

"Vamos," he says, tossing one of the guns behind him and resting the barrel of the other on the window ledge.

Coco looks at Andrés before pulling away, expecting the same crazed laughter as the night the man called Jorge died. Only this time, there isn't any laughter in his eyes.

This time, all he sees is black.

———

Sofia opens her eyes and all she sees is white light, screaming at her through her bedroom window.

Meanwhile, the banging noise coming from the front door, the one that woke her up, continues to amplify. There's only one person out of their mind enough to knock on her door like that this early, and for as much as she loves him, the temptation to rip open the door armed with a butcher knife persists.

She rolls out of bed and walks down the hall, foregoing the weapons but rehearsing the string of expletives she'll be hurling at Santi with each step. She unbolts her front door and swings it open. It's then that she realizes that the reason Santi was knocking so loudly on the door was because he wasn't knocking on it at all. He was kicking it.

He has a shoebox tucked under his arm and a plate of pastries clenched in his teeth, with a cup of coffee in each hand.

"Help," he mumbles.

She smirks and takes the plate from his teeth and a cup from his hand. Then she uses her free hand to smack him.

"What's wrong with you, don't you know what time it is?" she asks.

"Sorry," he says, pushing his way inside, "couldn't wait." He walks into the kitchen and sets the shoebox down on the counter and takes a sip of coffee. "There," he says. "All moved in."

"You're telling me everything you own is inside that shoebox?"

"What? Of course not. I'll go back for the rest later, this is just the important stuff," he says, patting the box, a boyish grin spread from ear to ear.

She looks at him with crooked eyes and follows him into the kitchen. She reaches to open the box, ready to laugh at just how unimportant its contents really are, when Santi slaps her hand. She cocks it back and turns her head to look at him, her eyes wide.

"Sorry!" he grimaces. "Shouldn't have done that. But no, you are not allowed to open that."

She lowers her hand. "Keeping secrets, are we?"

"Only good ones," he says, grabbing her hips and pulling her into him. "Promise."

———

Riiiiing

Sofia presses the phone harder against her ear.

Riiiiing

Her breathing deepens and she twists the cord around her index finger, watching the skin under her fingernail grow darker and darker.

Riiiiing

She pulls the phone from her ear and reaches to hang it back on the wall.

"Alo," a voice on the other end says.

Sofia's heart stops.

"Alo?" they repeat.

She turns the phone around and looks at it, her eyes brimming with memories triggered by the sound of her voice.

"Sofia?" her mother says.

Her eyes narrow. How does she know who it was?

"Sofia? Is that you?"

Oh. She doesn't know. She only thinks it's her. Still, how?

"Sofia, I don't know if you're there or if this is even you calling, but if it is, please listen," her mom pleads.

She puts the phone back to her ear.

"Your father is gone," her mom says. "Dead, actually. He died two years ago. Heart attack."

No. That can't be true. Can that be true? And of all the ways for a man like that to go, it had to be a heart attack? He couldn't have been hit by a car or pushed off a cliff or anything more deserving?

"You can come back now, dear," her mother says, her sobbing audible through the phone. "You can come home."

She twists her sweaty palm on the receiver until she finds a better grip. The words burn themselves into her eyes as if they were being scratched onto her retinas by a sharpened piece of iron pulled from a furnace.

Home. What is home, really? Is it a place? A person? A feeling? Sofia can't answer that. She's never had one.

"Sofia," her mom whimpers, "I'm sorry. I'm so sorry."

Click.

She hangs up the phone before her mom says anything else. She wipes her eye with her knuckle, walks across the room to her couch, and throws herself onto it. That isn't how that phone call was meant to go. Her mother wasn't supposed to answer. She wasn't supposed to sob or apologize or beg her to come home. Her father wasn't supposed to be dead. They were supposed to be there together, the same level of terribleness as they were inside her head. As they always had been. Her father was supposed to cry out in shock at the sound of her voice and in anger when she told him she had found someone to treat her the way she deserved.

Someone who could make her happy. Her mother was supposed to take the phone and attempt to say something halfway decent, only she wouldn't get the chance to because Sofia was supposed to hang up before she got a word out, leaving her with nobody to talk to but the evil man she chose to love.

That's how it was meant to go.

But then, when has anything ever gone the way it's meant to for Sofia?

CHAPTER 16

CHRISTMAS EVE 1986

"Do you even own a serving spoon?" Santi asks, rummaging through Sofia's kitchen drawers, most of which are filled with anything but what one would normally expect to find in a kitchen drawer.

"Who am I ever serving that would require me to own a serving spoon?" she responds back from her seat at the table where she's twirling a strainer in her hand waiting to pull the last of the buñuelos from the fryer in front of her.

"But I'm guessing you have every reason to own these?"

He reaches into a cabinet beneath the sink and pulls out a small bucket of paint brushes. Sofia shrugs.

"A couple years ago, I made plans to paint the kitchen."

"And when exactly are you planning on doing that?"

"Right after I use those brushes to remind you what happens when you go all smart-ass on me."

He laughs and his hand moves to the tiny circle protruding from his jean pocket. He traces it with one finger, then goes back to searching for something to serve the natilla he's prepared.

"You know," he says, "if I'd known you were such a slob, I don't think I would have ever agreed to move in here."

"Well, if I'd known you were going to be such a constant pain in the ass, I never would have let you."

He laughs again.

"Remind me again why we're doing this?" she asks, scooping out a pair of over-fried buñuelos from the oil with the strainer.

"Ah-ha!" he exclaims, throwing one hand up in excitement holding a large spoon. "Found one." He looks at her as if expecting to receive a prize or be made the King of England, but instead she looks at him the way a cat looks at its owner. "What did you ask me?" he says, reading her face.

"I asked you why we're making all of this food instead of going out to eat like normal people."

"Buñuelos and natilla are a Colombian Christmas tradition," he starts.

"That doesn't mean they're *my* Christmas tradition. I don't even like buñuelos. Or natilla, for that matter."

He laughs and shakes his head. "That just means you've never had a good batch."

"And this batch will be?" she asks, raising her eyebrows.

"Definitely not," he replies, walking across the kitchen and kissing her on the top of her head, "but you're going to tell me it is anyway, because you love me."

"That, or I'm going to take one bite and throw the rest in the trash," she says and pats him gently on the cheek, "because I love you."

He takes her hand in his and with the other he reaches down and again traces the circle protruding from his pocket. He runs his finger over it a few times, then digs his hand in his pocket and closes it around the ring, turning it over and over between his fingers.

"Where'd you put that spoon, let's get this over with already," she says, jumping up from her seat.

He pulls it from his back pocket and hands it to her, and she scoops him a large portion of natilla from the dish on the table and a significantly smaller dose for herself. Santi lifts the napkin covering the buñuelos and takes two for him and one for her and sets it on her plate.

"Buen provecho," he says, diving into his own food.

"Sure," she nods sarcastically, then takes a bite. "Yeah, that's not happening," she says, spitting the mouthful of natilla back onto her plate before tossing the whole thing in the trash.

"You didn't even give it a chance!" he exclaims, his mouth full.

"If the devil walked in with a hot bowl of shit and a spoon, and asked you to give it a chance, would you do it?"

Santi throws his head back in laughter, his finger reaching again for his pocket. "That is *not* a fair comparison, but I'll let you get away with it this year. Wait, where are you going?"

"Hold on," she responds, walking down the hall to her bedroom. When she emerges, she's carrying a box, wrapped in green and red striped paper. "Here," she says, handing it to him, "Merry Christmas."

He smiles at her and shakes his head as he peels back the wrapping. "You didn't have to get me a gift, amor. You know that."

"I know," she replies, "but I love you, so I did. Now shut up and open it."

"Right, right, right."

He finishes pulling off the paper, lifts the lid to the box, and chuckles to himself.

"Do you like it?"

"How could I not?" he asks, pulling out a brand new, black leather belt.

"I don't ever want to see you wearing that brown belt with black shoes again," she warns. "No more excuses."

"Ay ay," he agrees.

"So what'd you get me?"

"Oh, I... Well, I..." his finger draws fast circles around the ring poking through his jean pocket. He feels a drop of nerves trickle down his back as his mind races through the half a dozen or so questions that have played on repeat since he first brought the ring home from the jewelry store.

What if she hates it? What if she says no? What if she never wanted a ring? Or the big one: What if he isn't good enough?

"You didn't get me anything, did you?" she asks, her eyes narrowing at the same rate as her smile widens.

"No, I did. I just, I don't really know how to say this," he starts. He reaches his hand inside his pocket and closes it around the ring, same as before. Then he drops it, and pulls his hand back out and runs it through his hair.

"I left it at the office yesterday, so I'll have to run in tomorrow and get it. Sorry."

She shakes her head. "Are you always this forgetful?" she asks.

"I can't remember," he smiles.

"Guess you'll have to find some way to make it up to me." She grabs his hand and pulls him up from his seat and doesn't stop pulling until they reach their bedroom. "Merry Christmas, Santiago," she whispers in his ear.

"Merry Christmas, amor," he whispers back.

―――――

The clock strikes midnight, and Abuela picks the plates of buñuelos and natilla up off the table and slides them into the trash, asking herself the same thing she asked last year. *Why do I even bother?*

Of course, she knew Santi wouldn't be here. He called and told her so, just as he had the year before, and the year before that. He originally told her it was because Sofia felt uneasy about traveling so far during the holidays with the way the cartel was monitoring all major highways. After some digging and a few choicely-placed expletives, however, she discovered it was actually because his boss expected him in the office both on Christmas Eve and the day after Christmas. Which of course led her to spout off a good deal more expletives, significantly less creative than the others, detailing exactly where she recommended his boss put his Christmas decorations this year. The tree included.

The one decent thing Santi did on that phone call was tell her he had seen Coco a week or two prior and had encouraged him to come home for Christmas. Coco always loved Christmas, more than other boys his age and with his temperament, and so Abuela responded by doing the worst thing imaginable. She got her hopes up.

Voices of children, parents, and grandparents all celebrating what for them is the happiest day of the year drift up through her open window like the scent of a home cooked meal, further deepening the aching pit in her stomach. For everyone down there, today is the one day they get to be together without other commitments or prior engagements calling them away. For her, it's the one day she's forced to focus on the fact that what she wants and what she has have never been more at odds.

In a past life, she would have taken the food she made down the stairs to share with her neighbors, accepting their compliments with a wave of her hand and laughing with them until her lungs folded in half. Instead, she stands on her own in her kitchen, an empty plate in each hand and a pile of uneaten food in the trash, with no other plan than to lie on a couch she hates staring at a phone that doesn't ring while she waits for knocks on the door that never come. Because there's no such thing as past lives. There's life, and there's the past.

She shuffles towards the sofa but stops when a thought pops into her head as her eyes catch sight of her coat hanging by the front door. It's a terrible, awkward, inappropriate, out-of-place thought. One that makes her pause.

She shifts course and walks to the door, taking her coat from the hook and sliding it over her thin shoulders. She takes a deep breath and grasps the door handle, but something within her keeps her hand from twisting it and pulling it open.

What am I doing? she asks herself.

The answer to which, like most things in her life, is both

incredibly simple and impossibly complicated. What she's doing is asking for help. That's the simple part. The complicated part is that in all her years, she can't remember ever doing that.

With her hand still on the doorknob, she hears what sounds like the scuffling of a pair of shoes on the staircase on the other side. The thought of Coco standing outside injects a shot of adrenaline into her system and she's tempted to rip the door open, but the fear of finding nothing but empty stairs holds her back.

She stands without moving for several minutes, waiting for a knock or for someone to call out her name. When nobody does, she decides she must've imagined it and lets her hand slip from the handle.

She walks to the couch without taking her coat off, her eyes searching the floor for answers that are never there. She lies down and pulls her jacket tight around her, allowing the sounds of merry voices below to taunt her while she falls asleep.

———

The day Javier decided to buy a kitchen table for the studio apartment behind the store, he bought four chairs to go along with it. It's a decision he regrets every morning. Nothing makes a man feel lonelier than the eyes of three empty seats staring at him as he drinks his morning coffee.

Today is Christmas Eve, something he likely would have forgotten had Rosa not loaded her basket that morning with her usual items plus the extra ingredients she needed to make her annual Christmas natilla.

"Expecting company?" he asked her when she came to the counter.

"Wouldn't be Christmas without it," she responded.

He honestly didn't know if that meant yes or no, but one look into her eyes told him she was preparing herself for another year of disappointment. He wanted to tell her right then that he also was anticipating spending the evening alone but refrained, not because it wasn't true but because he didn't want to be the reason that whatever hope she was holding onto of her boys showing up escaped her grip and shattered across the floor.

As soon as she stepped out of the store and went upstairs, he closed up and spent the rest of the day sipping limonada at his kitchen table and arguing with the three chairs in front of him, all of whom made the same case and refuted any counterpoint he proposed by repeating the same word.

"Go."

He's never listened to them before, but as one comes to find out, loneliness and love are a potent combination. One that makes a man do crazy things, like put on his coat at midnight on Christmas Eve to go knock on his neighbor's door and invite himself in to eat her food before it gets tossed in the trash. Which is where he is now.

He tugs on his jacket in a failed attempt to smooth its many wrinkles, pushes a few loose strands of hair behind his ears, and balls his fist, raising it an inch in front of her door. That's as close as it will ever get.

For one vanishing moment, he thinks he hears her walking to the door and allows himself to imagine her throwing it open before he can knock and inviting him in with open arms. He pictures her taking him by the hand and offering him a plate, not taking no for an answer, and begging him to stay just a few minutes longer when he checks his watch and tells her he better be off.

When she doesn't, his fist falls to his side and curls into a ball inside his pocket. He turns and walks back down the stairs, taking each one gingerly so as not to lose his balance. Back in his kitchen, he sits at the table and drops his chin to his chest to avoid eye contact with the three chairs surrounding him. A tear crawls down his cheek and drops from his chin, and he watches it spread and darken as it seeps deeper and deeper into the raw wood tabletop.

Right here is where he'll spend the rest of the night. He won't move; he won't sleep. If he does, he's afraid the emptiness might weigh too heavy on his heart and keep him from waking up. So he can't, not because he's scared of dying but because tomorrow morning she'll be here to buy groceries and so he needs to be here too. To prove to her she isn't alone.

She never will be.

CHAPTER 17

NEW YEAR'S EVE 1986

TODAY IS New Year's Eve, a day for fireworks, celebrations, and resolutions. Sofia sits on the porch, alone, rubbing the same spot on the fourth finger of her left hand and watching children run up and down the street waving sparklers that highlight the euphoria in their faces. She turns and glances through the window behind her at the clock on the kitchen counter.

11:55 P.M.

Behind the same counter, Santi paces the kitchen, mumbling to himself. He came home from work earlier today very clearly burnt out. With a boss like his, she can't blame him. Still, she wishes he could put all that stress aside for one night and come sit with her.

She turns back to the street and counts the seconds left until the new year. At a minute to midnight, she stands up to go inside. When she reaches for the door, it opens from the inside, and suddenly she and Santi are standing face-to-face, less than a step apart.

"Hola," he says.

"Where's the phone?" she replies.

"The phone?"

"That's right."

"It's New Year's Eve, who are you calling?"

"Your boss. I'm going to see if I can't ruin his night the same way he ruined ours," she mutters.

He smiles. "I love you," he says, after a moment. He pulls his fist from his pocket and at the same time takes her left hand in his, "And I'm never going to not love you. From the moment I saw your face, all I wanted to do was find all the things that make you happy and do them over and over and over again for the rest of our lives."

He opens his fist without taking his eyes off hers and slides a ring onto her finger.

"Marry me."

With one sentence, he steals her breath and all her words.

She nods slowly, her smile growing with each bob of her head. He takes her face in both hands and kisses her, as if doing so was the only thing that ever mattered.

Fireworks explode into the air around them, sprinkling color onto a black midnight canvas. Sofia doesn't see them. She doesn't hear them.

But she feels them.

Oh, how she feels them.

————

Coco carefully lifts an arm off of his chest that belongs to the woman sleeping next to him, naked save for a blanket over her legs and the arm of a second girl draped over her stomach. He pulls a t-shirt from the pile of clothes at the foot of the mattress and walks outside to the balcony, his usual breakfast of arepa and scrambled eggs replaced by a cigarette and a cool breeze.

Last night, Andrés took him to a party in a mansion outside the valley thrown by one of Pablo's higher-ups. The place was overflowing with exotic food and expensive alcohol being served by even more expensive women. It was everything he once dreamed of, and yet standing there in the moment, the only things he wanted were the people he gave up to get there. If you'd asked him growing up if he ever thought he would miss climbing onto the roof of Abuela's house with Santi on New Year's Eve to watch the fireworks together while she was asleep in her room, he'd have answered with a convincing, "Hell no!"

And yet, here he is.

The balcony door opens behind him, and Andrés steps outside wearing nothing but a pair of golden boxer shorts.

"Shit, it's cold out here," he says, rubbing his palms together, then plucking the lit cigarette from Coco's fingertips and pressing it to his lips. "Two at a time?" he smiles, signaling with his head to the two women asleep inside. "How was it?"

"Best night of my life," he replies, stealing his cigarette back. "I hope we didn't keep you up."

"Something kept me up, parce, but it was not you three, I can assure you of that," Andrés laughs. He reaches for the cigarette again, but Coco pulls it from his lips and holds it in his left hand away from him. Andrés drops his arm to his side. "Can you believe that party last night?" he asks, bobbing up and down to keep warm. "I mean, what was that place? Can you even imagine having so much money you just go out and buy yourself a hippo? A fucking hippo! Shit. Makes you realize how much ladder we still have to climb."

Coco nods, moving his eyes to the ground in front of him.

"Hey, what's Abuela up to these days?" Andrés continues, leaning against the railing around the patio.

The question catches him off guard and he takes a sharp pull off his cigarette, making himself cough.

"Shit, you alright?" Andrés asks, smacking him on the back.

"Yeah, yeah, I'm good," he responds, his eyes puffy. "I haven't talked to her in months. Or years, I guess."

"You think she's dead?"

"Are you kidding? You could shoot that woman in the face and she'd spit the bullet back out and shout something at you about how 'Your aim is piss!' or 'You shoot like my grandmother, and she was a bitch!'"

Andrés howls with laughter. "She would, wouldn't she," he breathes. "God, I love her. You ever think about going over to visit?"

"Sometimes."

"Same," Andrés nods. "The old man too."

"Your dad? Why would you want to see him?" he asks.

"Nah, not him," he shakes his head. "The actual old man. Javier."

Coco taps his cigarette on the railing and smiles.

"Hey what about Cris?" Andrés goes on. "You think he still goes to the cancha every day and smokes by himself now that we're here?"

Coco doesn't answer.

"Can you believe he turned all of this down?" Andrés says.

Coco takes a pull and spits the smoke towards the sky. *Which part?* he thinks. *The money and the women? Or the rest of it?*

"I do kind of miss him, though," he continues, not waiting for Coco to respond. "It was nice always having an easy target to shit on, you know?"

"Yeah," Coco says, forcing a laugh and dragging a toe back and forth on the ground.

"Hey," says Andrés, standing up straight and smacking him on the shoulder, "I'm proud of you."

"Are you my dad now?"

"I'm serious, parce. You took care of business in Bogotá. You had my back and I appreciated that." He pats him gently on the cheek three times and opens the door to go inside. "I'm gonna see about getting us another job."

"Hágale."

Andrés smiles and steps inside, closing the door behind him. Coco looks at the cigarette between his thumb and forefinger with a heavy dose of skepticism, then flicks it over the railing and into the street.

Chapter 18

January 1987

Resolutions are for young people, because for some reason, young people think that just because there's a different number at the top of the calendar, suddenly anything can change. That they can be different. Better. The longer you're alive, the better you understand that hoping things will change simply because it's a new day or a new year is pointless. Why? Because people don't change. Not really.

———

Riiiiing.

The sound wakes Abuela from her afternoon nap, but she refuses to open her eyes. She knows she must be hearing things and doesn't see the point in opening them if all she'll be is disappointed. So she closes them even tighter and covers her ears for good measure—anything to keep the crazy out.

Riiiiing.

She opens one eye and squints at the phone, daring it to ring again.

Riiiiing.

She watches it sound and sits bolt upright, sending rippling shockwaves of pain spiraling down her spine.

"Son of a bitch," she says, grabbing at her back as she picks up the phone.

"Wow," Santi laughs on the other end. "I'll admit I was not expecting the profanity to make an appearance so early."

"Santi," she says, whispering his name.

"Hola, Abuelita," he says.

"H-how are you?" she asks, twisting the cord around her hand and clutching it like a support line.

"Good, good," he responds. "Great, actually. You remember Sofia?"

"Of course, of course."

"Well, I proposed to her yesterday," he says, "and she said yes."

"YOU'RE ENGAGED?" she shouts, surprising both of them.

"I guess I am, yeah," he says. "She's incredible, Abuela, she is."

"She better be if she's going to steal my baby boy from me."

"You're going to love her," he says. "Nobody has ever made me feel so..." he pauses, leaving her hanging on for the last word. "...happy."

She smiles and blinks back moisture from her eyes.

"And I'm happy for you," she says. "When do I get to meet her?"

"Soon. I promise."

"Good."

"Abuela?"

"Si, mijo."

"I miss you."

Her heart skips, and the phone slides an inch lower in her palm as her grip slips. She closes her eyes, takes a breath, and says, "Of course you do. Who wouldn't?"

Her voice is steady, but her eyes tell a different story, a silent army of tears marching through wrinkled trenches until they drop from her chin to the floor below. She opens her eyes and watches each small circle spread and darken at her feet and clenches the phone until she feels her knuckles start to ache to keep herself from shouting the words her eyes are begging her to let out. *I miss you too. I need you. Please come home.*

Santi laughs. "Hey, did Coco end up coming home for Christmas?"

"No, mijo," she answers. "I haven't seen him."

"Hmm. I guess I shouldn't be too surprised. He's always struggled a bit keeping his priorities in check."

She tightens her grip on the receiver and nods.

"Anyway, I gotta run. I'll call again next week, I promise," he says. "Ciao, Abuela."

She hears a click on the other end. Inside her chest, her emotions are at war. She stands up to give them more space to battle it out and sees her coat hanging by the door. She might not want it, but she needs someone to tell her what to do, and there's only one person she knows who enjoys advising people who haven't asked for advice, so she puts on her coat and goes downstairs to see him.

Outside, she sees Javier's broom lying on the sidewalk. She stoops down, picks it up, then steps inside the store, leaning it against the counter. She peers down each of the two narrow aisles but finds no one.

"Odd," she says to herself.

She takes a last look around before resigning her search, then steps out onto the sidewalk where something catches her eye. Something that's hung on the wall every day for decades but that she hasn't paid attention to for several years.

The answer is always love, it reads.

Had today been any other day or had the words come from anyone else, she would have dismissed them with a wave of her hand and an emphatic, "Ha!"

Today they take her heart by storm.

In the past, anytime anyone ever pushed her away, even just a little, Abuela reacted by pushing back. Harder and harder until they were no longer in the picture. Until she was alone.

Is she angry at Santi for leaving her for so long? Maybe. Upset with herself for letting him go? Sure. Is she heartbroken? Terrified? Of course. She's also annoyed and ashamed and jealous and anxious and a handful of other emotions she never bothered learning the names of, but this time, there's only one thing she's going to do about it.

She's going to love.

———

It's always the things you expect the least that hit you the hardest. This is true of everything from pop quizzes to head-on collisions. It's truest of love.

Javier dropped his broom when he heard the phone ring through the window of the apartment upstairs. His jaw fell at the same time, and he looked up at the open panes as if they had just begun singing him a song or making fun of the way he dressed. He bent down and picked up the broom only to drop it again moments later when he heard Abuela shout, "YOU'RE ENGAGED," at which point he left it be and walked straight through the store to his kitchen without bothering to lock up.

Now he's sitting at his kitchen table in front of three empty chairs all watching him turn the same object over and over between his fingers.

When Rosa comes to the store tomorrow for groceries, he already knows what she'll do. She'll tell him about the engagement and use her eyes to ask for his advice on what she should be feeling, not because she wants to but because she has to. Because it's annoyingly difficult to be happy for someone close to you when the thing you're expected to be happy about only takes them further away.

He also knows how he'll respond. He'll tell her that the only way to love somebody is to do it unconditionally, because love with contingencies isn't love. It's captivity. He'll say it with a smile on his face and an offer of groceries on the house, but on the inside, he'll be battling to follow his own counsel. Why? Because in the five years they spent together, he never left Luz's side long enough to buy her something he could surprise her with.

Except for once.

He drops the ring into his palm, unable to take his eyes off it. It's a beautiful ring. The simplest of gold bands with the tiniest of emeralds. He bought it on a lazy morning from the only jeweler in a coastal town neither of them had ever been to before. That ring was supposed to be the beginning of the greatest chapter in their perfect love story.

She never got to wear it.

He should be happy for Santi. He wants to be happy for him. But he isn't, because jealousy and love aren't capable of peaceful cohabitation.

He can't be happy for Santi because Santi has the only thing Javier wants, and all he has is an eternal reminder of the earth's cruelest morning. The morning everything changed.

He kisses the ring and puts it back in his breast pocket where it's lived since the morning he bought it, then switches off the lamp and rests his head on his forearm on the table, the eyes of three empty chairs fixated on the top of his balding head without blinking all praying for the same thing.

That he has strength left to wake up.

CHAPTER 19

JANUARY 1987

FEW RELATIONSHIPS LAST FOREVER. It's knowing that that makes so many of us look for ways out of them before they go too far. Before we give so much of ourselves to another person that when they leave they leave us empty. Hollow. It's why instead of saying the things we mean, we lie to ourselves and to the ones we care about. We lash out, act up, and do things we know we shouldn't, all so the other person will leave first, and we can go on pretending it was their fault things fell apart. That it's their fault we're alone.

Maybe that's why Coco left. Maybe he had to. Maybe he was afraid.

Maybe.

Cristian repeats the word in his head as if by doing so he could convince himself it was true. Coco didn't leave because he was afraid of caring too much. He left because he didn't care at all. Because Andrés offered him the world he always wanted, and all he had to offer were listening ears and open arms, two things no twenty-four-year-old in Medellín ever gave a shit about.

He drags a toe across the concrete without looking down. The cigarette between his fingers has lost its appeal, and he stubs it out on the block wall before flicking it into the bushes and shoving a balled fist into his pocket. The last visible sliver of sunlight drops behind the mountains on the opposite end of the valley, and he sniffs and raises his shoulders to keep from shivering.

Even though it's been more than seventeen years since he came to Medellín from Sincelejo, the chill that accompanies the evening breeze still sneaks up on him. When he moved here, he was a lost eight-year-old boy with more baggage than a passenger train and less enthusiasm for life than anyone save the grim reaper himself. He came alone to live with his aunt because his parents were incapable of raising him themselves.

Cristian's dad was a good man. He was also dead. He hates himself for wishing it had been his mother that was killed, but he hates himself for plenty of other reasons too, so he wishes it anyways. For his entire life, he has felt like he never belonged anywhere. He told his dad that once and his dad responded by telling him that it was impossible for anyone to belong everywhere or to everyone.

"All you need is one person," he said, putting his finger on Cristian's chest, and Cristian believed him, even if he misunderstood what he'd really meant.

When he died, Cristian took his anger out on his mamá until his persistent rebelliousness drove her into a spiraling addiction from which there was no coming back. Before she lost herself completely, she did the one good thing she'd ever done for her son. She made a phone call, then shortly afterwards she put him on a bus bound for Medellín to live with her sister.

His aunt took him in and put food in his mouth and clothes on his back, but that was where the favors ended. There was no love on either side, each simply completing their own separate prison sentence.

He never called or wrote to his mother and never saw her again until her ashes arrived in the luggage hold of a long-distance bus inside a cardboard box with his name on it. Nobody bothered to tell him what had happened to her, nor did he ask, afraid if he did, he would learn it had somehow been his fault.

A week later, his aunt took him by the wrist, dragged him across the street, and forced him to join a soccer game he didn't belong in, claiming she couldn't stand to look at his depressed face for another second and warning him not to come back until he had lightened up a bit. He didn't mind her dragging him out of the house so much, but he hated soccer, and so he hated her for it.

For forty-five minutes, he did whatever it took not to touch the ball or get in the way of the other boys on the court. He would have succeeded had the ball not chosen to roll to a stop directly in front of his right foot. When he saw it, he panicked and did the first thing he could think of. He kicked it out of bounds. That's when one of his teammates walked up and punched him in the nose.

He cried, not because it hurt but because it was the first time in a long time he had felt anything at all. As if that single punch from a pissed-off eight-year-old kid had somehow pulled away a dark, heavy blanket covering him from head to foot and somehow reminded him he was still alive.

The boy who hit him apologized and ran away, and the rest of the boys quickly realized the game was over and one by one drifted home, leaving Cristian sitting by himself on the short wall surrounding the court with his hand cupped under his nose to collect the blood dripping rhythmically from each nostril.

At least the game's over, he found himself thinking.

He never expected to see any of those kids again, but a few minutes later, he saw Coco sprinting up the street towards him, breathing harder than a bank robber at a police picnic and holding a melting pile of ice wrapped in an old hand towel.

He came back, so Cristian kept coming back too.

He drags a toe across the ground and closes his eyes, his lungs taking advantage of the unusually smoke-free air to collect some much-needed clarity.

"Sorry I'm late," a voice says cutting through whatever impending epiphany was headed his way.

Cristian looks at his former best friend with relaxed shoulders and a furrowed brow. "What are you doing here?" he asks as Coco plops himself down next to him. The words come out flatter and harsher than he intended, but he makes no effort to amend them. He looks him up and down, taking note of the invisible price tags on everything he's wearing, from his shoes to his coat. "Come back to do a little poor-person sightseeing or what?"

Coco doesn't answer right away. His eyes are stuck on the horizon, and he bites the inside of both cheeks, making them appear thinner than they already are. He blinks slowly as if each one were a conscious decision.

"I need help, Cristian," he says finally, his voice hardly more than a whisper. He scrapes a sneakered toe across the sidewalk and shakes his head. "I'm completely lost."

"I'm sure they sell maps around here somewhere," Cristian snaps pulling a fresh cigarette from his pocket and a lighter to spark it with.

"Ha," Coco laughs, sliding his hands in his pocket, "nice one." He drags his toe along the sidewalk again and opens and closes his mouth again and again until the words he came to say spill out on top of each other. "I screwed up, okay," he says. "That day I left with Andrés. I screwed up."

Cristian exhales hard out of his nose and rolls his eyes, pressing the newly lit cigarette to his lips.

"I should have listened to you. I should have stayed. I was wrong, Cris, I–"

"Don't call me Cris," he snaps.

"Right, shit. Sorry."

Cristian blows a pillar of smoke and bites his bottom lip to keep it from shaking. "What is it you really want?" he says, facing Coco.

"I–I don't know," Coco responds, his eyes bouncing in all directions. "I guess I was hoping for someone to talk to."

"I'm not your fucking therapist."

His words are sharp and he can see the effects of each one as it slices Coco deeper and deeper.

Coco takes his hands from his pockets and wipes them on his pant legs. "That's fair," he says. He looks at Cristian, hoping for a response but gets nothing. "I think part of me thought that if I came back here, we could pretend things were normal for a bit. That's all."

"If you wanted things to be normal, you would have come back a long time ago."

"You don't think I wanted to?" Coco asks, raising his voice and shaking his head.

Cristian scoffs.

"You don't understand anything about the world I'm wrapped up in, do you? What do you think, I can just walk into Pablo's office and say, 'Hey boss, I decided this isn't really for me, so I'm gonna go now, is that okay?'" he says in a mocking voice. "This shit doesn't work like that. Not once you've seen what I've seen. If I try to walk away, he'll pull me back in. If I turn around, he's right in front of me. If I run, I... I..."

He trails off, and Cristian looks him in the eyes for the first time since he arrived. The light, the laughter, and the life that once came standard are gone. All that's left is fear. For one second, he's tempted to put an arm around him and tell him he's sorry. Tell him he'll always be there for him. That he can come to him for anything, anytime, no matter what.

But he doesn't.

"Sounds like you better get out here," he says instead.

Coco opens his mouth to respond but closes it again. The two best friends look at each other for several seconds without recognizing who they see until Coco breaks the silence.

"Okay," he says. He glances once at the letters just in front of Cristian's shoe, then walks away.

Cristian waits until he's gone, then drops his cigarette and stomps the ashes into the grooves of the fading initials below to keep them from staring up at him.

Few relationships last forever. That's something we all know, even if we are too stubborn to admit it. That's why so many of us look for a way out before a relationship goes too far. Only sometimes it's too late. Sometimes, we're left empty.

———

Sofia spins the ring on her finger faster with each minute that passes until finally, she sees Santi emerge from his office building and start meandering toward her, flipping through a thick stack of documents as he goes. She slides a crate towards the back of the bodega and wipes her hands on her apron. Her back is to the door when he arrives, and she keeps it that way, pretending not to hear him approaching.

"Sorry I'm late," he says, opening his briefcase on the table and adding the papers in his hand to it.

"Again," she corrects without turning around.

"What?"

"Sorry I'm late *again*," she repeats. "That's what you meant, isn't it?"

"That feels unnecessary," he says.

She rolls her eyes. "It's the third time this week, Santi. The fifth in the last two weeks. At what point am I allowed to start getting annoyed?"

He shakes his head and pulls the last empty crate from beneath the table, and starts filling it with fruit. "I have a lot going on at the office right now; you know that."

"I do know that. I also know you have important things going on outside the office," she says.

He leans his head to one side.

"Me!" she says, pointing to herself. "You have me. Or had you forgotten?"

"Of course not," he apologizes and walks forward to hug her.

She hugs him back but not for very long. She pulls away and covers the crate he's just filled with a towel and slides it to the back of the room with the others, then steps outside and starts to close the bodega door, causing Santi to snag his briefcase and scurry underneath before he gets locked inside. She closes the padlock and starts walking without waiting for him.

"Sofia," he says, hurrying to catch up. He grabs her by the hand and spins her around to face him. "I'm sorry."

"I know."

"Work has just been so busy."

"I know that, too."

"As soon as I get this next promotion, we'll have enough money to do whatever we want, whenever we want. I promise. You should see how much the executives at my office make, it's unbelievable."

"I'm sure they have all the money in the world," Sofia retorts, "but do you know what else they have? Hookers and drug addictions and pissed off wives and kids who call them by their first names. Is that what you want?"

"What? Of course not. I do want us to be happy though, and I want our future kids to have the things I never had growing up."

Sofia looks him in the eye and nods slowly. "Me too," she says, "but the things I didn't have growing up were a mother who loved me, and a father who gave a shit. That's what I want. Not money."

She pulls her hand free of his and turns back up the sidewalk, walking the rest of the way home two steps in front of him.

When they get home, he'll apologize quickly and they'll make up slowly. In the morning, he'll wake up and go to work, and she'll wake up alone, spinning the ring on her finger faster and faster.

Few relationships last forever, even the ones we're all rooting for.

CHAPTER 20

JUNE 1987

COCO SITS on a stool at the kitchen counter, the half-drunk bottle in his hand just a few drops away from joining a dozen empty comrades piled at his feet. The entire apartment reeks of stale beer and sweat-stained sheets, but he has either grown too accustomed to it to notice or stopped caring enough to do anything about it.

"C'mon," Andrés says, walking out of his bedroom and into the living room, "let's go." He picks up Coco's jacket from a musty heap at the foot of his mattress and throws it at him, knocking the bottle from his hand and spilling its contents across the counter.

"Hey whatthe hell s'wrong with you?!" Coco shouts, each word stumbling over the one in front of it as if they were ten bottles deep themselves.

"I said, let's go."

"And *I* said, what the hell is wrong with you?" he repeats, using the counter as a crutch as he makes his way around the kitchen in search of another bottle. He finds one on top of the fridge and pops the cap off on the corner of the countertop then slumps back into his stool. "Where are you even going anyways?

We got more beer right here." He holds up the bottle in his hand proudly.

"Not me," Andrés shakes his head. "Us. We haven't had a real job in months, it's time to be proactive."

There's a knock on the door, and Andrés opens it.

"Q'hubo pues, Guzano," he says.

Andrés's friend Gilberto Guzman, known to most as Guzano, stands outside, leaning forward against the doorframe spinning a pair of silver and blue sunglasses in circles between his forefinger and thumb. He looks at Andrés, then sees Coco, and the pencil-thin attempt at a mustache sitting gingerly on his upper lip curls upwards into a smile.

"Hola Coco," he says, stepping inside and slapping Andrés on the back.

When Coco met him, one of the first things Guzano told him was that he would happily murder his own mother if it came with a paycheck. "I love that gordita, but she ain't paying my bills," he said, and Andrés laughed. He has hated him ever since.

"What are you doing here?" he asks Guzano, who pulls a toothpick from behind his ear and slips it into the corner of his lip.

"Good to see you too, mi amor," he responds, puckering his lips and blowing Coco a kiss.

"He's my insurance policy," Andrés clarifies, "just in case you decide to go off and do something stupid. Put your jacket on; we're leaving."

"Where are we going?"

"I told you, we're being proactive. Pablo upped the purse this week for dropped uniforms so..."

"We're going to go shoot some hijueputa policia and make some money, marica," Guzano spits. "You like money, don't you?"

Coco ignores him. "It's four o'clock in the afternoon," he says to Andrés.

"Este marica," Guzano mutters. "Vamos, Andrés. We don't need him anyway."

"You heard the man, Andrés," Coco says, lifting the bottle to his lips. "You don't need me now you got your boyfriend here."

Guzano balls his fist and steps at Coco before looking at Andrés, who shakes his head.

Coco spins in his seat, turning his back to both of them. Andrés sniffs and swipes the back of his forefinger under his nose, then crosses the room to the kitchen and takes Coco's beer bottle by the neck. He lifts it above his head and brings it crashing down onto the counter.

"Listen to me," he says, pointing what's left of the shattered bottle inches from Coco's forehead. "I only brought you into this shit because I thought you were serious about two things: getting shit done and making money. So if you're not, then get out. See how far you make it before it's your picture in my pocket with dollar signs underneath it."

Coco squints at the bottle in his face and swallows.

"Otherwise," he continues, "get up and let's go."

Coco looks back and forth from the bottle to the door, weighing his options. Eighteen months ago, he would have considered the bottle in Andrés's hand an empty threat. That was then, this is now. And while Andrés himself is evidence that a broken bottle won't kill you, Coco decides he'd rather live with whatever emotional scarring will accompany their afternoon plans then have his face match Andrés's.

"Fine then," he says, stooping down to pick up his coat. "Lead the way."

He follows them outside, where they pile onto the back of Guzano's motorcycle with Coco in the middle. Guzano kickstarts the bike and rides away from the house, zigzagging his way through the eastern hills of Medellín past groups of kids playing soccer in the street and mothers hanging laundry out to dry or beating hanging rugs with the end of a broomstick. They zip past bakeries, convenience stores, parks, and churches before they find what they're looking for.

On the corner, two blocks in front of them, laughing and kicking a crushed can back and forth between them, stand three men in coffee-colored uniforms.

"About time I won the lottery," Guzano shouts over his shoulder.

Andrés laughs. Coco swallows the spit in his mouth and silently hopes the level of drunkenness he achieved this afternoon will be enough to forget whatever is about to happen. He considers jumping off the side of the bike and making a break for it but knows that even if he manages to avoid a hospital visit from the fall, he'll likely end up there anyway with a pair of bullets in his back, one from Andrés's new best friend and one from Andrés himself, so he decides against it.

Guzano pulls to a stop in front of the cops and flashes a friendly smile, the toothpick in his mouth poking out to one side. Andrés wastes no time on pleasantries, immediately pulling his pistol off his back and pulling the trigger four times. He shoots the first cop in the throat and the second in the cheek, sending a million minuscule drops of blood and bits of splintered bone showering onto the asphalt behind them. He turns to the third and shoots him in the arm before he can get his rifle off his back. The officer drops and clutches at the bloody tear in his uniform. Andrés shifts his aim from the man's arm to his leg and puts a second round in his kneecap.

"Let's get out of here," Coco shouts, nudging Guzano in the side.

"Not yet," Andrés says to him. "Get off the bike."

"What?"

"Get off," he repeats, singeing the fabric on Coco's jacket by pressing the tip of the hot gun into his back. "Now."

Andrés steps off the bike onto the sidewalk and pulls Coco off by the arm. Guzano drops the kickstand, swings his leg around, and pulls a gun from his waistband, pointing it at the face of the last officer, bleeding silently on the ground. Andrés spins Coco around so he's facing the man on the ground and pulls the pistol from his belt. He shoves it into Coco's stomach.

"Shoot him," he says.

Coco's hand closes around the pistol grip, and he looks at Andrés with crooked eyes.

"C'mon, Andrés, I ca–"

"Shoot him."

"I–I...Why don't you have Guz shoot him? You guys split the cash between the two of you. Forget I was even here," he suggests, raising his hands above his head.

The street is silent save for the accelerated pound in his chest.

"Shoot him," Andrés repeats, "or I'll shoot you." He raises his gun and points it at Coco the same way he had the broken bottle at home.

Coco hears the sound of sirens in the distance growing louder and wonders how much time he would have to buy before Andrés decides to finish the job and get out of there. Only he isn't sure if finishing the job in that scenario would mean one more bullet, or two.

He takes the gun from Andrés's hand. The cop grimaces and looks up. The blacks of his eyes expand and form a mirror, enveloping Coco in his own reflection. He sees the gun in his hand and the hatred in his gaze. The pounding in his chest stops, replaced by a calmer *thump thump thump*.

He inhales slowly, exhales sharply, and pulls the trigger.

BANG!

———

BANG!

"Put. Me. Down," Sofia warns.

"Sorry, sorry, sorry!" Santi says, trying not to laugh at the fact that he just ran his newly pronounced wife's head into the side of the doorframe. "I've never done this before, obviously, only seen it in movies," he says, contorting his body in a new direction and carrying her across the threshold, kicking the door shut behind them. "It's supposed to be good luck, I think."

"You better hope so because that's the only way you're getting lucky tonight," she responds, rubbing the emerging knot on the back of her head with her palm. "Now will you put me down?"

"Never!" he answers, running through the kitchen and into the bedroom with her still in his arms.

He drops her onto their bed and throws himself on top of her. Her ensuing giggles are infectious, exploding their way between every crack in his soul and forcing a smile to his lips he's sure will never straighten. He wraps both arms under her back and flips her on top of him.

"Wait, wait, wait," he says as she begins tugging at the buttons on his shirt.

"Really?"

"Just one minute," he says, pushing her onto the pillows and holding up one finger. "I have to do something first."

He stands up at the foot of the bed and digs a hand in his back pocket, from which he pulls a neatly folded sheet of paper.

"If you're working on our wedding day, I might have to murder you," she says, crossing both arms over her chest.

He grins and finishes unfolding the note in his hands.

"Sofia," he reads, clearing his throat before going on. "The first moment I saw you, I thought you were beautiful. The first time we spoke, I thought you were indescribable. The first night we kissed, I thought you were brave. The first morning I woke up next to you, I thought you were radiant. Now, as I write this, on the day before we sign our marriage papers in some dirty downtown notaría in front of a couple of strangers, I realize that all the while I was thinking those things of you, there was one thing I knew. I knew you were everything. Everything I want, everything I need, and everything that, until I met you, I never thought would be possible to find in a person."

He glances up from the paper and sees her biting at her

bottom lip. He folds the paper, returns it to his pocket, and continues, "There are a million promises I could make to you today and a thousand ways of saying each of them. Instead, I'll make one and hope it's enough. I promise to love you. For the rest of forever, I promise to love you."

"Santi," she says, her voice unsteady.

He kneels on the bed and crawls towards her, and she opens her arms to him.

"Te amo," he says, pressing his forehead to hers.

"Y yo a ti," she whispers back.

They're simple words, but then again, love itself is a pretty simple thing once you're in it. It's finding and losing it that gets complicated. Especially when that loss comes as unexpectedly and as harshly as it will for Santi and Sofia.

Because perfect love stories don't exist.

Everybody knows that.

———

"Tell me something beautiful."

Those are the words Luz said to Javier anytime the silence between them stretched too long, to which he would respond with more silence while his brain dizzied itself putting together a string of words beautiful enough for her. Usually, what came out was a simple phrase related to love or life or family or earth, but on occasion, it would be about heartache or loss or longing for the impossible. Because beauty and happiness aren't always synonymous, something they both understood and tried to appreciate.

If he had known exactly how their story was to end up, he might have spent less time picking his words and more time using them. On the other hand, he might have spent even more time picking them to ensure not a single one got wasted. Either way, he would have held her closer and whispered them quieter so she knew that every word belonged to her and her alone.

"Tell me something beautiful," she said to him immediately

after the accident, blood seeping through her clothes, and he paused, tears spilling down his cheeks.

"You," he told her. "You are my something beautiful."

He glances at the blank chalkboard on the wall outside the shop, silently reminiscing on the day he found it. It was the only thing that was left behind by the previous owner of the apartment he now calls home. He found it shoved inside a cupboard in the kitchen. It looked like it had never been used, perhaps not even touched. He took it out of the cupboard and immediately threw it in the trash before a voice made him pull it back out.

"Tell me something beautiful."

The morning of Luz's accident may have been the last time she ever said those words aloud, but he still hears them every morning, and every morning he pauses until he finds words beautiful enough for her. When he does, he scribbles them onto the chalkboard and hangs it outside the shop, where he hopes she'll stop by to read them.

Today, the board is blank. Today his words all stuck together.

The broom passes back and forth on the sidewalk as he stares at the blank chalkboard on the wall, his brain in knots from its many attempts to pull apart the words all clumped inside his head. He turns away in resignation and looks up at the sky. That's when it hits him.

He leans the broom against the wall and grabs the board. He carries it inside, scribbles a few short words, and takes it back out where he slides the loop of twine back over the nail in the wall and reaches again for the broom. He rests his chin on his interlocked hands atop the stick and rereads what he's just written.

"Love is too beautiful a thing not to be celebrated at every opportunity."

PART FIVE

ACCEPTANCE

CHAPTER 21

OCTOBER 1988

IF THE LIGHT inside you dies, darkness has no choice but to take its place, slithering from the shadows to stand center stage and present a self-composed arrangement of misery, pride, and denial, reaching out at the climax and stealing the color from behind your eyes. When the light inside of Coco died, it was no different.

If Coco were anybody else, or if today were any other day, the drive might be relaxing. Twisting roads wind their way through the mountains in front of him like a snake carving a path through tall grass. A thin layer of fog hovers inches off the road, rising steadily with the sun. The air outside his open window runs erratically in all directions threatening to extinguish the cigarette dangling from his fingertips. He turns his wrist over on the steering wheels and checks his watch, then gives Andrés a nod. Andrés looks to his right and does the same to the driver of the mud-caked Jeep parked beside them.

Both cars pull away from the secluded ranch house they've been parked in front of since the earliest hours of the morning and accelerate down the corkscrewing dirt road in front of them until it merges with the highway. Coco leans into each curve as it comes, one hand lightly gripping the steering wheel, the other resting on the gear shift. He looks up and finds the Jeep in his rearview mirror to ensure they're following at the right distance, then shifts his eyes back to the road just as a pair of tail lights belonging to a white Mercedes sedan appear around a bend.

He pushes in the clutch and shifts gears, pressing harder on the accelerator as he lifts his left foot off the pedal. He uses the extra power to pull to within a few feet of the Mercedes driving ahead of him. A grin creeps across his lips.

One year ago, he stood on a street corner and watched blood pour from a dime-sized hole in a man's forehead. He watched him tip over backward before lowering his gun, lighter now that it was missing a bullet, and took a few shortened breaths, his chest heaving.

"How's it feel?" Andrés asked.

"Powerful," he answered.

Andrés laughed and slapped him on the back. "My boy," he said. "Plenty more where that came from, I guarantee you that."

Then they climbed on his motorcycle, Coco, Andrés, and Guz, and rode home. As if nothing even happened.

Coco wipes the grin off his face and pushes the accelerator the rest of the way to the floor. His eyes are dark as he maneuvers the car into the left lane and pulls even with the white sedan. He gives the driver of the Mercedes two seconds to realize what's happening before he throws the wheel to the right, sending the other car crashing into the steel barricade lining the highway where it skids to a stop, the front right wheel snapped clean from its axle.

He punches the brake and jumps from the car before Andrés has time to open his door. He pulls a mini Uzi off his hip and sprays the doors of the totaled car with bullets, sending shattered glass and shards of metal shooting off in all directions. The driver's head falls against the steering wheel, his face rendered unrecognizable in an instant by a slew of bullets ripping through cartilage and bone, like an eager toddler unwrapping a Christmas present. A second man unwisely opens the back door and he shoots him twice in the chest.

Moments later, the Jeep pulls behind the Mercedes, and a group of four men pile out onto the street, led by Guz, who slips from the passenger seat and approaches the sedan, a toothpick sticking out of one corner of his smiling face.

"What's the move?" he shouts at Coco.

"Grab him and let's get the hell out of here," he yells back, signaling to the backseat of the Mercedes.

Guz nods, then turns to the three men standing behind him and gestures with his head towards the crashed car. "You heard the man," he says. "Go get him."

Two men rush to the opposite side of the car and pull out the final passenger from behind the passenger seat. His head hangs limp, and a steady stream of thick, dark blood oozes from his shoulder. Together they drag him towards the lead car and throw him inside, sitting him up in the backseat.

"You," Andrés says, pointing at the one closest to him, "put these on him." He tosses him a pair of handcuffs and a burlap sack, and the man does as he's instructed, shutting the door when he's finished and jogging back to the Jeep.

Andrés nods to Coco who whistles and spins a finger in the air. "Time to leave," he says.

The men obediently pile back inside the Jeep and Guz does the same. Coco and Andrés take their seats in the lead car where Coco throws it in gear and whips around to head back in the direction they came. Andrés bounces in the passenger seat, laughter bubbling up from his gut. Coco's eyes are steady on the road ahead of them, both hands on the wheel.

The man in the backseat with the burlap sack over his head makes a whimpering noise and Coco jerks the steering wheel to the left, slamming his head against the window.

"Cállate," he says, with a wink to Andrés, "hijueputa."

———

"I'm not mad. Do I look mad?" Sofia asks, struggling to tie her apron behind her bulging belly that, in recent days, seems to her to be growing larger by the minute. The bodega door hangs halfway open, and her customers have begun lining up on the other side.

"I'm not even going to answer that," Santi responds, untying his tie to tie it again. "Why didn't you tell me this was way too short?"

"I did," she snaps. "Twice, actually, before we left the house." She slips the apron off her head and crumples it into a ball. "Piece of shit," she spits at it before throwing it into the corner. "Look," she says, turning back to him, "all I'm asking is for you to tell me *why*. That's it. That's all I want."

"And I've told you already," he says, straightening his collar and picking his coat up off the slicing table, "it just doesn't make sense so early in my career to be turning down opportunities like this." He slides both arms in his sleeves and throws them forward, pulling his jacket up onto his shoulders. "Besides, you'll love living in Medellín. The weather is amazing; the people are friendly. Even the fruit tastes better." He picks up a pineapple from a neat stack on the table in front of him and waves it at her as if to further illustrate his point.

"And I've told *you* already that that isn't the real reason. We both know that," she chirps back, plucking the pineapple from his hand and slapping it down on the table. She picks up her machete and points it at his nose. "You've already been promoted three times in two years; this is far from the last opportunity you'll get to move up. The real reason is that you want to move home, and you think your work is more important than mine."

"No seas tonta, amor," he says, both hands in the air. "Of course, I like the idea of being closer to my family, but that's like *this much* of why this job makes so much sense." He holds his forefinger and thumb towards her and pinches them close together. "If we weren't having a baby, I might not even suggest it, but how are you expecting to keep the shop open with a newborn?"

She opens her mouth to respond, but he cuts her off and keeps going.

"Plus, the timing really couldn't be any better. They told me they'd give me six months before the transfer is official, which means we have plenty of time to find a buyer for this place *and* figure out this parenting thing a little bit before we move."

She twists the machete in her hand, her eyes on her husband, then raises it and brings it down across the top of the pineapple, dropping its head to the floor.

"This *place* is my *home*," she says.

"And I understand that, but sometimes good things have to end to make room for even better ones. I'm doing what's best for us as a family. What's going to allow us to be together the most, in the long run," he says, picking the pineapple head up and slipping it into an empty trash bag he then clips to the side of the table.

"If it's about being together, why not quit your job and come work here with me? That way, we'll be together every day," she says, chopping a second pineapple on the table and tossing the severed head over the trash bag and onto the floor.

"And lose all of my income? Now how does that make any sense?"

"What about my income? Last time I checked, all those people out there are lined up to give me money, not rob me blind. But I guess that doesn't matter?"

"No. I mean, yes. Yes, of course, it matters," he stammers, "but it's different, okay? I love this place too. It's where we met. It's where I fell in love with you. But it just doesn't make sense to keep it if it means derailing my career." He bends down again and picks up the fallen pineapple head, flipping it around in his hand before dropping it in the trash. "Our life is changing, Sofia, and like it or not, we have to change with it."

A tear squeezes its way into her field of vision and he sees her blink it away, something he's noticed happening more and more often in recent months.

"I just want to do what's best for our family," he repeats, his hands falling to his sides.

She takes a deep breath and steps closer to him, raising a hand to his cheek. "And *I* just want to get it through this thick skull of yours that what's best for our family will never be more money or a fancier job title," she says. "What's best for our family is you. You're all I need. All we need." She takes his hand in hers and presses it to her stomach.

He looks at her eyes and squeezes her hand and swallows the words he knows he ought to say.

"Amor," he says instead, "I'm taking the job. I know you think that's wrong, but someday I hope you'll understand why I did it." He drops her hand and bends down to collect his briefcase. "I'll line up some potential buyers for the shop over the next few weeks," he says, sliding the bodega door the rest of the way up to leave. "Te amo."

"Y yo a ti," she says, her voice a whisper.

The walk between the bodega and his office is longer than usual. When he arrives at his building, he takes the elevator up, goes straight to his boss's open door, and knocks.

"Santi!" his boss says, spinning in his chair to face him, "Have you had time to consider my offer?"

"Yes, sir," Santi says. "I'll take it."

CHAPTER 22

OCTOBER 1988

As a parent, nothing makes you feel safer than knowing your children are okay. At the same time, nothing scares you more than thinking they may not be.

When she was young, nothing scared Abuela. Not spiders or heights or bullies or the dark. Not even death. At least not before she laid eyes on those ten impossibly small fingers and one scrunched-up nose that too closely resembled her own. That was when she learned just how frightening death could be. Holding María in her arms instantly shortened her breath and put a pound in her heart she never quite learned how to control, because she knew as well as anyone that the world is an incredibly cruel place, and this child had no choice but to trust that she would protect her from it. From all of it. And what would happen if she couldn't?

On the day Santiago was born, the doctors escorted her from the delivery room without answering the only question she had. The one she repeated louder and louder the further they dragged her down the hall, and that she continued to shout from the waiting room chair they sat her down in—the question whose answer scared her more than anything else in the world.

Is she okay?

Abuela woke up this morning with a smile on her face. She smiled making breakfast, smiled listening to the news on the radio, and even smiled when she went downstairs and found Javier once again sweeping dangerously close to her front door.

She smiled bigger when her phone rang and bigger again when her grandson held the receiver against his wife's belly, giving her the chance to share a few secrets with her great-grandbaby.

Her smile lasted all day, but behind it lurked the same feeling of fear as the day she left the hospital all those years ago with two new sons but without a daughter. When she got home that day, she laid a sleeping newborn on a mattress on the floor and knelt in front of a two-year-old boy, tasked with the impossible responsibility of explaining to him that his mother, the person he trusted to always come back, was gone. As she spoke, she saw his eyes dim and watched as he struggled to comprehend why his entire world just got darker.

Abuela woke up this morning with a smile on her face that lasted all day, but behind it lurked a question. The same question she asked herself of that two-year-old little boy with tears on his cheeks and two tiny fists clenched in fury at the universe. The one that kept her from sleeping on countless nights as she waited for him to come home.

Is he okay?

She doesn't need to see him to know the answer, and as a parent, nothing could scare her more.

CHAPTER 23

CHRISTMAS EVE 1988

IT'S CHRISTMAS EVE AGAIN, the day lonely people feel the loneliest. Javier sweeps the ground outside Abuela's front door, the rhythmic swishes of the broom synchronized with an incessant tap on his chest. The door opens and Abuela steps outside, pulling her coat tighter around her and tucking it under her chin before she sees him.

"Buenos dias, Doña Rosa," he says to her with a curt bow.

"Javier," she responds, stepping past him and inside the store where the wind can't reach her. She takes her usual items from the shelves and stacks them inside her basket along with a few others.

"Expecting company?" he asks, following her inside the store and leaning the broom in the corner.

"I am, although I'm not sure how much confidence I can place in that answer," she responds as she carries her basket to the front and places it on the counter. "Santi told me weeks ago he would be here, but with how that boss he has controls his life, I don't think I'll fully believe him until I hear the knock at the door."

She raises her eyes and rests her hands on the countertop. Javier watches her without responding.

"He'll come," he says finally. He stretches his fingers towards

167

hers but can't quite bring himself to close the gap between them, as if each fingertip were a magnet flipped the wrong direction. Instead, he raps his knuckles on the counter and says, "And what about Don Sebastián?"

"Coco? Who knows. At least Santi has the sense to call once in a while, even if it is less than he ought to. Coco hasn't called or been home in years, you know that."

"Of course of course of course," he apologizes. "I take it you still don't know where he is or what he's up to then?"

"Santi told me a year or so ago he saw him and Andrés in Bogotá. They went to visit him on their way to a job of some sorts. Knowing Andrés, that tells me all I need to know about what Coco is up to."

"Andrés is a good boy. He got dealt a crooked hand is all."

"That's one way to look at it," she responds with a curt laugh. "I'm sorry. I should speak more kindly, I know he's been like a son to you ever since... well, ever since his mother and father separated."

"No need to apologize," he says with a wave of his hand. "Even I know Andrés has a certain undeniable knack for finding trouble."

He watches Abuela drop her gaze to the counter and immediately regrets having a voice.

"Head up, Doña Rosa," he says, "I'm sure he and Sebastián are just fine. Plus, Santi comes home tonight, remember?"

"We'll see," she says, and raises her head.

"He'll be here. And if he isn't, you know where to find me."

"Of course," she responds with a quick smile. She lifts one hand and puts it on top of the basket. "Any chance these are on the house today?"

"Of course, of course, of course," he blurts out, gesturing with his arms towards the shelves behind her as if begging her to rob him of whatever she'd like.

"Maybe next time," she winks. She pulls a few bills from the breast pocket of her coat and drops them on the counter, then picks up the basket and hooks it inside her elbow.

Javier watches her go and feels a pinch in her chest when he hears the door shut.

It's Christmas Eve, the day lonely people feel their loneliness, and for the first time in a very, very long time, he has hope he might not be one of them.

———

Sofia closes her eyes and shifts her weight, looking for a comfortable position that doesn't exist. She hates driving in general, but being eight months pregnant and seven hours and five pee breaks into a ross-country road trip has increased that hatred to a much more dangerous level.

It was Santi's idea to spend Christmas in Medellín. He suggested it months ago, right after Sofia learned she was pregnant, and she agreed. At the time, she was excited about the chance to finally meet Abuela and see the place where he grew up. She's less excited now, because at this point she has no way of knowing whether he suggested the trip as a fun getaway and opportunity to meet his family, or because he was anticipating a job transfer and saw this as a headstart at convincing her to get on board. That paired with the fact that the entire country is being quietly controlled from above by a druglord puppeteer, and she almost wishes she had gone into labor two months early so she could've had a reasonable excuse to stay home.

The car passes over an exceptionally large pothole, and the car shakes violently, causing Sofia to shut her eyes tighter and flex her fingers resting on top of her belly button.

Yesterday was her last day at the fruit stand. She hasn't told Santi that yet. The day before last, he told her that he had a handful of interested parties coming by to "take a look and make sure things are up to scratch before they make any kind of offer." As soon as he told her that, she decided that yesterday would be her last day. That way instead of chasing away each greedy businessman with her machete as they arrived, she could simply lock the door and refuse to turn over the key.

"Amor," Santi says, reaching across and shaking her leg gently for her to open her eyes.

On the side of the road ahead of them, a group of men controls the flow of traffic passing in either direction, all in their early twenties with an assortment of firearms tucked into their jeans or slung across their chests.

"It's nothing to worry about," he says, his hand still on her leg. "I'll take care of it."

He stops the car at the signal of a skinny, patchy-bearded teenager with a toothpick in his mouth. Sofia catches sight of the pistol grip hanging over the edge of his belt, and immediately each breath she takes grows shorter and harsher.

Santi rolls his window down and nods at the young man standing inches from the side of the car.

"Get out," the man says.

Santi swallows and unbuckles his seatbelt. He looks at her and gives her a warm smile of reassurance, then opens the door and steps onto the street.

"Her too," the man nods.

"She's pregnant; does she have t–"

"You think I give a shit?" he spits. He squats down and eyes Sofia through the open door, pulling the toothpick from his mouth and sliding it behind his ear. "You. Get out."

Her fingers fumble to grasp the door handle, and she pushes it open and climbs out, walking around the hood of the car to stand beside Santi. The man looks her up and down with a smile on the left half of his mouth, then reaches his hand inside the car and removes the keys from the ignition. He uses them to pop open the trunk, rifling through the bags inside, and returns to where Santi and Sofia are waiting. He pulls the toothpick from behind his ear and snaps it between his fingers, flicking it to the ground.

"A que vas a Medellín?" he asks.

"Visiting family," Santi responds, straight-faced. "I grew up here, in Villa Hermosa."

The man nods slowly before responding. "Welcome home," he says. He tosses the car keys back to Santi and spins on his heel to walk away.

Santi and Sofia climb back into their seats, and he takes her hand as they drive away.

"Are you okay?" he asks her.

"With you," she grips his hand tight, "always."

Growing up, Christmas was the most magical twenty-four hours of the year. Abuela made natilla and buñuelos every Christmas Eve morning and the boys helped by throwing ingredients at each other until one of them missed on purpose and hit her instead. Then she would kick them out of the house with strict instructions not to come back until they had learned to keep their hands to themselves and their heads out of their asses. Every year they nodded and left, each attempting to push the other down the stairs on their way out, then ran to the soccer court up the hill, grateful to have it all to themselves. They spent hours switching off taking shots on goal until their shirts were dark with sweat and their feet were swollen and aching, at which point Coco would tuck the ball under his left arm, put his right arm around Santi's shoulders, and list off all the evidence as to why he would always be the better soccer player.

Christmas Eve night, Abuela would read stories until both boys fell asleep, only to wake them up a couple of hours later at midnight to see what El Niño Jesús had brought for them. It was never anything spectacular–some secondhand clothes, a few pieces of chocolate, or a toy or two–but they loved and appreciated it anyway. It was a day they looked forward to all year. A simple, quiet party for three.

This is not that.

Coco smiles and pulls a shot glass from a tray carried by a woman with braided purple hair wearing nothing but a shimmering silver bikini bottom. He leans against the fence in the center of the immense courtyard and watches a pair of show horses trot in dizzying circles, directed by the men seated in the saddles wearing fresh-pressed uniforms and carrying short whips tucked under their arms.

On the patio surrounding the horse arena, dozens of men, each drunker than the next, laugh at crude jokes and pass an assortment of drugs between them and the half-naked women sitting on their laps.

Feliz Navidad, Coco thinks before tossing the shot in his hand into the back of his throat. He winces and sets the glass down on a cocktail table next to him.

"Can you believe this place?" Andrés asks, approaching from behind and smacking him on the back with a stack of bills. "I just won a thousand lucas betting whether or not some drunk bastard could jump over a stack of four chairs."

"And?"

"And he's either on his way to the hospital, or they just carried him inside and left him there so they could keep partying. Either way," he laughs and flips the stack of cash in Coco's face. "Oye," he says to a woman walking past them with a tray of drinks. He swipes one from her and downs its contents in a single motion, replacing the glass to the tray, then grabs her by the arm and waves his winnings at her. "This is all yours if you give me fifteen minutes."

"Maybe next year, sweetheart," she winks, pulling a bill from the pile and tucking it into her top. "Thanks for the tip, though," she says, kissing him on the cheek before walking away.

"Damn," he whispers, his fingertips pressed to the place where her lips were, "I thought she was the one."

Coco laughs.

"Then again, maybe it's that one," he points at a woman across the arena from them. "Hey!" he shouts and starts to march towards her, stopping when everyone around him stands and applauds in his direction. Andrés looks around him, wondering what he's done to deserve such praise, and discovers that they aren't clapping for him but the person standing behind him.

Pablo Escobar.

"Holy shit," Andrés whispers, the words falling from his mouth before he can stop them.

Coco does a better job of composing himself and nods at Pablo and the entourage of men around him as he approaches. "Don Pablo," he says, "a pleasure to finally meet you." He smacks Andrés on the shoulder, spurring him back to his senses.

"Patrón," Andrés says, his voice at least two octaves deeper than normal, "it is an honor." He starts to bow but stops himself midway down when he realizes the stupidity of the act, resulting in his standing with his head awkwardly close to Pablo's chest and his eyes strained upwards to look him in the face.

Pablo sidesteps him and holds a hand out towards Coco. "Coco, right?"

"Sí, Patrón," Coco responds.

"Andrés Merlano, Don Pablo, again, such an honor to meet you." Andrés sticks his hand out towards Pablo, who ignores it.

"You led the Hoyos job back in October, cierto?" Pablo asks Coco.

"That's right, Don Pablo, we–" Andrés starts, but Pablo holds a hand up to stop him.

"Sí, Patrón," Coco says. "That was me."

Andrés glares at him.

"That was clean work," he replies. "Well done." He turns and nods to his men behind him and starts to walk away, but after just two steps he turns back around. "I'm having a meeting next week to discuss the state of the business. Join us."

"Sí, Patrón."

"Bien," Pablo nods. He raises both arms to the house's grounds around them. "Welcome to the family," he says, then excuses himself silently.

Andrés watches him leave, a scowl growing across his face, before shoving Coco in the chest. "What the hell's wrong with you, huh?"

"What are you talking about?" Coco answers.

"I'm *talking* about you telling the boss it was *you* who led the Hoyos job."

"I did lead the Hoyos job," Coco says coolly.

"*We* led that job! Both of us!" Andrés shouts. "Shit, Coco." He shakes his head and kicks a fallen glass against the wall behind them, shattering it. "At least he gave us both the nod to come to that meeting next week. Otherwise I could fucking kill you."

"Good thing," Coco says to avoid the argument of correcting him. He knows Andrés will end up coming with him to that meeting regardless. Plus, his mind is still stuck on the last word Pablo spoke before he left. *Family*. It reminded him of the first time he met him, seven years ago. Only that time, instead of "Welcome to the family" it had been "La familia va primero."

Family comes first.

No matter what.

CHAPTER 24

CHRISTMAS EVE 1940 - CHRISTMAS EVE 1988

"MERRY CHRISTMAS, JAVIER," Luz whispers in his ear, plopping herself onto the bed beside him, the morning sun dripping in through the cracks in the window curtains and lining the floor with light.

"Mmmm," Javier hums, rolling to his side and draping an arm across her waist. "Merry Christmas, amor."

"Aren't you going to open your present?"

"Give me a few minutes to wake up, and I promise I'll open my present all day long," he responds, his fingers wandering confidently along the curvatures of her bare skin.

"Not the present I was talking about," she laughs, slapping at his fingers before they can reach their destination, "although I like where your head's at." She pulls his hand from her back and places a perfectly wrapped gift in his open palm. "Here. I hope you like it," she says, leaning in and kissing him on the cheek.

She hops up from the bed and dances to the opposite side of the room, where she pulls a red dress out of a weathered leather bag on the floor and slips it over her head, tying it behind her back.

Javier opens his eyes, sees the gift in his hand, and tilts his head. "When did you even find time to buy this?" he asks.

"Stores are open late here," she replies, "and you're a heavy sleeper." She crosses back to the bed and sits down next to him. "Now open it."

"You're sure there's not something you'd rather I unwrap first?" he asks, snaking a hand around her back and tugging at the string to her dress.

"Javier," she warns, "open it."

"Whatever you say," he says, both hands raised in surrender. He rips away the paper, throwing the scraps to one side, and is left holding a tan leather wallet with a phrase stamped onto the front cover. "Family is forever," he reads aloud, flipping it open and thumbing through the empty photo sleeves inside.

"Do you like it?" she asks, biting at her thumb. "If you hate it, you can throw it away. I won't be offended."

"Hate it? I could never hate anything that comes from you," he says. She looks at him, unconvinced. "But this? This I love. Really."

"And what about the words on the front?"

"I love them too."

"Oh good," she breathes. "I went back and forth a few times with a handful of different options, then I decided to scrap them all together until the photo holders got to me because I started thinking about all the different adventures we could fill them with, and then I thought, 'Pictures aren't for places, they're for people', and what better people to fill them than our family, you know? You, me, our kids."

"Our kids?" he interjects.

"Oh," she blushes, "shit, I've said too much. Why do you always let me ramble like that?"

"Because it's adorable."

She slaps him on the arm, then leans in for a kiss. "But," she says, "you do want kids, don't you?"

He puts a finger beneath his lip and looks up at the ceiling. "Let me think," he says, tapping his chin. "Do I want to have kids with the most gorgeous woman in the world? You know what? I think I do."

She laughs and sighs at the same time.

"You're not..." he starts, shooting her an insinuating look.

"Not what?"

"Pregnant. Like right now, you're not, right?"

"What? No, of course not. Although someday, maybe."

"Not maybe," he corrects. "Definitely."

"Really?"

"Really," he answers. "More of you to love, less of me for you to focus on."

"Don't be stupid," she quips.

"You know," he says, lifting a finger in the air, "if we're serious about this whole kids thing, we probably ought to get some practice in."

"I have no idea what you mean by that," she grins.

"Oh really?"

"Really," she says, leaning in. Then, just before their lips collide, "Javier, tell me something beautiful."

He pauses to look her in the eye. "To live a life alone is not to live at all, but to endure. To live you must first love, and who better to love than you?"

Luz smiles bigger with each word he speaks.

"Merry Christmas, Luz," he whispers.

"Merry Christmas, Javier."

———

"Are you ready for this?" Santi asks as the car rolls to a stop in front of the familiar old chalkboard on the wall. He yanks on the parking brake as he pulls the key from the ignition.

"The way you keep talking makes me feel like I'm on my way to meet the Pope or be interrogated by the police," Sofia responds, clicking off her seatbelt and opening the car door.

He laughs and steps out onto the street, jogging around the

trunk to help her. "Closer to the latter than the former, I'm afraid," he says. "But you're right. Nothing to worry about. She's going to love you. Here." He offers her his hand.

"I don't need help," she says, taking his wrist with a white-knuckled grip and pulling herself to her feet. "Are all cars this damn low to the ground?" she asks. She leans back, pushing her belly out towards the house in front of them. "That's beautiful," she points at the chalkboard. "Who do you think wrote it?"

Santi turns to read the phrase scribbled on it. *Christmas is about the who, not the what*, it says.

"That'll be Javier," he answers. The door to the shop is pulled shut and he wonders if Abuela has finally invited him for Christmas Eve dinner. Why else would he close the store?

"Who's Javier?" Sofia asks.

"He's..." Santi starts, then pauses. "He's some combination of good friend and father figure. Or, grandfather figure."

She gives him a questioning look.

"Because he's old," Santi clarifies.

"Ah," she laughs, "I see. Will I get to meet him?"

"I hope so," he says, escorting her past the board and pulling open the door leading upstairs. "I'll come back for the bags in a bit. After you." He gestures to the staircase, and she nods and starts her ascent, one labored breath at a time. He follows close behind, his hand hovering an inch or two behind her lower back in case she stumbles.

They reach the second-floor landing, and Sofia puts both hands on her hips, her breath heavy. "Are you... ready... for this?" she asks between inhales.

"With you," he smiles at her, "I'm ready for anything."

Then he raises his fist and knocks on the door.

———

Tap, tap, tap, tap.

Abuela looks at the stack of empty plates on the table and

pretends not to feel the gentle drip of loneliness drilling into her heart.

"He'll be here," she whispers.

Tap, tap, tap, tap.

She shifts her weight in the chair to keep the ever-present aches of old age from sending bolts of discomfort down both legs and out through her toes. The clock in the boys' bedroom beeps once, signaling 10 o'clock, and she contemplates going to bed rather than waiting up for more disappointment to arrive.

He'll be here.

Tap, tap, tap, tap.

Piles of food stare at her from the kitchen counter, but she ignores them. She should eat. She knows that. But she isn't hungry, hasn't been in days. Weeks, maybe.

Knock, knock, knock, knock.

Abuela puts a hand to her chest when she hears it, the persistent tapping immediately replaced by a steady *thump, thump, thump* as she stares at the door. Classic Santi, showing up late but doing it with a smile on his face so big it makes you forget how to tell time.

She stands up and moves quietly across the room, afraid her shuffling footsteps might scare away whoever is out there. She reaches the door and places the palm of one hand on the cold metal surface.

Knock, knock, knock, knock.

"Knock again and you'll lose a finger," she warns. She slides back the bolt lock, takes two deep breaths through her nose, and opens the door.

"Finally!" Coco says, stepping inside. "I'm sorry, but if that's how long it takes you to walk from the table to the door, I think it might be time to consider a wheelchair or euthanasia or something."

"Coco?" she says, tilting her head ever so slightly to the side, her jaw hanging open after she speaks. She steps towards him and holds his head in her hands. She looks him up and down, examining him as if she were a formerly blind woman seeing him clearly for the first time. "You're okay," she breathes.

"Course I'm okay, what did you think? That I ran off and got myself shot?" he says, kissing her on the top of the head before making a beeline for the kitchen. "Beautiful," he says, grabbing a spoon and diving into the overflowing dish of natilla, shoveling it into his mouth.

"There's Coca-Cola in the fridge," Abuela says, pointing. She gives the empty stairwell another glance, then closes the door.

Coco nods, his mouth too full to respond, and takes a beer from the fridge before plopping himself down in a chair.

"So," he exhales, flipping his feet onto the table, "miss me?"

"Not for one single second," she answers, smacking his sneakers back down to the floor where they belong.

"Me neither," he grins.

Knock, knock, knock, knock.

Coco stops mid-drink and cocks his head at the door. "Are you expecting someone?" he asks, wiping his mouth with the back of his hand and reaching behind his back, touching his fingertips to the outline of the pistol grip hidden beneath his coat.

"At this point," she says, "I'm not sure what to expect."

She pulls the door open and Santi immediately rushes inside to embrace her..

"Merry Christmas, Abuelita!" he exclaims.

By the time he lets her go, she's grinning from ear to ear.

"This is Sofia," Santi says, turning towards his wife standing on the landing outside and gesturing to her to come in.

"Hola Sofia," Abuela says, taking her hand and wrapping her in a bear hug. She kisses her lightly on the right cheek, then steps back and places a hand on her stomach. "Hola chiquito," she smiles.

"Feliz Navidad," Sofia says. "It's so great to finally see your face instead of just hearing your voice over the phone."

"Likewise," Abuela confirms.

"Wow," Sofia says, looking at the walls around her, "Santi has told me so many stories of this place it almost feels like I'm the one who grew up here."

"I'm sure they were all lies," Abuela says with a wave of her hand. "Or at the very least a bunch of sugarcoated bullshit to make me look better than I am. But that's Santi. I could stick a knife in his hip and he would somehow find a way to thank me for it."

Sofia laughs.

"Q'hubo hermanito," Coco says from his seat at the kitchen table. "You gonna introduce me or what?"

"Coco!" Santi says, looking back and forth from Abuela to his brother to Sofia as if he were walking into some elaborate surprise party they had all been in on. "What are you doing here?"

Coco takes a sip from the bottle in his hand and shrugs. "It'd been a while since I saw Abuela. Figured I ought to stop by and make sure she wasn't rotting on the floor or stuck on the toilet."

This time it's Santi who laughs and Abuela whose cheeks grow red.

"Grab me a drink, would ya?" Santi says, sliding Sofia's coat off her shoulders and hanging it on the hook by the door. He puts one arm around her and the other around Abuela and walks with them to the kitchen.

Coco stands up and takes a pair of bottles from inside the fridge, twisting off the caps and dropping them on the counter, and hands one to Santi and the other to Sofia. Abuela brings the plates of food from the counter to the table and sits down in the chair between her boys.

"So," she says, "considering you both left me here alone for the past seven years, whose ass should I kick first?"

They all laugh. Even her. The perfect transition into a night of complete and utter joy. A night of family.

The last one they'll ever get.

"Shit," Coco says, looking at the clock on the wall during a temporary lull in the conversation, "I gotta go. It's late." He stands up from his chair and kisses Abula on the top of her head.

"Where could you possibly have to be this late on Christmas Eve?" Santi asks.

"Can't answer that, little bro," he winks, ruffling Santi's hair with his hand as he walks past. "You're still too young."

Santi straightens his hair and stands up to say goodbye. "Pase lo que pase," he says, reaching out his hand.

"Pase lo que pase," Coco repeats back.

They slap hands and pull each other into a brief embrace.

"Sorry," Sofia says, "but what's that about?"

"That," Abuela smiles, "is how you say 'I love you' in brother."

"I thought this meant 'I love you' in brother?" Coco says, flicking Santi in the crotch with the back of his hand.

"Argh," Santi mutters and keels over with both hands on his abdomen while Sofia covers her mouth to keep from laughing, and Abuela slides off her sandal and proceeds to turn any part of Coco she can reach black and blue.

"Is that all you got?" Coco laughs, his hands covering his face. "You've lost a step."

Abuela stops the barrage and points her sandal at him. A smile tiptoes across her lips, then disappears.

"Before you go, hijo," she says, "I need to tell you something." She swallows, takes a deep breath in and out, and casts a glance over to Santi who gives her a nod of encouragement. She shifts her eyes back to Coco and continues, "I need to tell you that this is your home. It always was and it always will be, and I should never have thrown you out the way I did."

Coco raises an eyebrow and leans his head towards her. "And..." he says.

"And anytime you need a place to stay for a night or a year or forever, you can come home."

"And..."

She raises her shoe again. "And don't get smart with me or I'll be forced to smack it out of you."

Coco shakes his head. "Try again."

She sighs. "And I'm sorry."

Coco grins and embraces her. "I'm sorry too," he says. "Te quiero, Abuelita."

"I love you too," she responds. She hugs him back, her energy replenished to a level she had long ago deemed unattainable. When she finally lets him go, the sandal in her hand catches on something on his back, and she stops. "What is that?" she asks.

"What is what?" he says, taking a step back towards the door.

"On your back. What is that?"

"Nothing."

"Let me see it." She drops the sandal and holds out an empty palm.

Coco looks at her hand, then reaches behind him under his coat and pulls the gun from his waistband.

Her eyes narrow to slits the second she sees it, her smile pulled straight. "Why do you have that in my house?"

"If it helps, I can put it outside."

"Coco," she stops him. "I'm serious."

"Relax, okay? It's a safety precaution, that's all," he says, tucking the pistol back behind him.

"Are you in trouble?"

"No, I'm not in trouble. Why do you always assume I've done something wrong?"

"I didn't ask if you did something wrong; I asked if you were in trouble?"

"Isn't that the same thing?"

She doesn't answer.

"I'm not in trouble," he says, "*and* I didn't do anything wrong. The opposite, actually, I'm doing pretty well for myself. Can't share too many details, though. Pablo prefers we keep our mouths shut when it comes to work-related matters."

"You're working for Pablo Escobar?" she asks.

Coco pauses. "I am," he says, straightening his back. "Is that a problem?"

"Of course it's a problem, Coco, do you know what that man is capable of?"

"Funny, I don't remember you having a problem with him when he gave you all that cash a few years ago," he says.

"Don't be stupid."

"I'll do my best, but genetics are genetics," he shrugs.

Abuela's cheeks glow red hot, but she ignores him. "Have you used it?" she asks.

"What?"

"The gun. Have you used it?"

"Once or twice to light a cigarette," he jokes.

Abuela looks at him unamused.

Coco swallows. "Of course, I haven't used it," he says.

Abuela stares at him as she decides whether or not to believe him. "Good," she finally says. "If that ever changes, if you ever shoot someone, I'll kill you."

"You have to see the irony in that," Coco laughs.

"Do I?"

He bites his cheek and sniffs, scrunching his nose. "You're doing it again, you know," he tells her.

"Doing what?" she asks.

"Same thing you've always done: Tell me how to live my life because you think I'm doing it wrong.

Abuela's back stiffens and her shoulders curl backwards. "Well," she says, "maybe I wouldn't have to if you stopped making stupid choices and instead tried being a little more–"

"A little more what?" Coco cuts her off. "A little more like Santi?"

Santi perks up at the mention of his name, then does his best to shrink into his seat.

"I didn't say that," Abuela utters.

Coco shakes his head and laughs. "You didn't have to. You never have to," he says. "I can see it, right now, in your eyes."

Abuela blinks furiously, then she squares her feet and shifts her weight to her toes. "So maybe I do think that," she says, "but would it kill you to be a bit more like your brother? Look at him."

She points to Santi, still frozen in his chair.

"He's married, good job, starting a family," she goes on.

" I don't want any of that!" Coco says, his voice raised.

"Sometimes, Coco, life isn't about what you want. It's about what's best for you. What's going to keep you safe."

He shakes his head at the floor, then raises his head and looks her in the eye. "I don't need you to keep me safe."

Abuela looks back at him and opens mouth.

"Abuela," Santi cuts in. "Hear him out. Please?"

She looks at him and nods.

"I'm sorry I am not exactly who you think I should be," Coco continues "but I'm me. Life might take me a little longer to figure out than it did for Santi, but I'll get there. I'll be okay. I promise."

She looks at him, breathing slowly, her eyes glistening..

"Okay?" Coco asks.

"Okay."

He smiles. "Te quiero, Abuelita."

"Y yo a ti."

"Am I free to leave now, your honor?" he says with a bow.

"Where did you learn to be such a pain in the ass?" she answers.

"From the best," he says with a wink in Santi's direction. "Sofia," he says taking her hand, and kissing it gently, "pleasure meeting you. And if I didn't already mention it, kudos for being patient with my brother long enough to teach him how to make a baby. That can't have been easy."

"Shut up," Santi says, swinging a punch that Coco dodges.

"Still haven't learned any new moves, huh?" he says, backpedaling toward the door. "Hey, try not to bore her to death too quickly, okay? I like her."

Santi smiles and shakes his head.

Coco opens the door, but Santi grabs his arm before he steps out.

"Hey," he says. "Be careful, okay?."

Coco puts his hand on Santi's. "Don't worry, hermanito."

He steps onto the landing and closes the door behind him. Abuela inches closer to the door, listening to the sound of his footsteps until they disappear.

"Are you okay, Abuelita?" Santi asks behind her.

"Si, mijo," she answers. She wipes her eyes with her palm and turns around. "Siempre."

CHAPTER 25

CHRISTMAS EVE 1988

SANTI DROPS the suitcase next to the mattress on the floor and stoops down to smooth the nonexistent wrinkles from the bedsheet, causing a million previously invisible dust particles to dance under the light of the moon shining through the window. His coat is draped over the inside crook of his elbow and he hangs it on the rusty nail sticking out from the wall above the bed.

For the first seventeen years of his life, he thought he would never leave this bedroom. Now he's back and wondering if he had made the wrong choice, being gone for so long. Not for himself, but for them. For Abuela, and Coco. If he had stayed, would they be happier? Would they be better off?

The other half of the room is empty save for the second mattress pushed into the corner, and a handful of orphaned cigarettes tucked halfway beneath it.

"So," Sofia asks from the doorway, "this is where the magic happened."

"If by magic you mean attempting to study while Abuela shouts at the neighbors from the balcony," he quips, "then yes. This is where it happened."

She laughs, and he blushes. Even now, her laugh still does that to him. Catches him by surprise. He brushes the redness from his cheeks by running a hand through his hair, then reaches that same hand towards her, inviting her closer.

"So that was kind of crazy in there," he says.

"Maybe a little. Then again, what's family without a little crazy?"

"If you actually believe that, you're in luck. We've got plenty to go around."

She laughs, touching his chest.

"Santi?" she says, inching her fingers up to his chin and pulling his eyes onto hers.

"Yes, amor?"

"You know how much the bodega means to me, right?"

He feels his cheeks growing warm again. "I do," he answers.

"Good," she says. "That makes what I'm about to say a little easier."

He squints at her, confused, and she takes a short breath in and out.

"I think I'm okay now."

"What do you mean?"

"I mean," she exhales, "I'm okay. I'm ready. Let's move to Medellín."

Santi smiles. "Are you sure? What changed your mind?"

He sees her eyes sparkle with moisture and squeezes her hand.

"Santi, I would kill to have a mother who cared about me the way Abuela cares about you. I would kill to have a mother who needs me the way I can see in her eyes that she needs you. And I would *kill* to have a mother capable of being not just a competent, but a strong, adoring grandmother to our daughter. The type of grandmother who will be there for her anytime, anywhere, and in any way she needs." She smiles at him. "You have all of that here That's why I'm willing to give up the bodega. Not for you. Not for me. For this. For her."

She pulls his hand onto her stomach. He feels something sharp poke into his palm and he turns his wrist and sees that she has slipped the small brass key into his hand.

"I trust you," she says.

He grins. "It's going to be wonderful," he says, "I promise."

He has every intention of keeping it too.

It won't be enough.

———

Abuela throws the remaining scraps of food into the trash and flicks off the light in the kitchen. She drags her index finger along the wall as she walks down the hall, pausing outside Santi's and Coco's bedroom and peeking through a crack in the curtain at Santi and Sofia, their arms wrapped around each other, their chests rising and falling like the ocean kissing the shore. Wave after wave, second after second.

She smiles, then shuffles off to bed.

———

"Merry Christmas, Javier."

Javier's eyes spring open, and her face dissolves into the darkness of the room around him. The voices and laughter coming from upstairs have stopped, and the street outside is silent, telling him it's well past midnight. He tugs his bedding tighter under his chin and shifts his weight from hip to hip, looking for some semblance of comfort he hasn't found in years.

Finally, he settles on one side, his face towards the wall, his hands tucked under his left cheek. A pain in his stomach that's been there since before he went to bed intensifies, and he grimaces, closing his eyes. Tonight, like every Christmas Eve since he's lived here, Javier skipped dinner, not wanting to spoil his appetite in case he was invited upstairs. Which means that tonight, just like years past, he went to bed with a terrible stomachache.

That's what he tells himself anyway.

You see, the more times a heart's been broken, the harder it is for its owner to convince themself they'll one day find someone capable of putting it back together. At a certain point, it gets easier to tell yourself the pain in your heart is really something else, a stomachache, for example, rather than trying again to sweep up all the pieces.

That's why Javier chose to go to bed tonight with a horribly intense pain in his stomach. Because he's been sweeping all day.

"Merry Christmas, Javier," whispers a voice inside his head.

"Merry Christmas, amor."

PART SIX

CHANGE

CHAPTER 26

OCTOBER 1989

SANTI AND SOFIA used to walk to work together. Side-by-side, step-for-step. Now, Santi walks alone.

The wind dries the roll in his hand before he takes a bite, and he drops it to the curb. He takes a sip of tepid coffee and throws the half-full cup into the nearest trash receptacle nailed to the side of a telephone pole. The fist around his stomach tightens, and Santi throws his hands in his pockets and brings his shoulder up towards his ears to ward off the wind. It doesn't help.

On the day he and Sofia arrived home from Medellín after Christmas, he was the happiest he could remember being in months, the pieces of his life finally falling into place.

During their first two weeks home, he capitalized on that happiness by bringing in a handful of interested buyers to the bodega until he found one Sofia agreed with. A nice enough man with a nice enough look who promised to treat her customers with the respect they deserved and continue to sell the quality of fruit they had grown accustomed to.

He took a day off of work the day before the sale was finalized to work the fruit stand with her. After all, the bodega was her first true home, and he felt that deserved a proper goodbye before locking it up for good.

The baby came a little less than a month later and for two days afterward, Santi felt like a blind man on a roller coaster, never knowing which way was up or what was coming next and doing it all with a white-knuckled grip and smile on his face fighting back the nausea.

Forty-eight hours later, he got a call from his boss.

"We need you back."

So he went back.

Before the baby had arrived, Santi subtly pestered his boss to make his Medellín transfer official, but without any luck. When his boss called him into his office on Santi's first morning back, the first thought that ran through his head was, *"Talk about shit timing."*

However, when he walked into his boss's office, he was told that the transfer wasn't going to happen. No, he hadn't done something wrong. If anything, the opposite. There would be plenty of other opportunities like this one in the future but for now, his boss needed to keep him close to the vest.

"Bullshit," Santi spat at the floor that morning walking back to his cubicle.

That was almost eight months ago, but the sentiment remains.

He kicks a bottlecap off the curb and lifts his head. Less than a half block in front of him is the bodega, her bodega, and outside of it a man wearing an apron the same shade of green as hers was on the day he met her. The man is smiling and handing cups of fruit to a steady flow of customers, who in turn drop coins and bills into a large glass jar on the table. The fist around Santi's stomach tightens again, threatening to return the single sip of coffee from earlier.

When he found out the transfer wasn't happening, he waited a few weeks before breaking the news to Sofia. When he told her, she smiled and said all the right things to his face, but he heard her tears fall silently behind closed doors for weeks afterward, the happiness she experienced after their Christmas outing to

Medellín replaced by the type of happiness you feel when you have everything you need but are without one thing you desperately want.

The bodega had been her home for years before Santi barged into her life. Now it was gone, and for no good reason. Seeing the mixture of sadness and anger in her eyes drew emotions out of Santi he didn't know existed. Equal parts shame, guilt, and fear. Like he was walking on eggshells and struggling to breathe at the same time.

Fortunately, the tension between them was eased by the existence of one pincushion nose and two honey-colored, almond-shaped eyes.

Their little girl brought them laughter and joy and a place to direct their frustrations without worrying about them being thrown back in their faces. But one thing she couldn't provide was an outlet for the unspoken truth left hanging between them. The fruit stand was the first thing Sofia had ever loved and because of Santi, it was gone.

Maybe it's for the best. There's no way she could've kept up at work with how busy she is with the baby, he thinks as he approaches the bodega.

But as much as he'd like to believe that, he knows it's a foolish thought. Could she have done both? Of course. She's Sofia. Women like Sofia accomplish whatever they want simply by telling themselves they will.

No way she could've kept up. What a stupid thought.

He walks past the bodega and the man behind the table catches his eye and gives an understanding nod. Santi has tried to buy the place back from him on three separate occasions but each time, the answer has been the same.

"Sell it back? I'm still trying to figure out why you sold it to me in the first place."

Santi nods back to him and walks the rest of the way to his building, stepping into an empty elevator that soon fills with men wearing itchy suits and smelling strongly of coffee or a cheap hooker's perfume. The bell dings on his floor, and he shoves his way out into the hall. He stands by the elevator doors, waiting for the feelings of claustrophobia to dissipate, pushes his shoulders back and his chin up, and walks directly into his boss's office without knocking. Then he says the words he's been swallowing for eight months.

"I quit."

Without waiting for a response, he walks to his own office, picks up his phone, and dials a number.

Riiiiing

"Alo," a voice on the other end says.

"Coco?"

"Q'hubo, hermanito."

"I need a favor."

———

"Are you gonna help me or what?" Andrés asks, walking into the house with a stack of boxes in his arms as Coco hangs up the phone.

"I thought about it, but then I remembered that when I moved all my shit in two weeks ago, you weren't around to help because you were too busy doing...what was her name again? Veronica?" Coco smirks.

"Her name was Victoria," Andrés corrects, "and she was worth it."

Coco waves his hand at the growing pile of boxes in the middle of the room. "What is all of this stuff anyway?"

Andrés drops the boxes in his arms next to the others and twists sharply to both sides, cracking his back. "Don't worry about it," he says. "Who was that on the phone?"

"Don't worry about it."

Andrés tilts his head. "Are you being smart with me?" he asks.

"Hard not to be smart around your dumb ass," Coco quips back.

Andrés laughs. "Go get some boxes out of the car," he says. "Marica."

He picks up the top box from the stack on the floor and walks to the master bedroom at the back of the house. Coco steps outside and walks around the back of the open hatchback parked with one wheel popped up onto the curb. He ducks and pulls out a long skinny box from on top of both rows of seats, the last two feet of it sticking through the passenger side window, and removes it from the car along with a pair of smaller boxes he tucks under one arm, then heads back inside.

Their old apartment might have been shit, but that didn't mean it hadn't been bigger and nicer than any place Andrés or Coco had ever lived in before they started working for Pablo. Still, with the amount of money they had made recently, sizing up almost felt obligatory.

"One big enough to impress the expensive legs," Andrés said when he handed Coco the second set of keys.

When he first saw the place, he thought it was a bit over the top, then he remembered whose name was on the lease, and he counted his blessings that Andrés hadn't splurged on a three-story penthouse somewhere in downtown Poblado.

"What the hell is this?" he says, walking into Andrés's bedroom and tossing the long, skinny box at his feet.

Andrés smiles and rubs his hands together while bending down to slice it open with a knife he pulls from his pocket. "This," he says, struggling to free whatever it is from it's packaging, "is what's going to make this house a home."

He slides it out and lifts it in the center of the room.

"Really?" Coco laughs, staring at the shining silver pole before him and shaking his head. "Classy choice. Very classy. Where do you want these?" he asks, gesturing to the boxes under his arm.

"Throw them anywhere," Andrés says, his eyes glued to the pole in his hand as if it were a crystal ball revealing his future. "You should get one of these, parce."

"I think I'm alright," Coco responds, dropping the boxes and turning to leave.

"I'm serious. You want one? I know a guy."

"One is plenty," he says with a smirk. "Although, I appreciate the sentiment."

"Your loss."

The phone rings in the kitchen, and Andrés throws the pole onto his mattress and runs to answer it.

"Hola?" he says. "Oh, hey boss! No, this is Andrés. Hey, I had a couple of ideas I wanted to run past you I think el Patrón might..." He stops mid-sentence and twists the phone cord around his finger as Coco walks into the kitchen behind him. "Coco?" he says into the phone. "Of course. He's right here, let me get him for you." Andrés turns to him, his face flat. "For you. It's el Flaco."

El Flaco. One of Pablo's most trusted men, and Coco's and Andrés's boss. Skinnier than a cat with the runs, and twice as slippery.

He takes the phone from Andrés.

"Alo?" he says. "Sí. Claro que sí. I'll talk to Guz, of course. Andrés también, cierto? Ok. We'll be there." He hangs up the phone and leans against the counter.

"What did he say?" Andrés asks, picking at his fingernails.

"Meeting in two days," he replies. "At the hacienda. Call Guz and let him know."

Andrés nods and grabs the phone off the wall, pausing before dialing Guzano's number. "Did he say what the meeting's about?" he asks.

Coco shakes his head. "Nothing specific. Just that Pablo said it's time we sent a real message."

Andrés grins. "Excellent."

CHAPTER 27

NOVEMBER 1989

THE HOUSE IS CLEANER than it's ever been and likely ever will be. Sofia can't even remember the last time she didn't wake up exhausted and with her clothes flecked with dry flakes of baby food, both spilled and regurgitated, making neglecting to clean the kitchen or sweep the floors feel more than justified. Those marginal messes have compounded over the past eight months, however, reminding her each time she pays attention to it that no matter how well she thought she was managing to balance the jobs of mother and homemaker, all she had really been doing was treading water and calling it a new style of swimming.

She peers out the kitchen window at the first stripes of morning sunlight painting the street. She leans the broom in her hand against the kitchen table and sinks down into a chair. She should be out there right now. At the bodega. Lopping the heads off the last few pineapples while the line on the sidewalk grows.

Instead, she is here. Giving her husband a makeshift birthday present in the form of a clean house. He'll love it, of course. She knows that. Perhaps more than any other present she could have bought him. Even for all his striving and obsessing over titles and salaries and status, what makes him happiest are the simple things. A kitchen floor devoid of crumbs. A freshly folded stack of clean laundry. A perfectly smoothed bedsheet. If he'd only been able to realize that about himself, maybe things would be different.

When they came home after their Christmas trip to Medellín, all Santi could talk about was how excited he was to move. Sofia didn't share that excitement. The best, and maybe the only, word she could find to describe her feelings was that she felt ready. Ready to have a baby, ready to start a new life in a new home, and, most significantly, ready to say goodbye to the bodega.

That readiness changed with time.

The closer it all came, the more fear crept in. The reasons she'd had for signing off on the move, the ones that once seemed very real, felt significantly less so. Especially when it came to selling the bodega.

"What if we just locked it up instead of selling?" she asked one morning. "I just can't stand the thought of anyone else owning it."

"That wouldn't make any financial sense," Santi replied without looking up from the newspaper.

"I thought the whole point of taking this promotion was so that we didn't have to worry about finances so much anymore?"

Now he looked at her. "Don't do that, Sofia," he said, then went back to the paper.

In the end he convinced her. Or she gave in. Hard to tell which. He found a buyer for the bodega who Sofia liked well enough and that was that.

She allowed her mind to focus on other things, like the kicks in her ribs and the hiccups in her stomach, until she found herself counting the days until she got to meet her little girl. She was ready again.

Until, of course, Santi came home after work one day, took one look at the dozen or so half-filled cardboard boxes littering the family room, shook his head, and said, "We need to unpack all of this. It isn't happening anymore."

"What do you mean?" she asked.

"I mean we aren't moving. The transfer isn't happening, they gave it somebody else."

"What? Who? Why?"

"Can we not talk about it right now? I'm really tired."

That was it. She gave up the thing she loved the most only for him to tell her it had been for nothing, then refuse to give her any kind of explanation because he was tired? *Tired?*

She rests her head on the table and closes her eyes.

"Whoa," Santi says, emerging from the hallway several minutes later and taking in the scene in front of him. He hears Sofia snoring lightly, a thin string of drool drawing a line from the corner of her mouth across her fingers and down into a small pool on the table, and smiles. He picks up a neatly folded blanket from a small stack beside the couch and lays it out flat on the floor beside the front window. Clinging to his neck is an eight-month-old girl, her chubby fingers grabbing and pinching at any part of him they can get to, and he peels her away from him and sets her down on the blanket. "Amor," he says, crossing the room and kneeling beside the kitchen table. He brushes a fallen lock of hair from Sofia's cheek and leans in, so their faces are millimeters apart when she opens her eyes.

"Happy birthday, Santi," she says, her voice stumbling from her lips, still half asleep.

He takes her hand and stands up, pulling her up with him, and kisses her three times on the forehead. "Well," he says, "I would be lying if I said I'd ever gotten a better gift than this. Seriously! Look at this place! I've never seen anything this clean with you in the middle of it."

She laughs. From behind them comes a high pitch squeal and they turn to see their baby girl babbling on in happy gibberish, apparently engaged in rivetingly entertaining conversation with the corner of the blanket she's managed to grab and is shaking excitedly. Sofia giggles into Santi's chest and wraps her arms around him, slipping her hands into the back pocket of his pants.

"What's this?" she asks, her fingers closing around a folded piece of paper.

He takes a quick step backward, but she pinches the paper and pulls it free.

"What is this?" she repeats, holding it up.

"Don't be mad," he says.

"Poor start."

"Let me finish," he says, holding his hands up at her like a cobra tamer who dropped his flute. "Don't be mad, but I have a surprise for you. A big one. I was going to wait until after breakfast to tell you, but since I'm assuming you won't be able to wait that long," he plucks the paper from her fingertips and flattens it on the table, "I guess now will have to do."

She turns to see what he's just unfolded, and her confusion grows.

"A map of Medellín?" she says, her left eyebrow raised.

"That's right."

"Why do you have a map of Medellín in your pocket?" she asks. "And what are these red stars you've drawn on it?" She points at a pair of stars added to the map in red marker.

"I'm glad you asked. This one," he points to the first star, "is our new house. And this one," he slides his finger to the second star, "is a corner bodega perfectly suited for Medellín's newest premium fruit stand. A fruit stand that you are going to own and where we are going to work. All three of us. As a family." He looks up to gauge her reaction and sees her eyes actively working to connect the dots between what he's saying. "It isn't Calle 72, but you and I both know the fruit is always fresher in Medellín."

Sofia looks at him. "What are you talking about?" she asks.

"I'm talking about our new home. Or, homes, technically. I know the bodega here was like a home to you; hopefully this one can be too. Also, you might want to start packing because we leave in two weeks."

"We're moving to Medellín?"

"We are moving to Medellín."

"And you're going to sell fruit with me?"

"Every day until you beg me to leave you alone."

"What about your job?"

"I quit," he grins.

"Without telling me?"

"That's right. But in my defense, I wasn't actually planning on quitting when I did. It just sort of...happened." He pulls a seat back from the table and drops himself into it.

Sofia stares at him in disbelief. "What did your boss say?"

"Mostly curse words at first. Then once he ran out of those he told me I had to stay on for a while longer to transition my accounts, which I agreed to because, let's face it, we could use the money if we're going to move across the country. Plus I didn't want to burn any bridges."

Sofia puts her hands on her hips and shakes her head, biting her thumb. "And so when did... Where did you... How did you manage to find an empty corner bodega in downtown Medellín in two weeks' time?"

"I called Coco," Santi shrugs as if the answer should have been obvious. "He found the place in two hours. Although it wasn't *technically* empty until a day or two ago. Some guy was using it to sell bags or lamps or something, I forget, but he was ancient and more than happy to take the cash and run off to some finca to retire on or a strip club to die in. Anyway, I sent the money yesterday afternoon, so it's official. No going back now."

She looks into his eyes and sees the reflection of her smile. "Thank you," she says. Then she takes his face in her hands and kisses him.

It's the happiest she ever remembers being. It's also the happiest she ever will be again.

———

Four people sit on either side of the stretched table, all silently staring the same man in the eye as they internalize what he's just said to them. Sunlight pours through the open windows in buckets, coating everything and everyone in a dewy layer of perspiration. Coco wipes both palms on the legs of his jeans before clasping them back together on top of the table, his forearms slippery against the leather armrests of his chair. His eyes point towards the man at the head of the table, drilling a hole in the center of his forehead as they work tirelessly to avoid making direct eye contact.

Beside Coco, Andrés sits with an off-center smile on his face stretching from ear to scar, a disturbingly accurate metaphor for the information they've been given. His arms are folded across his chest, and he's leaned back in his seat, his head bobbing slowly like a fishing lure in mildly turbulent water. On the other side of Andrés is Guz, also smiling and scratching at his molars with a toothpick.

"Any questions?" Pablo asks, leaning back and locking his hands over his belly button. His eyes swivel around the table, waiting for somebody to respond as his thumb taps out the rhythm of the ticking second hand on his wristwatch. "Good. Así será pues," he says, satisfied with their silence. He slaps his hands down on the table to push himself up to his feet but is stopped by a shaky voice from the far end of the table.

"Patrón?" a man says, wiping beads of sweat from his hairline with the back of his index finger. "Forgive me for asking, but don't you think there might be a better way of going about this?"

"Éste huevón," Coco hears Andrés mutter to Guz.

Pablo settles back down in his chair and inhales, his inflated chest pushing his shoulders backward. He pauses before responding, perhaps giving the man an opportunity to take it back. "We've tried other ways," he says finally, his voice steady and low. "Nothing else will deliver the message that needs to be sent. Unless you have a suggestion?"

The man gulps. "I just think, and forgive me if I'm overstepping, but I just think, when we consider how the country has divided itself over our...management of things of late, that carrying out another operation that kills innocent Colombians may not be our wisest move." He stops speaking and looks around the table at the others, his eyes begging for someone to back him up. When nobody does, he continues, sitting up straighter with the kind of faux confidence you'd expect from a housecat cornered by a group of famished dogs. "I mean, we're talking about killing people for no reason. Women and children and..."

"And you think I give a shit about that right now?" Pablo asks, his voice loud enough to keep the man from saying another word but not so loud it gives off the impression he's lost his cool. His eyes are black marbles inside their sockets. "I love Colombia more than anyone in this room, but a message needs to be sent. A message strong enough to make every last hijueputa who lives here understand that this is my country." He taps his finger against his chest. "Mine."

The man says nothing. He sinks, dejected, into the back of his chair and shakes his head at his feet as though they were the ones to blame for him opening his mouth in the first place.

"Coco," Pablo says, swiveling in his chair, "can I trust you to make this happen?"

Coco perks up at the mention of his name. He'd stopped paying attention when the man at the opposite end of the table spoke, following his own spiraling thoughts. Were there other ways of sending a message? Of course there were. Does he want to be responsible for the deaths of dozens, hundreds maybe, of innocent people? Of course he doesn't.

Then again, he has something not many others do. A sidekick willing to do anything Pablo asks without batting an eyelid, leaving Coco to stand on the sidelines until the time comes to collect the paycheck.

He looks to his left and sees Andrés fidget uncomfortably in his chair and tighten his grip on the armrests.

"Claro que sí, Patrón," he responds. "We'll make it happen."

"Have at it then," Pablo nods. He claps his hands once in

front of him, and the meeting adjourns. All of the men but one stand up and push their chairs under the table, shaking Pablo's hand on their way out the door. Only the one seated at the far back corner remains.

As he walks out, Coco looks back at him and at Pablo, who stands up and shuts the door. The next time they meet in that room, there will be a new face at the end of the table. The unfortunate price of speaking your mind.

"Oye!" he shouts across the patio at Andrés, who is talking to the rest of the men from the meeting, or, more accurately, performing a one-man rendition of his weekend judging by his body language and the laughter on the lips around him. "Vamos. We have work to do."

Andrés looks at him and holds up a finger.

"Andrés!" he repeats. "Vamos. Bring Guz." He walks to the circle driveway and climbs into the driver seat of his car and waits.

"I was in the middle of something, you know," Andrés says, sitting down in the passenger seat.

Guzano opens the rear door and sits down behind him.

"Do you want to go back and keep trying to make friends?" Coco asks. "Or would you rather get to work so that next time we're here, your chair's a little closer to Pablo's?"

"Good point," Andrés agrees.

Guz smiles from the backseat, his arm hanging out the open window, smoke billowing off of a lit cigarette perched between his fingers and painting an abstract landscape of storm clouds on the horizon. "This ought to be fun," he says.

Coco nods and starts to the car.

"Vamos."

———

Riiii–

Abuela answers the phone before it's finished its first full ring, her patience having exhausted itself. For a fraction of a second, she contemplates singing a tone-deaf rendition of "Cumpleaños Feliz" over the phone, but refrains, knowing that the second a single note left her mouth, hell would freeze over, and she would drop dead. And if there's one thing Abuela hates more than anything, it's cold weather. So rather than risk it, she settles instead for a simple, albeit meaningful, "Feliz cumpleaños, mijito. Dios te bendiga."

Santi thanks her and relays a pair of saludos from Sofia and the baby, then tells her, "I have a surprise for you."

His smile floats through the phone and smacks itself onto her face. "You do know that people are supposed to surprise *you* on your birthday, right?" She asks, wiping her mouth with her hand.

"I know, I know, I know. Woke up in a good mood, I guess."

"So what is it then?" she asks.

"Are you sitting down?"

"Of course, I'm sitting down. What do you think I'm moseying around the house, twirling the phone cord around my finger? You're handsome but not that handsome."

She feels Santi grin.

"Abuela," he says, "we're moving to Medellín. In two weeks."

She drops the phone, and it bounces off her knee and falls to the floor. "Dammit," she mutters, rubbing her knee, then shouts at the receiver laying face up on the ground, "You're coming home? Did I hear that right? You're coming home?"

"Abuela, pick up the phone," she hears him respond and bends down to retrieve it.

"This better not be some kind of joke or I'll get on a bus tonight so the first thing you see tomorrow is me smacking the nonsense out of you."

"Not a joke. We're really moving."

"What about your job? I thought you said they gave that promotion to some shit-nostrilled, no-deserving wannabe?"

"Your words, not mine," he interjects.

"I might have said it, but I didn't hear you disagree," she clarifies. "Which reminds me, I still need to get myself a sturdy pair of slippers and come have a chat with that boss of yours."

"There's no need for that anymore," Santi laughs. "I already quit."

"Oh," she pauses. "Good for you. I always thought you were too good for that lifeless job anyways. So, when do you get here? I'll have to find a bigger mattress for the two of you to put in your bedroom."

"We come in two weeks," he says, "and don't worry about the mattress. We actually found a place of our own already."

"You were in town house-hunting and you didn't bring that baby girl to meet her grandmother?"

"Relax," he responds. "We weren't in town. Coco found the house for us."

She lets out an unintentional grunt of air when she hears his name.

"I take it you still haven't talked to him?" he asks.

"The phone works both ways, you know that."

"Abuela, it's been almost a year. Just call him."

"Why should I?"

"Abuela..."

"No really," she says, sitting up straighter, "why should I? He's so busy turning himself into a blood hungry maniac he can't so much as call his own grandmother to make sure she's still alive and now *I* have to call *him*?"

There's silence on the other end and she hears her own heart thumping.

"Please call him," Santi says, finally. "For me?"

She scrunches her nose and lowers her eyebrows. "Fine," she yields, "but only because it's your birthday."

"Gracias, Abuelita."

"Yeah, yeah," she says.

In the background, she hears a crash followed by a screaming baby and Sofia shouting, "Well, now how is that my fault? Huh? You dropped it on your own face!"

"Oh no," Santi says. "I gotta go before a fight breaks out over here. But I'll see you soon, okay? Two weeks."

"My money is on the baby," she winks, "if you're collecting bets."

"I've got 50 pesos on her myself," he chuckles.

"See you in two weeks, mijo. Te quiero muchísimo."

"Y yo a ti."

Click.

Abuela hangs up the phone and stands to open the door. Then she heads downstairs to tell Javier the good news. Her babies are coming home.

CHAPTER 28

NOVEMBER 1989

DEATH IS FAIR. It is also entirely unfair. Never is death more unfair than when it separates a parent from their child, stealing one for itself and leaving the other to gasp for every breath they'll ever take for the rest of their life.

———

Swish, swish, swish

Javier sweeps from side to side in quick motions, the joints in his elbows and shoulders creaking in the wind like the doors to an abandoned saloon. It's colder than usual today. The chill in the air that normally nips at his fingertips today bites off chunks of him at a time until it's ripped a hole large enough to wiggle inside his chest.

The door to Abuela's staircase pops open suddenly, and she trots outside with the enthusiasm of a person thirty years younger and a smile on her face that makes him jealous of whoever put it there. Then he remembers. It's Monday. The day Santiago moves home.

"Good morning, Doña Rosa," he says, leaning the broom against the wall and shuffling towards the store.

"Good morning, Javier," she responds with a friendly wave of her hand. "I'll come back for my usual things. I'm headed out."

"Of course, of course, of course," he replies, shaking his head as if he's just made an incredibly foolish mistake in assuming she would do the same thing this morning as she has for forty years. "And where are you off to, if I may ask?"

"El Centro," she says, buttoning the top two buttons of her coat to protect against the wind. "Santi and his family arrive tonight, and I'd like to have something special waiting for my granddaughter when she comes to visit tomorrow."

"You're more than special enough yourself if you ask me," he says, confused at the confidence with which he says it.

"That's kind of you to say," she says. She steps to the curb and turns her head in either direction in search of a cab.

"Would you like some company?" he asks quietly, slipping his hands into his pockets and wiping his palms on the inside of his pant legs.

"What's that?" She looks at him.

"Oh nothing, I just asked, if it isn't too much of a bother, if you might like some company? My company," he clarifies.

"I can't ask you to close the store all morning just to run errands with me."

"No, no, no, I'm happy to do it. Happy to." He picks up the broom and tosses it inside the store, pulling the door closed as it bounces noisily on the tile floor. He takes a faded, brass key from his pocket and locks up before she gets another word out.

"Well, alright then," she says, eyebrows raised in bewildered amusement at his sudden, apparent energy. "Just promise me you won't babble in my ear the whole time, alright?"

"Of course, of course, of course."

Abuela gives him a final nod of approval before turning her attention back to the street. "TAXI!" she yells, loud enough that every cab driver in a six-block radius perks up and looks in her direction. A block away on a perpendicular street, a taxista stands on his brakes and screeches to a stop, then backs up to make the turn up the street to collect them.

Javier climbs in after her and closes the door, sitting as close to the door as he can, the door hand digging uncomfortably into his upper thigh. They drive for several blocks and he keeps quiet, stuck in a hopeless loop of wanting to talk to her but not wanting to annoy her, his mouth opening and shutting and opening and shutting like a blind, hungry goldfish.

"Doña Rosa," he says, finally.

"Sí?"

"Gracias."

"What for?" she asks, her eyes glued to the windshield.

"For letting me come with you this morning," he answers. "It's nice to get out of the house."

She grins and looks at him, then puts her hand on top of his, giving it a gentle squeeze. "You're always out of the house," she says, "with that damn broom in your hands."

He laughs.

She does too.

"That's true," he says, "but this is much, much better than that."

———

"Santi!" Sofia shouts from the living room loud enough for him to hear her over the cries of the wailing baby on the couch. "What on earth could be taking you so long? If we don't leave soon, we're going to have to drive the last few hours in the dark!"

No reply.

"Santi!" she yells again. "Did you hear what I said?" She looks at her daughter, whose wails have turned to impossibly high-pitched screams, and plugs her ears. "And have you seen Azulita? She's going to scream like this the entire way if we don't find that damn blanket!"

She lifts the baby off the couch and sets her on the floor, then weaves her way through the living room and down the hallway, poking her nose into each of the remaining cardboard boxes dotting the floor. She opens her mouth to shout again but stops when she notices the phone cord running the length of the wall from the kitchen into their bedroom. The door is cracked, and she peaks through it to see Santi tying his tie with one hand and slipping his shoes on with the other, the phone wedged tightly between his ear and shoulder. She shakes her head.

Everything in the house was packed into boxes on Saturday morning. The car was loaded the same afternoon, a full two days before they were scheduled to leave for Medellín. Santi being Santi, he wanted things ready to go early so there would be no last-minute surprises or delays. His last day of work was meant to have been Friday, and yet all weekend their phone rang off the hook with people calling to ask a question about one of his accounts or fill him in on an issue with an upcoming project or tell him that somewhere someone's shit had hit somebody else's fan and he was the only person in the entire company capable of cleaning it up.

Bullshit.

Two hundred people working in that office, and not one of them knows how to do anything besides cause problems and bitch about the weather. That's what she thinks, at least. She only wishes he would have let her pick up the phone a time or two so she could have told them that herself.

"You let me talk to one of them, any of them, and I guarantee the rest'll stop calling," she said, and he laughed.

She turns around and goes back to digging through boxes until she finds what she has been searching for. A thin, deep-blue blanket patterned on either side with tan-spotted cows. A gift from Javier that their daughter hasn't let go of since she first got her chubby little hands on it. Blue because it's Santi's favorite color. Cows because they are Sofia's favorite animal.

She takes it to the living room and uses it to scoop her screaming child off the floor, her shouts subsiding the second her fist closes around the blanket and pulls it against her amber-colored cheek.

"There there, cariño," she whispers, wiping the tiny pool of tears from under the baby's eyes whilst bobbing up and down and side to side like an ocean buoy in the breeze. "Mama's here. I'm right here."

Santi walks out of the bedroom and into the living room with his briefcase tucked under one arm. He straightens his tie and smoothes his hair on either side, and says, looking at her, "Don't hate me."

"Never a good way to start a conversation," she says, still bouncing, "but go on."

"The office called."

"Of course they did."

"One of my biggest clients is in crisis mode, and they need me to help out for a few hours this afternoon."

"Curious," she says, "how long are you going to call them that?"

"Call who what?" he asks, confused.

"*Your* clients. You don't work there anymore, remember? They're not *your* anything."

"Well, I mean..."

"I suggest you call back and tell them to solve their own problems because if they keep asking you to do it for them, your wife is going to drive down there and give every last person there a problem so big it'll take a team of doctors and probably a pair of therapists to sort them back out."

He laughs and kisses her cheek. "Last time," he says. "I promise you. Both of you." He pinches the baby's cheek, and she smiles up at him, proudly showing off a pair of white corn kernel teeth. "After this, it's just us. Deal?"

"Deal," she concedes. "But we're leaving first thing tomorrow morning. I'm done living in a house full of cardboard landmines." She nudges a box in front of her with her toe, and it tips over, emptying itself of a sizable pile of unmatched socks.

"So, one more *tiny* detail I forgot to mention," Santi says, holding up his thumb and forefinger a half-inch apart and squinting at her through the gap. "My client is in Cali. I'm flying over there this morning and can't get a flight out until tomorrow afternoon."

"You're telling me I have to live like this for two more days? Where's the phone? I'm calling your boss's secretary to get his address so I can go fill his living room up with boxes full of human sh–"

"Ex-boss," he corrects with a grin.

"What?"

"My *ex*-boss's secretary."

"Not funny," she warns.

His smile widens. "Listen, why don't you two leave today, just like we planned, and I'll fly straight to Medellín tomorrow and meet you."

"Nope," she responds immediately. "Uh-uh. Not happening. You know how I feel about driving alone, especially between cities with the cartel doing whatever the hell they want these days. No way."

"I know, and normally I would share those feelings but I talked to Coco already and he promised he would make sure you don't have any problems" Santi says, pulling the car keys from his pocket and dangling them in front of her.

"Pays to have a brother in the cartel, I guess," she scoffs.

Santi smiles and kisses her forehead. "You'll be fine."

"You already bought your plane ticket, didn't you?"

He doesn't answer and instead gives the keys a little shake until his daughter grabs them and shoves them into her mouth along with half her fist. "Coco will be at the house when you get there. He'll let you in and help you unload things and make sure you're comfortable." He sets his briefcase on the floor and holds her shoulders. "The drive will be fine. I promise."

"Don't promise things you have no control over," she replies.

He pulls the two of them into his chest. "Fair enough. C'mon, let's load these boxes so we can get going."

Together they load the last of their things into the back of the car, Santi carrying one box at a time and Sofia somehow balancing three boxes in one arm and holding the baby in the other. He locks the house and slides the key beneath a loose tile on the front porch for their landlord to collect later. He opens the car door and places the final box on top of a crooked pile on the passenger seat.

"See," he says, "We wouldn't have all fit in there together anyway."

"There's always the roof," Sofia says, leaning over in the backseat as she buckles the baby into her car seat.

Santi smiles at the thought of her strapping him onto the roof and speeding away. "I'll pass, but I appreciate the offer." He looks at his watch. "Shit, I'm late. Drive me to the airport?"

"Sorry," she says with a straight face, opening the driver's side door and spinning the keys around her knuckle. "No room."

———

The car pulls up to the airport with Sofia behind the wheel and Santi crammed into the backseat underneath and in between a jumble of various sized boxes, each of them jabbing and poking at a different spot on his body like a group of in-training acupuncturists. The drive from their house wasn't long, but it was long enough for him to have complained one too many times about his lack of legroom, the outcome of which was Sofia making sure to round each ensuing corner faster and sharper than she otherwise would have.

She leaves the car running and steps out onto the curb outside the departures wing of the airport. Santi pushes his way out of the back seat to join her, his briefcase tumbling to the pavement at her feet. She stoops down and picks it up, weighing it in her hand and contemplating whether or not she could throw it far enough into the street for him to miss his flight going to retrieve it. Ultimately, she decides to hand it back to him, and he takes it and sets it immediately on the ground, and wraps his arms around her.

"Be safe," he says, kissing her on the forehead.

She turns her head, so one ear is pressed to his chest, the controlled *thump, thump, thump* inside, tugging at the reins of her own racing heart and slowing it down. "I will be," she whispers back.

He takes her by the shoulders and looks into her eyes, his face swimming in their reflection. "I know you will be," he smiles. "Call my hotel when you get there, okay? I told Coco to get the phone hooked up for us."

"Of course you did," she smiles. "I will."

He picks up his briefcase and leans his head and shoulders through the open back window to get a better look at the chubby-cheeked face bubbling behind the passenger seat. She looks back at him, her honeycomb eyes spilling out and gluing his feet to the sidewalk. The temptation to climb back in the car and spend the entirety of a nine-hour drive doing whatever it takes to make her smile grows inside his chest but he forces himself to suppress it.

"Be nice to Mamá," he says to her. "That means no screaming and no pooping. Got it?"

She giggles and kicks her feet happily against the seat. Santi nods, accepting her answer, and kisses his hand and presses it to her cheek. He stands up and straightens his tie in the window's reflection, giving Sofia time to wipe her eyes before he turns to face her.

"Don't go," she says when he does.

"This is the last time," he responds. "I swear."

She shakes her head. "Please," she repeats, "don't go. Don't."

He opens the car door for her and leans in to give her one last kiss. "I love you," he says.

She stops shaking her head and instead nods once, closing her eyes briefly and opening them back up brighter. She takes a deep breath in and lets it out slowly. "Y yo a ti," she says.

He starts to walk away but doesn't make it a dozen steps before he turns around. "I almost forgot," he says, "is my tie too short?" He pulls his suit coat away from his tie.

Sofia looks him up and down and shakes her head. His tie, of course, is knotted to the perfect length, but that isn't what he wanted her to see.

He's got on a pressed tan suit, freshly shined brown shoes, and a black belt. The same one she bought him for Christmas when they were dating.

"Didn't anyone ever tell you not to wear a black belt with brown shoes?" she asks, her words tripping over the emotion in her voice.

"No, but someone told me something similar once," he shrugs. "A few years ago. Only, I couldn't find my brown belt anywhere this morning. Too many boxes."

He winks, then turns around. She laughs and slides the car into gear. As the car rolls away from the curb, a wave of fear washes over her, drenching her in uncertainty as the smile drips from her chin.

How did we get here?

Dark spots begin forming at the corners of her eyes, and she realizes she's holding her breath as she accelerates onto the highway adjacent to the airport. She exhales and blinks away the black spots, her fingers wrapping tighter around the steering wheel.

"You'll be okay," she whispers to herself, refocusing her gaze. "I promise."

————

Coco pushes the table an inch to the left, then two inches to the right, then takes half a step back to check his work.

"Bien," he says, with a self-approving nod.

He has a lot going on today. Or, more accurately, people he is in charge of have a lot going on today that he is on the hook for.

He should be there with them. Or, maybe not *there* but *near there*, just in case things go sideways. He absolutely should not be here, worrying so much about whether or not the table with the TV on it is perfectly centered on the wall.

He walks into the kitchen to reorganize the pile of food he's prepared for Santi and Sofia's arrival. He picks up a fallen banana and replaces it to the top of the stack. It's going to be nice having Santi close again. He's the most particular person Coco knows, hence the thrice-reorganized pile of food, and yet, he's also the only person in his life who never made him feel judged for making mistakes.

Of course, the type of mistakes he's opened himself up to in his new line of work aren't the type you worry about being judged for.

Take today, for example. If things go wrong today, it won't matter who might be judging him. All that will matter is who is going to want to kill him.

————

The drive is as uneventful as anyone embarking on a long road trip can hope for. The baby sleeps through honking horns, hums happily during stops for gas, and chatters to herself as they carve their way through the mountains. Sofia, meanwhile, does a good job of keeping her thoughts on the road and off anything else, only once slipping into wasted wishes for Santi to be there keeping her company despite his promise of a safe trip coming to fruition.

It isn't until the sun ducks out of sight behind her, and the first of the Medellín city lights illuminate the mountainsides ahead that she thinks about him again. Only this time, she isn't wishing for him to be there. She's begging.

Fifty yards in front of her, a half-dozen cars are parked haphazardly along the side of the road. A group of men with assault rifles on their backs or long blades strapped to their hips stand with their backs to her, leaning against a wooden barricade stretching from end to end across the highway. Smoke pirouettes from several of their fingertips as they engage in animated conversation that is put on pause when one of them notices Sofia approaching and points out her arrival to the others.

She rolls to a stop a good distance away from the barricade and two of the men drop their cigarettes to the asphalt and walk toward her car. The first man bends down until his eyes pull level with hers He glares at her through the window. She hears a quiet whimper from the backseat and almost echoes it with a cry of her own but stops herself, choosing instead to collect enough courage to look back at the man outside.

When she does, he returns her stoic look with a twisted smile, the left side of his mouth pulled at an uncomfortable angle thanks to a thick, dark scar running the length of his face from the tip of his eyebrow to the corner of his lip. Behind him, a man with a pencil-thin mustache twists a toothpick between two fingers. The first man taps the glass three times with the tip of his pistol.

"Out of the car," he says. "Now."

––––––

"Nine, ten, eleven." Santi counts each row out loud as he searches for his assigned seat. "Excuse me," he says to a young woman sitting in the aisle seat. "Sorry to bother you, but it looks like I'm the window." He holds up his ticket and ID card to her as if he expected her to ask for proof.

"Oh," she says, "right, yeah, right. Go ahead."

She stands up to make room for him to pass, and he does, sitting down in his seat as the woman falls back into her own, her knees bouncing up and down like a kangaroo on speed.

"First time flying?" he asks her.

"What?" she says, looking at him. The color in her eyes looks small in comparison to the white around them. "Oh, yeah. It is. Yours too?"

"No," he replies. "I wish I could tell you the nerves go away after a few times, but..." He points to his own knee, bouncing up and down in unison with hers.

"Ha," she laughs. "I guess that's helpful, in a very traditionally unhelpful sort of way."

"Right," he says. "Sorry. It does get better once we're up in the air. I promise."

The woman swallows when he speaks the words "up in the air," and he takes that as his cue to stop talking before he says anything that might make her throw up. He pulls his wallet out of his coat pocket to replace his ID card in its appropriate slot. He takes his time flipping through the photographs inside while they pull back from the gate and taxi to the runway. The plane accelerates, slowly pushing Santi's entire body back into his chair, and he folds the wallet shut, running his thumb over the lopsided words stamped onto the front.

You may not see them now, but family is forever.

Now more than ever, he needs that to be true.

The plane gathers speed and lifts off the runway. Santi closes his eyes and grips the armrest next to the window as tightly as he can without his knuckles popping through his skin. The other armrest he leaves open for the woman beside him, and she accepts it in silent, shaking gratitude. The plane dips as it works its way up to cruising altitude, making Santi's stomach drop, and he turns his thoughts to Sofia to distract himself.

God, I hope they're okay, he thinks, shooing the opposite possibility away before it can poke anything more than a toe inside the door to his mind. *Of course they're okay. They have to be. Right?*

The plane shakes violently, and his eyes fly open. He sees the woman next to him with a death grip on both armrests, a look of pure terror spread from forehead to chin.

"Nothing to worry about," he says, forcing a smile. "Just a little turbulence."

He closes his eyes and leans back in his seat.

Then the plane explodes.

PART SEVEN

LOSS

CHAPTER 29

NOVEMBER 1989

SOFIA STEPS out of the car holding the top of the door with both hands until she's sure her knees won't buckle beneath her.

"Where are you headed?" the man with the scar on his face asks Sofia, his breath smelling strongly of cigarette smoke and tooth decay.

He holds out an open palm, and she obediently drops her keys into it without being asked. The man standing to his right sniffs audibly and pulls a toothpick from on top of his ear, slipping it between his teeth while twirling it between his thumb and index finger.

"Medellín," she answers, standing up as straight as she can and looking him in the eye.

"I gathered that much, sweetheart," he snarks. "Where in Medellín are you going?"

"Aranjuez."

"You live there?"

"We're moving there, from Bogotá. My husband is from Medellín originally."

His eyebrow twitches slightly at the word husband and the man next to him spits on the asphalt at her feet, wiping his mouth with his forearm. "Your husband?" the first man says. "And where is he?" he ducks down to look through the driver's side window at the passenger seat full of boxes. "I don't see him," he says, standing up.

"He's on a business trip."

"So you're alone," the second man says. He nudges his partner on the arm with his elbow, a twisting smile creeping to his mouth.

Sofia locks her knees to keep them from shaking and slowly clenches her fists at her sides.

The first man ignores his friend and stoops down, this time looking through the back window of the car where he sees two miniature feet bouncing harmoniously. His face straightens and the twitch in his eyebrow returns.

"How old is your daughter?" he asks.

Sofia swallows a full breath of air, and her throat tightens, constricting itself around her words. "Eight months," she manages.

The man looks at her, then at the car window, then back at her. He nods and stands up straight, then whistles at the rest of the men standing in the road ahead, signaling for them to clear the way. His friend's mouth hangs open as he looks in disbelief at his partner as if he'd just donated a month's salary to charity or tossed the only food they had to the neighborhood dogs.

"Andrés," he says, "let's think about this for a second. She's young, she's fit, she's alone," he counts on three fingers. "Could be a lot of fun, and no harm done."

"She's not alone," Andrés responds. "Don't you see she has a baby back there?"

"That's an easy fix," his partner says, reaching for his waist-band and stepping towards the car.

"No, Guz," he grabs his arm and pulls him back. Then he turns to Sofia and hands her back her keys. "Have a safe trip."

"Gracias," Sofia breathes.

She opens the door and slides down in her seat. She drives until the men at the barricade are out of sight behind her, at which point she pulls over and buries her face in her hands on the steering wheel. Her shoulders quiver with each breath she takes, and for several minutes she does the only thing that at that moment her body feels capable of. She cries. She cries until her fingers are pruned and her heavy sobs are replaced by inconsistent, shuddering breaths of emotion. Minutes pass before she can gather and steady herself. She blinks away the moisture from her eyes until her vision clears, and looks at the highway ahead of her, darker now that the sun has disappeared.

She reaches up and adjusts the mirror to give herself a better view of her daughter.

"Damn you, Santi, for making me do this alone," she says. She pushes her foot down on the gas pedal and accelerates slowly, putting more and more distance between herself and the men behind her. "I miss you," she whispers.

She means every word; she just has no idea how much.

———

Coco unlocks the door and lets himself inside. He turns to the kitchen and sees that a banana, the same one from that morning, has fallen from the top of the stack of food. He puts it back, then faces the living room. He walks around the couch and pushes the table with the TV on it an inch and a half to the left. He crosses the room back to the front door where he slides off his coat and hangs it on a nail in the wall.

"Whew," he exhales, taking a seat on the couch and kicking his shoes off before lifting his feet onto the coffee table. He grabs the TV remote off the arm of the couch and turns it on, flipping through channels until something catches his eye.

There's a fútbol match on, a rerun of the Colombia national team from the Copa America a few years back. What stops him though, is the thin, scrolling banner at the top of the screen. The one that reads, "Breaking: Attempted assassination attempt on presidential candidate César Gaviria this morning in Bogotá. For more details, turn to channel 03."

"Attempted?" he whispers.

He turns the channel to Channel 03 where a female news anchor answers his question.

"If you're just joining us, today's top story is an explosion that took place earlier this morning on a commercial flight out of Bogotá. National Police are saying the explosion was an assassination attempt on presidential candidate César Gaviria, who officials say was due to be onboard, but for unknown reasons abandoned his plans at the final hour."

Coco's eyes grow wider with every word she speaks. His hands grow numb one finger at a time and a bead of sweat spills down his spine. The remote slips from his grip and tumbles to the concrete floor, causing one of the two batteries inside to pop out and roll beneath the couch. Coco doesn't notice.

He's too busy staring at the TV. More specifically, he's too busy staring at a number on the TV.

"One-hundred and seven," he says.

That's when it dawns on him. He was just responsible for one-hundred and seven deaths. Men, women, children. Colombian citizens. Innocent people. He isn't just a murderer anymore, he's a terrorist.

What's worse is that he knows Pablo isn't going to take the fall for this. No way. He'll do everything in his power to pin it on somebody else.

"Shit," he says, and jumps up from the couch. He grabs his coat and opens the door. "Shit shit shit," he repeats, not stepping outside.

He closes the door again and takes off his coat, replacing it to the nail in the wall. He takes a deep breath. Santi will be here soon. He'll know what to do.

And if he doesn't, at least Coco will get to say goodbye.

How did this happen? he thinks. *How could I have let this happen?*

CHAPTER 30

NOVEMBER 1989

TWO SECONDS. What can happen in two seconds? Not much. Then again, how long does it take to pull a trigger? Or to say "I love you"? How about to step off a chair? To wave goodbye?

Two seconds. What can happen in two seconds? Not much. Only everything.

———

By the time Sofia finds the house at the address Santi gave her, she's as exhausted physically as she is emotionally. She sees a light on inside when she pulls up and prays he was telling the truth when he said Coco had things set up for them inside and that one of those things is a mattress and a blanket, so she doesn't have to spend valuable sleeping hours digging through boxes. She takes the top box from the passenger seat and tucks it under her arm, wary not to waste a trip.

She opens her door and rounds the back of the car to collect her now sound-asleep little girl. She scoops her into one arm, admiring her tiny head cocked awkwardly to one side and hands clutching the blue cow blanket draped unevenly over her belly. Sofia is careful not to let the blanket slip as she pushes the car door shut with her foot and navigates the uneven walkway leading her to the front door.

The house itself is nothing special. It's on the first floor of a three-story building tucked neatly into the middle of a crowded block, typical of downtown Medellín. Across the street, a large family is laughing around an enormous pot of what she imagines can only be sancocho and telling stories she figures will only get louder as the night wanders on. A few of them wave to her and smile when they see her looking in their direction and she nods back. She notices a couple of miniature soccer balls on the balcony above her new front door and hopes they belong to a neighbor girl so her daughter has someone close by she can look up to.

She knocks twice on the steel door with her elbow, and Coco throws it open immediately as if he'd been sitting, waiting all day with his hand on the latch on the other side.

"Finally!" he exclaims. "Did you guys drive the whole way in reverse or what?"

"Hi Coco," she responds with a smile.

"Hey, sis. Hola chiquita." He gives each of them a kiss on the cheek and steps out of their way. "Come in, come in."

She steps inside expecting to be greeted by an empty house with at most a mattress on the floor in the center of the living room. What she finds instead is a pair of cloth couches pointed at a small table with a television on top, a round kitchen table with four chairs surrounding it, and a kitchen counter piled high with rice, bananas, arepa, and a host of other food Sofia can't quite make out through the exhaustion clouding her vision.

"Not bad on short notice, huh?" he says. "There's a bed in the back bedroom for you guys and another little mattress on the floor in this first one." He gestures at the door closest to them in the hallway.

"It's perfect," she says. "Thank you."

"Nah, it was nothing," he responds, waving his hand.

Sofia drops the shoebox under her arm onto the first couch and walks into the first bedroom, where she lays her lightly snoring angel on the mattress in the corner, gently tucking a corner of her blanket under her cheek and draping the rest over her legs and torso.

"Seriously though, what took you so long?" Coco asks when she emerges back into the living room. He opens the front door again and pokes his head outside, looking in either direction. "And where the hell is Santi? Did he get lost out there or did you ditch him on the side of the road somewhere?"

"Shit," she responds and starts digging through her pockets, "I need to call him."

"Call him?"

"He had a work thing come up this morning so we came without him. We would have gotten here sooner, too, but we ran into a few friends of your boss's."

"Yeah," he says, scratching the back of his neck, "sorry about that. They didn't give you any trouble, did they? I told Andrés to keep an eye out for you, but that would have been harder for him to do, considering he's only ever met Santi and Santi is..." He pauses. "Wait, you said he had a work thing? I thought he quit his job like a month ago?"

"He did," she replies, clearly perturbed as she rifles through the pockets of her coat until she finds the scrap piece of paper with the hotel's phone number on it. "There you are. Is there a phone hooked up somewhere?"

"In the kitchen," he says, his eyes narrowing at the paper in her hands. "So, how long is he staying in Bogotá?"

"He isn't in Bogotá," says Sofia, crossing in front of him to the kitchen and taking the phone off the wall. "He's in Cali."

"Cali? Why Cali?" he asks, shifting his weight from one foot to the other and back again and reaching up to scratch at his chest.

"Couldn't tell you. All he told me was that he had no choice but to fly over there this morning and that he would meet me here tomorrow."

"Fly?"

"Yeah," Sofia answers. "He caught a plane early this morning and is flying here tomorrow."

"Santi hates airplanes," he says.

"Not enough to tell his boss, apparently," says Sofia as she dials the number on the paper in her hand.

Coco's eyes bounce around the floor. "I need to leave," he says. He takes his jacket off the back of one of the kitchen chairs and speeds out the door, closing it sharply behind him.

Sofia stands in the kitchen, looking at the door for several seconds. "Weird," she says to herself. She shrugs it off and presses the phone to her ear, listening as it rings four times before a woman on the other end picks up.

"Hotel Solana, Marina speaking."

"Hola, can you please connect me to Santiago Gonzalez's room?"

"Un momento, por favor."

"Gracias." She twists the phone cord around two fingers while she waits to be connected.

"I'm sorry," the woman says when she returns, "but it looks like Señor Gonzalez has yet to check-in."

"That's odd," she says, looking back at the front door. "You're sure?"

"Si, Señora."

"Okay. Could you give him a message for me when he does arrive? Just tell him his wife called and that we made it safely to Medellín."

"Of course. Anything else I can do for you?"

"That's all, thank you. Buenas noches."

"Buenas noches."

Click.

She hangs up the phone and walks to the couch, sitting down with a *thud*, her body too exhausted to lower itself down slowly. She picks up the television remote and flicks on the news where a woman in a pantsuit is in the middle of reporting that no survivors have been recovered after a bombing earlier that morning that many are now speculating was an unsuccessful attempt carried out by Pablo Escobar to kill the frontrunner in the country's upcoming presidential election. Who, as luck would have it, had decided at the last minute not to board the plane.

"The plane?" she mutters to herself.

That's when she sees it. The bomb in question hadn't been placed in a building or hardwired to a car ignition or hidden in a parking garage. It was put on a plane. A plane that departed this morning from Bogotá's El Dorado Airport. Flight number 203. Departure time: 7:15 A.M. Destination: Cali, Colombia.

One. Two.

That's all it takes for Sofia's brain to piece together what's happened.

Two seconds for her world to stop spinning and her life to crumble into pieces of sand so fine they'll only ever escape faster the harder she tries to hold onto them. Two seconds for nothing to ever be okay again.

What can happen in two seconds? Not much. Only everything.

———

Coco climbs onto his motorcycle, blinking hard and shaking his head. *There's no way,* he thinks. *Right? There must be a dozen flights a day between Bogotá and Cali, there's no way Santi was on that one.*

"Right?"

He says it out loud as if hearing it that way would change the answer. He kicks on the engine and looks back in through the window at Sofia talking on the phone. He blinks hard again and accelerates down the street without a clue where he's going.

He pushes a hand through his hair as he speeds through a stop sign and turns up a street that climbs the mountain in random twists and turns like a balloon string in the wind.

Santi wasn't on that flight. he thinks. *He can't have been, because if he was, that would mean he'd be dead. And it would be my fault.*

My fault.

My fault.

He shakes away the echo and pulls over behind a parked taxi on the side of the road, and buries his face in his hands. His thoughts pound on the walls of his skull with desperate fists like prisoners entombed on a sinking ship until finally, they relent. An unmarked mass grave slipping silently into the darkness below.

"What are you doing here?"

The voice brings him back to life, and he gasps for air, looking around for the one he knows it belongs to.

Cristian exhales a pillar of smoke and flicks a cigarette towards him. A silvery-gray cloud floats in place around his head, framing his face like the glow of a painted saint, and he looks at Coco with sunken cheeks and raised eyebrows.

Coco slides off the motorcycle and takes two fumbling steps forward. His eyes are bloodshot and his mouth is dry, his bottom lip clenched tightly in between his teeth to keep it from trembling. He shakes his head, and the hairs on the back of his neck stand up straight as he opens his mouth once, twice, three times before any words come out.

"He isn't dead," he says. "He can't be dead. He can't be dead."

Cristian looks him up and down, his fists balled inside his pockets. "What are you talking about? Who's dead?"

Coco takes a few more steps toward Cristian, who does the same, closing the gap between them. Cristian opens his mouth but doesn't get a sound out before Coco collapses into his chest, and he reacts by wrapping his arms around him.

"Tell me it isn't true. Tell me it isn't my fault," Coco repeats quieter. The next words come out as hardly a whisper, almost as if they were attached to the very air he was breathing. "Tell me it isn't my fault that he's gone."

Cristian almost swallowed his cigarette when he saw Coco pull up. He watched him arrive and saw his head drop like dead weight into his hands. He saw his shoulders rise and fall with each jerky, uneven breath, and still, his first thought was to tell him to go to hell because apparently, he hadn't made that clear enough the last time they spoke.

It wasn't until Coco looked at him that he understood why he had come. He saw it in his eyes. The light was gone from them, the darkness too. The laughter, the joy, the anger, the fear, the anxiety. All gone. That's when he knew Coco wasn't here because he wanted to be. He was here because he had nothing left.

He was also here because someone was dead and, despite his whispered denial, it's likely his fault. But who is it? Andrés? He smiles a bit at the thought but wipes it off with the back of his hand.

With the weight of Coco's head on his chest, Cristian squats down until the two of them are sitting on the ground. He leans his back against the short, block wall between them and the fútbol court on the other side and puts an arm around his shoulders until his breathing steadies and slows, and he sits up, his eyes stormclouds.

"Smoke?" he asks, pulling a crumpled box of cigarettes from his back pocket and offering it to him.

Coco slides one out and sets it between his lips. Cristian slips one out for himself and strikes a match for them.

"Who is it?" he finally asks.

Coco sniffs and bites his lip before responding. "Santi," he says.

"How did it happen?"

"A bomb. On an airplane. I helped put it there."

Cristian swallows, unsure of what to say. "Santi always wanted what was best for you, you know that, right?"

Coco nods.

"He wouldn't have wanted you to blame yourself like you are. He'd be a lot angrier with you if you didn't use this as a catalyst to finally become the version of you that he always knew you could be than he would be about himself dying."

Coco nods again.

"So, what are you going to do about it?"

With that, they sit there in silence, smoking until Coco falls asleep, his head tipping an inch at a time to the side before all at once crashing onto Cristian's shoulder. Cristian takes the burnt-down cigarette butt from his fingers and tosses it behind them, along with his own.

Cristian's breaths deepen with each minute that passes, his body using the extra oxygen intake to keep his lungs from coughing and sputtering emotions like a forgotten garden hose turned on after years of useless sitting. The muscles in his back pinch and twist, and he fidgets narrowly in either direction.

For as long as he has been alive, Cristian has always needed the people in his life more than they have needed him. His dad, his mom, his aunt, Coco. Each of them filled some part of him he was incapable of filling himself, and one by one, they all left, leaving behind them the open voids they used to fill along with newer, deeper ones they cut on their way out.

He looks at Coco asleep on his shoulder, and his back straightens. Every muscle he has aches, and his eyelids burn with sleep, but he fights off the temptation to move.

For the first time in his life, somebody needs him instead of the other way around. So he'll sit here for as long as he has to, fight through pain for as long as he's able. Because he knows what it would feel like if he left.

Minutes pass and roll into hours as the sky goes pitch black save for a speckling of stars that look like they were carefully placed one at a time from horizon to horizon. His blinking slows as the first hint of sunrise tickles the backs of the mountains behind him, and without even realizing it he drifts into sleep.

When he wakes up, Coco is gone.

He stands up and stretches his arms high above his head. With one hand, he rubs the fist-sized knot behind his shoulder, and with the other, he reaches into his pocket and pulls out the same wrinkled cigarette box from the night before.

He slips a single stick from the box and lets it dangle from his bottom lip while he lights it. He exhales with puckered lips and watches the thin tendril of smoke float in front of his eyes and disappear without a trace.

Almost as if it were never there.

CHAPTER 31

NOVEMBER 1989

ABUELA SWINGS her legs out of bed at exactly 6:24 A.M. and bounces down the hall, stopping just long enough to smile at the empty mattresses in the boys' bedroom, happy memories and anticipation of future sleepovers with her great-grandbaby dancing an elegant tango inside her head. She enters the kitchen and scrambles an egg, then pours a cup of coffee before turning the dial on the radio and plopping herself onto a chair at the table.

The woman on the radio speaks in the same monotone voice as ever and Abuela waits to hear what events from the day before will make her hair stand up and her heart pine for a happier, more peaceful past. A time when the name Pablo Escobar was synonymous with hope, not terror.

"We will now read the names of the identified victims aboard flight 203 which, if you aren't already aware, exploded yesterday morning just minutes after takeoff," the newswoman states. "Carlos Alberto Fuentes Rodriguez, Carolina López García,..."

Abuela sips her coffee and allows her mind to wander off and focus itself on things like what she'll make for lunch on Christmas Eve next month or which flavor of cake to have at Santi's baby's first birthday party. Her eyes travel the room until they lock onto the plush, purple and white stuffed tiger on the couch she bought when she went out with Javier yesterday.

He had tried convincing her to go with a teddy bear or a baby doll instead of the tiger, but her mind was made up the moment she saw it.

"No woman in Colombia makes it through an entire life without having her heart broken," she told him as they walked out of the store. "That's why we cannot teach our girls to play nice. We must teach them to be fierce. Beautiful, but fierce."

Abuela smiles picturing two tiny arms wrapping themselves around that tiger's neck, and takes another sip of her coffee.

"...Liliana Claudia Ramírez Díaz, Alejandro David Rojas Moreno," the woman on the radio continues, "Santiago González Navarro..."

The mug in Abuela's hand slips and crashes onto the floor, sending jagged-edged pieces shooting around the room. There must be a dozen men named Santiago González Navarro living in Colombia. A hundred, maybe. But this isn't any of them. No. It's her boy. It's her Santi.

Because since when has Abuela's story been the type to have a happy ending?

A single tear drops silently to her cheek. From there, they never stop. They're tears for Santi, of course, but at the same time, they are tears for so much more than that.

They're the tears she didn't cry when she found out she was pregnant and the life she had known and loved were taken away from her.

The tears of a grandmother thrown back into motherhood, carrying a baby boy in her arms while her baby girl lay cold some-where beneath a thin, white sheet. The tears of a mother failing to honor an unspoken promise to her daughter, one made in silence on opposite sides of a hospital room door, that she would keep her boys safe.

They're the tears she couldn't cry when Santi left for college because for as much as she needed him next to her, holding her hand, she knew she had to let him go. To let him create a life of his own. The tears she couldn't cry when Coco slammed the door that last morning because doing so would mean admitting to herself it was her fault he was gone, and her fault he might never come back.

They're tears for Sofia, now faced with two impossible tasks. The first being to raise a child alone and the second to do so without losing so many of her own broken pieces along the way that she falls apart completely. They're tears for a child whose only memories of her father will come from other people. Telling her stories of a man with kind eyes and a kinder smile whose laugh would move mountains of burden from anyone's shoulders and whose hand seemed to find its way to yours anytime you went down a set of stairs or a hill too steep to navigate on your own. A man she'll never get to remember.

The river of tears flows soundlessly down her wrinkled cheeks. Some of them are for Santi, but most are for much, much more than that. They are the tears from a lifetime of never having anything given to you, only ever taken away.

———

Swish, swish, swish

It's 8:04 A.M., and Javier has been sweeping for just over an hour with no plans of stopping. A handful of customers filter in and out of the store, and he gives them a nod, silently telling them to leave their money on the counter before turning his attention back to her unopened front door.

Something is wrong. He knows because in all the time they've lived here, he can count on one hand the mornings where Abuela's door stayed shut this far into the morning. That coupled with the sound of shattered porcelain he heard through her open window earlier, and his heart is at risk of pounding straight through his ribs and breaking down her door.

Another half-hour passes, and Abuela's door still refuses to open. He cranes his neck to see the time on the clock inside, and finally decides he's waited long enough.

He's going upstairs.

――――

The stuffed tiger under Abuela's head is a shade darker than when she lay down, and she clutches it until her already shaky hands quake even more violently, hoping that by exhausting what little strength she has left her body will have no choice but to tumble into a deep sleep. Her river of tears slows to a stream, then a trickle.

This isn't how today was supposed to go. Today she was supposed to be happy. Today she was supposed to be with her family.

She gives the tiger another squeeze and shifts her weight up and down her spine, then settles back into the same uncomfortable position as before.

Knock, knock, knock.

The taps on the door are quiet enough that she pretends not to hear them. More likely than anything, she's either imagined it, or else it's Javier coming to drop off her daily groceries and check that she's still alive. Neither of which she has the energy for.

Knock, knock, knock, knock.

The second set of knocks is louder and more erratic, like the person on the other side was gaining confidence but still hadn't mustered up enough to keep their fist from shaking. She sits up slowly and eyes the door.

"Santi?" she whispers. "Sofia?"

No. She can't give herself that hope. She stands up and walks to the door, her hand hovering on the latch until she hears the third round of knocks. She turns the lock and pulls it open.

"Hola, Abuelita," Coco says.

His eyes are puffy and bloodshot, the bags beneath them deeper and darker than she has ever seen. She looks at him, and he looks at her, and without saying a word to each other, the thing they've each been fearing separately cements itself as reality.

He steps inside, and the door swings shut behind him. She spreads her arms and pulls him in, squeezing him the way she always does, as if she were trying to get the last drops of juice out of him.

"He's gone," she whispers into his shoulder. "Isn't he?"

Coco nods.

"How could he be?" she asks, pulling away. "Why was he even on that plane to begin with? And Sofia? I didn't hear her name on the radio, was she not with him? What was he going to Cali for? He was supposed to be coming here. He was supposed to be coming home."

"Abuela," Coco starts.

"No," she stops him. "Maybe it wasn't him. Maybe it's..."

"Abuela," he repeats. "It was him."

"But what if it wasn't? What if..."

"Sofia got here last night without him. She told me he got called on for a business trip to Cali last minute."

She shakes her head furiously at him. "Can't be. He quit his job. It can't be him. It can't be my Santi."

"It was supposed to be his last favor to his boss, or something. One last trip, that's what he told Sofia," Coco rattles.

Abuela says nothing, now pacing back and forth between the couch and the kitchen table.

"If he had only told me he was going, I could have stopped it or, or warned him, told him about the bomb," he continues.

Abuela stops.

"Bomb?" she asks. "What bomb?"

He doesn't answer.

"I thought the plane crashed, the radio didn't say anything about a bomb?"

Again, he doesn't respond.

Abuela's eyes narrow. "What aren't you telling me, Coco?"

she asks, walking towards him until her face and his are no more than a foot apart. "If it was a bomb, how did you know about it?"

"Abuela, you have to understand, I..."

"For once in your life, Coco, answer me without the bullshit."

He takes a deep breath, holds it, and exhales. "I can't tell you anything," he says.

She looks him up and down, reading between the lines. "This was your fault?" she asks, begging to be proven wrong.

Coco winces, then smirks.

"You would like that, wouldn't you? If it was my fault?" he says, causing her to take a step back. "That's probably exactly what you want right now, isn't it? That way you can tell the whole world once and for all that everything, *everything*, is my fault. And you would be right."

Abuela cocks her head and bites hard on the inside of one cheek until she tastes blood. Then she stands up straight, and says, "My baby is dead because of you. Dead. And you want to turn yourself into some kind of martyr? To make this whole thing about you?"

"What if it had been me?" he asks.

"What?"

"What if it had been my name you heard on the radio this morning? Would you be this upset? Or would you be hugging Santi and rocking him back and forth telling him how grateful you are it was me and not him?"

"Spare me the hypothetical bullshit, Coco, please."

"Why should I?" he spits back. He raises his hands as if in his own defense, and then lowers them. "Your *baby*," he shakes his head. "Of course. How could I forget? Santi, the angel baby, and Coco, the family screw-up. That's how you see it, right? That's how it's always been. This isn't about me, and you know how I know? Because you never, not for one second, gave a shit about me."

"Don't start, Coco."

"Start what? Telling the truth?" He laughs and shakes his

head. "From the day she died, all I was to you was an afterthought. I saw it the second you came home from the hospital. The way you looked at him and held him all day long without caring where I was or what I did or whether or not I was even surviving."

"Coco."

"And there I was all along, gasping for air, screaming for help, but you never heard me. Did you? You never listened. Never cared."

"Not today, Coco, please," she begs, emotion welling up under her eyes.

"Why not? Why not today? Huh?" he asks, stepping towards her until they're standing face to face again. "He was her replacement, wasn't he? You can admit it now; it's okay. And what was I? I was the brat kid you got stuck with then, and you're stuck with now, because now he's dead too. Just like my moth–"

Smack!

The back of her hand strikes his cheek, and it flashes white before turning a deep shade of red. He stumbles backward and reaches his hand to his face, the black in his eyes turning the same shade of maroon as his cheek.

"Santi's dead," he says quietly. "But I'm still here. Can you see me? I'm right here." He raises both arms and pounds his chest with his fist, sending the tear hugging the tip of his nose in a freefall to the floor. "I'm right here, and I need you. I need you now, just like I needed you then."

Abuela's chest swells and crashes like an angry tide as she stares at him, her eyes caught in a tug-of-war between anger and heartache, until finally, she says, "And I need Santiago, but I'll never have him again. Because you took him from me."

Coco looks at her in quiet disbelief. His chest shrinks, and he says, "Took him? You think I took him? You think I stepped onto that airplane and shot him in the head? Is that what you think happened?"

"You might as well have," she says.

He shakes his head and looks around the room for the words to say next. When he finds them, he points a finger at her and continues, "You aren't the only one hurting right now. You aren't the only one who loved him. I loved him too. He was my brother. I would have strapped that bomb to my chest and ran as fast and as far away from him as I could if I thought he was going to be anywhere near it."

Abuela's eyes reach a tipping point and overflow onto her cheeks, and she shakes her head narrowly. "But you didn't. You didn't, and now he's dead." She reaches for the door latch behind her and pulls it open. "I want you to leave," she whispers.

"Abuela."

"Leave," she repeats. "Now."

He looks at her one last time, wiping the effects of betrayal from his eyes. Then he walks past her, through the door, and down the stairs.

The adrenaline coursing through her body speeds out through her fingertips when she slams the door shut behind him. Dark circles appear on the fringes of her eyesight and grow steadily towards the center of her vision, and she knows she needs to find something to lean on before everything goes black. She reaches again for the door, pulls it open, and collapses.

———

Javier sets the broom in the corner and steps out onto the sidewalk, stopping dead when he sees Coco. His face is white, and his eyes bloodshot, giving him the ominous appearance of an insomniac vampire, and giving Javier the same pervasive feeling as before. Something is not right. Coco doesn't seem him looking, just opens Abuela's door and walks upstairs.

Instead of following him upstairs, Javier steps back into the store, picks up the broom, and goes back to sweeping. His brain struggles to connect the scattered dots as he tilts an ear towards the open window above, hoping for some clue or insight into what's happening. At first, he hears nothing, then the sound of muffled voices filters out. Javier keeps sweeping from side to side but lifts the broom off the ground to make it easier for him to make out the words floating down.

A loud *smack* interrupts the garbled words, and the broom moves faster back and forth above the walk. Javier strains his ears and manages to make out a few words from their conversation.

Santi is dead. Javier doesn't know when or why or how, but he knows he hasn't made it up. His eyes flit briefly to the chalkboard hanging on the wall beside him, the message on its dirty face written for a close friend, his wife, and their daughter. All of whom were supposed to be here to visit later this morning.

"Family is forever. Welcome home."

The door to upstairs flies open and slams against the wall, and Coco rushes out. He wipes his face with both hands and climbs onto the motorcycle he left parked beside the curb, then speeds away up the hill and out of sight.

Javier drops the broom and is halfway up the staircase before it hits the ground, taking the steps two at a time like someone half his age. He reaches the landing and raises a fist, but before he can knock, the door opens from the inside. Rosa collapses into him, and his arms hold her with strength he'd long thought abandoned him, as if they'd been saving it all for the day they were truly needed again. He lifts her and carries her inside, laying her on the sofa and sitting with her head buried in his chest. He combs his fingers slowly through her thick, gray hair and absorbs each of her sobs as they come.

"Javier," she whispers.

"Sí, Doña Rosa?"

"Santi is...," she says. "He's... He's..."

"I know, Doña Rosa, I know."

She looks at him and blinks away the puddles pooling beneath her eyes. "Stay with me today. Please?"

"Of course, Doña Rosa, of course of course of course."

CHAPTER 32

NOVEMBER 1989

THE MEDELLÍN CARTEL IS AN ORGANIZATION. It isn't a club or a fraternity or some other group you join when you're young and immature, then walk out on with a wink and a tip of the hat once you've grown up and out of the lifestyle. It is an organization, and organizations have structure. They have rules, and where they have rules, they have consequences.

The first rule of the Medellín Cartel is trust. When trust is upheld, you are rewarded. When it's broken, you are removed. Rules and consequences. Black and white. Simple.

———

"Dónde está ese hijueputa?" Andrés spits under his breath. He looks at the door and wipes his palms on his pant legs.

The bomb went off twenty-four hours ago. That means it's been twenty-three and a half hours since he found out that the one person they had needed dead was also the only one who had survived.

For a moment, Andrés was happy about that. This had been Coco's job and he screwed it up. That would make it easier for him to leapfrog him in the pecking order. One seat closer to the head of the table. Unfortunately, that thought only lasted until he got home and Coco was nowhere to be found.

Everybody in the entire country suspects Pablo was behind the explosion. They were right, of course, but Pablo wasn't going to let them know that. No, there had to be a fall guy, and unless Coco miraculously reappears, that fall guy is going to be him.

Around him, the seats begin to fill as men file in from the courtyard or from the gravel driveway outside. Guz walks in and takes his seat across the table. He looks at Andrés, then at Coco's empty chair, then back at Andrés, silently asking the same question.

Dónde está ese hijueputa?

He wouldn't have run away, not without telling Andrés. That wouldn't be like him. Is it possible Pablo got to him already? Sure. This is Pablo Escobar we're talking about. Still, he doesn't see that as likely. If he was going to take Coco out that fast for messing this up, he would have done the same to Andrés. And Guz. After all, the three of them organized this whole thing together, and Pablo knew it.

So where is he then? Why would he disappear?

Did he get bribed? Journalists and politicians would pay a pretty penny for any information that could lead to Pablo's arrest right now. They might even offer him protection on top of a paycheck. Not that they could keep that kind of promise. Pablo has eyes everywhere. And triggers.

The door opens and Pablo walks in and takes his seat.

"Andrés," he says immediately. "Where is Coco?"

He clears his throat and wipes his forehead to buy himself a second to think. What are his options here?

Option one, he covers for Coco, who shows up in the next twenty-four hours and accepts responsibility for the fuck-up. Pablo punishes him however he sees fit and Andrés slides one seat to his left.

Option two, he covers for Coco who never shows his face again and Andrés not only gets blamed for the bomb, he also takes heat for lying about Coco's whereabouts.

Option three, he doesn't cover for Coco, at which point Pablo either decides to blame Andrés immediately for the whole situation, or he sends him to find Coco.

In other words, three options that are all varying degrees of "close your eyes, throw the dart, and hope you hit the board and not the man standing next to it because he'll take that dart and use it to slit your throat."

"Coco won't be coming this morning," he answers, looking Pablo between the eyes and wiping his palms on his pant legs again. "Stomach flu."

Pablo stares back at him, visibly chewing on his answer.

"Everybody out," he says. "This country just witnessed a horrible tragedy, we should be mourning with the rest of our fellow Colombianos."

The men at the table look at each other, then stand up and one by one exit the room.

"Before you go," he continues, "there are people out there saying I had something to do with what happened yesterday. Of course, everyone in this room knows that I played no part. That said, let's make sure anyone outside of this room who might possess sensitive information is taken care of. No loose ends. Entendido?"

"Ententido," the room echoes.

"Bien. Andrés, stay behind please," he instructs.

Andrés nods and sits back down. Guzano makes eye contact with him as he passes and ever so slightly shrugs his shoulders.

When the room is cleared, he stands and approaches Pablo, taking a seat in the chair closest to him.

"What happened yesterday was unfortunate," Pablo says.

"Very," he replies.

"What happened?"

He takes his time before responding. "I think I'd better let Coco answer that, Patrón. This was, after all, his operation."

Pablo crosses his hands and rests them on his stomach. "And if he never shows?"

"He'll show."

"For your sake," Pablo says, "I hope you're right."

He holds a hand toward the door, dismissing him, and Andrés takes the invitation. Outside, he finds Guz but doesn't say a word to him. Just nods. Guzano nods back.

Coco better have a good excuse for going quiet, he thinks, *or else I'm going to kill him.*

As if he'll have a choice.

Rules and consequences.

Black and white.

No loose ends.

Entendido?

———

As a baby, you trust your parents unconditionally. You have to. They are your voice, your strength, your oxygen, your life, and so you trust them, not out of choice but the absence of it. You trust them to do whatever it takes to keep you from getting hurt, not understanding that sometimes that's a lot to ask of a person. But you ask it anyway, because you have to, and so we try. We try and try and try to keep our children safe.

Sometimes we fail. We fail because we get distracted or because we fall asleep or because we take our eyes off of you for one second and suddenly you're slapping both palms down on the hot stove or throwing yourself down the stairs. Other times we fail because our own pain is just so damned painful we don't have room left for anything else. It's then that we let go.

Sofia stands outside the waist-high steel gate and stares at the house. Their house. Her house. A house that should have been filled with imagination and hope and laughter and a million happy memories, but that instead held nothing but pain. A house where trust had been broken. A house that was never given the chance to become what she needed it to be: A home.

She struggles to hoist her baby girl up higher on her hip. Her daughter responds with a signature two-toothed grin and Sofia answers with a pain-filled, close-lipped smile of her own.

She turns back towards the front door and relaxes her shoulders, then lifts the latch on the gate and steps through to the oblong cobblestoned patio. She slides closer to the door, her legs refusing to lift her feet off the ground.

A pudgy fist tugs on a lock of her hair and she closes her eyes, resentful at the pain for reminding her that her heart is still beating. She opens her eyes again and fights the urge to turn and run. After all, how can she willingly set foot inside a place where the pain in the air is so thick it feels palpable.

Even after all these years.

She shakes her head and raises her hand to the door.

Knock, knock, knock.

A woman with sunken cheeks and lost eyes opens it, her fragile frame hinting at what must have once been a beautiful soul before life came along and beat it out of her. The stench of alcohol and cheap cigarette smoke once tattooed to her are gone and for a moment Sofia thinks her mother may not recognize her without a haze of inebriation clouding her vision.

Seeing her makes Sofia feel a million emotions in a single moment, but she can't let emotion get in the way right now.

Before she came here, Sofia considered going to Abuela, but immediately decided against it. The simple reason being that right now, she needed someone she could ask to set aside their own pain to ease hers. The more complicated reason was that sometimes life leaves children without any other choice than to do what they did the moment they were born–Trust their parents unconditionally.

"Sofia," her mom whispers, more to herself than to her

daughter. Her eyes dart back and forth between her daughter standing in front of her and the infant girl nuzzling into her shoulder and her lips shake out a series of jumbled half-sentences. "What are you...? Is this...? Is she your...? Is she my...?" Tears dribble down her cheeks and she lets them run unobstructed, her hands trembling at her side waiting for answers.

"Hola, Mamá," Sofia says.

The two words are like a sucker punch to the woman's gut and she collapses to her knees on the doorstep. "Mijita. Mi Sofia," she cries, "forgive me. I made mistakes. So many mistakes. Too many. Too many..."

Sofia's mother melts into a puddle at her feet, her face hidden behind her palms and sheets of tears, and Sofia's back straightens with renewed strength. She reaches down and takes her mom by the hand, pulling her to her feet, then embraces her.

It isn't forgiveness. Not yet. Maybe not ever. But right now, she needs a mother.

"Come in, come in," her mom says, detaching herself from her daughter and wiping her eyes. She moves aside, making room for them to follow her inside.

The house is different than when Sofia was last here. It's emptier. Brighter. She looks around, taking it all in before she says something she never thought she would ever say again. "Mamá," she turns to look at her, "I need your help."

"Of course, mija. Anything, anything," her mother responds. "What is it? Food? Money? I don't have much but anything I have is yours. I'll manage." She marches to the kitchen and starts rifling through drawers, pulling out loose bills and change and dropping them on the counter.

Sofia shakes her head with wet eyes and looks at her daughter. "I don't need money," she says. "I need you to be a mother again."

A light sparks in the back of her mother's eyes when she says it. "Y-you mean that? Really?"

Sofia shakes her head. "Not to me," she says. "To her." She nods to her daughter sitting on her hip.

The spark disappears. "I don't understand," her mother says.

Sofia sniffs and wipes her eyes with her free hand. "I just have some things I need to work out and–"

"What happened, mija?"

Her mother puts one hand on each of her daughter's shoulders and pulls her face to her chest, but Sofia doesn't break. Instead, she melts.

The tears flow before she can stop them and her shoulders heave and quiver like an old car engine on a cold, wet morning.

"Was it a man?" her mother asks.

She nods.

"And was he…"

"The most incredible man I've ever known."

"What happened to him?"

She pulls away from her mother's chest and inhales with her entire body. "He's gone. He was killed. Yesterday."

"Oh, mija," her mother sighs, taking her hand. "I'm so sorry, cariño, I can't even begin to imagine. But are you sure you want to do this? Are you sure you want to leave her?"

She shakes her head again. "I have to. At least until I get my mind straightened out and figure out what I'm going to do next."

Her mother stares into her eyes for several seconds without saying anything. Then, quietly, she says, "Sofia, dear, don't do this. I know you're in pain but believe me, please believe me, when I tell you that no amount of pain you are feeling now will ever compare to the pain of losing your daughter. Especially when you know you didn't have to. When you know you could have done things differently."

Sofia believes her.

It doesn't matter.

No quest is as hopeless as searching for reason in a mind completely engulfed in grief.

She kisses her daughter's curly hair and hands her to her mother. "Te amo, chiquita," she says, pressing her thumb to her cheek one final time, then she turns and leaves without looking back.

Once she's outside, she breathes a sigh of exhaustion. She looks up at the sky and a breeze crosses in front of her, drying her eyes. "Damn you, Santi," she says. "I can't do this alone."

Death is cruel, but never is it crueler than when it separates a parent from their child.

PART EIGHT

CONSEQUENCE

CHAPTER 33

NOVEMBER 1989

EVERY FOLLOWER eventually reaches a point where they decide they're tired of being told what to do. Unfortunately, by the time that day comes, most are too worn down to do anything about it. That, or they're too afraid. So instead of standing out and making a scene, they drop their heads in defeat and self-loathing and fall back in line, marching to the same beat as before.

There are, however, a select few to whom this doesn't apply. Those who choose boldness over compliance. Freedom over habit. Risk over inevitability. The ones who don't fall back in line, but who instead grab a pistol and aim for the head.

———

Coco slides his key into the lock and opens the door. Behind him, the setting sun pulls a shadowy blanket over the city a mile at a time. He steps inside and flicks on the light without worrying about being seen. He needs to be quick.

He screwed Andrés yesterday by not going to that meeting. Left him alone to take the blame for their operation going sideways. He might feel sorry about that were he not so confident in

Andrés's ability to make a shitty situation look like a golden opportunity, even to Pablo Escobar.

No doubt he will have told Pablo everything he needed to hear to avoid getting a bullet to the brain right then and there. Told him that all signs pointed to Gaviria being on that plane, up to the morning of the operation. He'll have acknowledged that Pablo was angry, incredibly angry, as he should be, then explained to him that he can't get too caught up in emotion. Not when there were bigger fish to fry.

Right now, that meant damage control. Tying up loose ends. And the most obvious loose end of all?

He pulls a duffle bag from beneath a pile of dirty clothes on his bedroom floor and turns it upside down, emptying it of a pair of underwear and a few unmatched socks. Setting it on the mattress, he reaches behind the headboard and pulls out a stack of cash, throwing it inside. He moves methodically through the rest of the house, bouncing from room to room and taking similar stacks of bills from their various hiding places until the bag is full. He zips it shut, throws it over one shoulder, and is walking toward the front door when the deadbolt twists, freezing him in place.

If circumstances were different, he might have hid or run or thrown the bag behind the sofa and acted like nothing happened. But he doesn't. Santi is dead. Coco isn't, but he might as well be. So when he sees the door start to open, he does what he's been scared to do for far too long. He plants his feet and reaches his right hand behind his back. He wraps his fingers around the pistol grip sticking out of his waistband and pulls it out, raising it in front of him.

He isn't falling back in line. Not this time. This time, he's aiming for the head.

———

Andrés watches from the backseat of a parked car as Coco pulls up to the house and goes inside. Guzano sits next to him, scraping dirt from under his fingernails with the tip of a dull blade, his eyes slits, focused on the yellow light shining at them from the curtainless window. Andrés elbows him in the shoulder, and the knife slips, jabbing him and triggering a trickling fountain of deep, red blood from the corner of his middle fingernail.

"Hijueputa," he mutters, sticking the finger in his mouth to keep the blood from running.

"Let's move," Andrés says.

They climb out of the car and cross the street. He sees Coco's shadow moving down the hall towards the living room. He slips the key into the lock but before he twists it, Guzano grabs his wrist.

"What's the plan here?" he asks.

Andrés looks at him, his eyes red but emotionless. "We talk to him," he says. "If we don't like what he has to say, we take care of him. You heard the boss."

Guzano grins and steps aside, gesturing for him to lead the way. Andrés twists the deadbolt free and pushes the door open and immediately finds himself face to face with the barrel of a pistol aimed directly between his eyes. Behind the gun stands Coco, straight-lipped and steady as a bolder.

Guzano's smile disappears, and he slinks to his right, pulling the dull blade he had in the car back out of his pocket.

Andrés takes a step closer, looking at Coco through the barrel of the gun as if it were nonexistent, and says, "Where've you been?"

Coco doesn't move. "What's it matter to you?" he responds, spitting each word as though it had just insulted him.

"You know exactly what it matters," he replies. "We're wading in some pretty deep shit because of you. Me, you, Guz. All of us." He takes another step closer and clenches his fists at his sides. "That job goes sideways and you disappear without a word for two days? Then you ditch a meeting without telling anyone? I covered for you when the boss asked where you were yesterday, by the way, but I can't put my ass on the line like that again."

"Don't then," Coco replies with a half shrug of his shoulders. "Tell him it was my fault. The whole thing. I didn't do my homework and we missed our mark. The end."

Andrés laughs. "Missing the mark is just the tip of the iceberg, parce. Pablo's paranoid as shit right now that they're going to find some way to tie this all back to him. If I hadn't vouched for you, he would have already assumed you were gearing up to sell him out and would have every guy he's got out looking for you," he says. "You know how this game works, Coco. You get cold feet, the rest of you gets cold too. Or did you forget?"

"Are you here to kill me then?"

"Nah," he shakes his head. "Just here to talk."

"Why's he here?" Coco moves for the first time since they arrived, pointing the gun at Guzano before steadying his aim back on Andrés.

"Same reason he's always here," Andrés smiles. "In case you fuck up. Which, if you hadn't noticed," he points a hand at the duffle bag strap over Coco's shoulder, "you're kind of doing right now. Where are you going with all that cash?"

His shoulder dips, and the bag slides lower onto his arm, but he pushes it back up. "I'm leaving," he says.

"Where to?"

Coco doesn't answer.

"I know about Santi," Andrés says. The gun in Coco's hand twitches, and his eyes widen by a pair of millimeters when he hears his brother's name. "I saw his name in the paper this morning. Don't worry; I didn't tell Pablo yet. Or anyone, for that matter," he goes on, raising his hands like he's doing him a favor. "I'll have to tell him soon, though, if you can't snap out of whatever this is." He takes a step closer, and when Coco doesn't respond, he continues. "It's not your fault he died, Coco. It's part of the job. You gotta move on, put it behind you and get back to work, because if you don't, if you run, he'll find you. I'll find you."

"I don't care."

"No, I think you do care," he says, the muscles in his jaw clenching together as he talks as if he were being shot through the spine with a thousand volts of electricity. "Santi had a wife, didn't he? And a dau–"

"Don't," Coco warns.

"I wouldn't dream of it," he says coolly. "I'm here as a friend, remember? But Pablo? He wouldn't think twice."

Coco looks down at the floor without lowering the gun. He drags his toe back and forth on the ground, then says, "You're here as my friend?"

"That's right."

Coco looks up at him and a look of amusement spreads to his face. "I don't believe you," he smiles. "You know why? Because when have you ever *actually* been there for me as a friend? We've known each other for what, seventeen years, and yet I can't remember one time you were there when I needed you. You only ever showed up when it suited you." He pauses and shakes his head. "Don't kid yourself, Andrés. You're the shittiest friend I've ever had."

Andrés's nostrils flare, and his lips pull together tightly. "Watch your mouth," he responds quietly.

"Or what? You'll kill me?" Coco mocks. "That wouldn't be very friendly, would it?"

Guzano laughs, and Andrés gives him a look that immediately shuts him up. He turns back to Coco, and his chest, shoulders, and chin all rise.

"You know what?" Coco says. "I lied. Go ahead and kill me. Would be the first favor you've done me our whole lives." He spits on the floor and lowers his gun without taking his eyes off him. "I'm done with this shit."

Andrés stares at him, his fists clenching and releasing at his side like two hearts pounding the same slow beat.

"No, you're not," he disagrees. "You're not done with anything. You owe me. That money in there?" He points at the bag. "I got you that. Without me, you'd still have nothing. You'd still be nothing."

Coco steps up to him, close enough that they can feel the heat of each other's breath and the *thump thump thump* of the veins in their necks.

"Without you," he says, "I would still have my family." He cocks the pistol at his side and presses the barrel against the underside of Andrés's chin. "The only thing I owe you is a bullet. Just one. Right here."

Guzano moves to intervene, but Andrés raises a hand and stops him.

"Pull the trigger then," he says.

Both of their eyes are black, one with anger, the other hatred.

"Pull it," he repeats. "Go ahead."

Coco inhales, shifts his grip on the handgun, and squeezes.

The magazine slides from the bottom and topples to the floor, dancing from end to end before finding a final resting place at Andrés's feet.

"I'm done taking orders from you," he says. He puts the gun on his back, sidesteps Andrés and Guzano, and walks outside, tightening his grip on the duffle bag as he climbs onto his motorcycle and rides away.

"Do you want me to follow him?" Guz asks.

"No," Andrés replies, rubbing his chin. "I know where to find him. Besides, we should get the order from the boss first. That way at least we make some money off of him."

"I like the way you think," Guzano grins. "Although I doubt una rata like that will be worth much.

"Might not be worth anything at all," he smiles back. "C'mon, let's go get a drink."

———

By the time Sofia arrives back at the house, the sun has set and the needle on the dashboard is dangerously close to slipping below the final notch on the fuel gauge. She slept in her car last night after leaving her mother's, on a street she'd never been on before, far preferring feelings of anonymity to those of hopelessness that awaited her here. She wasn't sure she could face this place again, not after what it did to her. She still isn't, which is probably why she spent the hours between waking up and now meandering through the city, hoping that scenes of bustling downtown streets or lackadaisical urban neighborhoods would be enough to quiet the pain screaming and attempting to break holes in her ribs, desperately wishing to escape.

Her fingers tremble as she shuts off the engine, her body struggling to comply with even the simplest of requests, and she steps onto the pavement. She turns towards the front door and notices a light turned on inside. The last optimistic shards of her heart instinctively twirl and skip at the thought of Santiago waiting inside for her to come home so he can wrap her up and carry her to bed, burying her beneath mountains of kisses every step of the way. She almost smiles, but then the rest of her heart catches up and again begins to beat its hopeless song, a slow, disso-nant melody fading as it loses its grip on a newfound rescue line and disappears onto a black canvas.

Santi isn't inside. Most likely, she just left a light on when she walked out this morning. She takes a step forward and pauses again. And if she hadn't left a light on? Santi isn't inside, so who is?

She's heard the stories. Everyone has. Of Pablo Escobar not wanting to take the risk of some emboldened widow or orphan or childless parent whose loved one he had just murdered standing in front of a camera and hand-over-heart declaring that he, and he alone, was responsible and that they can prove it, so he sends a friend or two to find them and offer them a choice. Plata o plomo. Cash or firing squad. Either way, they keep their mouths shut.

She wants to run. Not away from whoever's in there, but directly towards them.

When she opens the front door, she does it with her chin high and her eyes wide open. Inside, she sees a man sitting on the couch with an open bag of cash between his feet. She's sure he has a gun behind his back or on his hip, but he doesn't take it out. Just looks at her, then at the bag, then back at her without saying a word.

"What do you want?" She asks, crossing her arms.

Coco's eyes are weighed down by deep bags, and his voice cracks when he answers. "I... I don't know. I just wanted to..." He trails off, his jaw still moving like a mute ventriloquist doll. He takes the bag from between his feet and stands up, walking towards her. "This is for you," he says, holding it out.

She tilts her head. "You think I want your money?" she asks. "Do you think that fixes something? You think it brings him back?"

"Please," he chokes. "Please, take it. Take it; it's all I can do. It's all I have. I feel..."

Sofia's fingernails find the familiar half-moon grooves in her palms, and she clenches her balled fists tighter. "You feel what, Coco? Sorry? Responsible? Sad? Do you feel sad, Coco? Is that what this is? Some sick way of clearing your conscience so you don't have to feel sad anymore, and you can go back to doing whatever the hell else your boss asks you to do without caring whose life you're changing or, or ending or ruining?"

"Please," he whispers.

"Stop saying please like I owe you something," she snaps. She points a finger at him. "You did this."

A tear drops to his cheek, and she watches as it falls to the floor.

"I want you to leave," she says. She drops her head to keep from looking into his eyes, afraid that if she does she might find something familiar in them.

He wipes his cheek, then walks past her silently. Before he leaves, he sets the bag on the floor by the window and turns back to face her. "You need to leave," he says. "I'll do whatever I can to keep them from coming after you, but still, you need to get out of here."

"Please go," she replies.

He nods and walks outside, closing the door behind him.

She hears the latch click as the door shuts and all at once collapses into a pile on the floor, and for the first time in years, there is no one there to catch her.

She lets herself cry. It's all she can do. Then, slowly, she sits up and looks around her, blinking away the film of moisture in her eyes. She sees the shoebox she dropped on the couch when she arrived the other night and notices for the first time the words scratched on the side.

Santi. Important.

They are printed in near-perfect penmanship and underlined with three parallel, even length lines. She crawls to reach it and pops off the lid. Inside is a collection of mismatched items that to anyone else would look like the results of a raccoon scavenger hunt. As she pulls them out, however, each one carves a deeper chasm into her already broken heart.

At the bottom, shoved into one corner, is a toothpick she recognizes as the same type she would put in every cup of sliced fruit she sold at the bodega. The same one that was in the cup of mango verde she gave to Santi on the first evening he stopped to help her close up. Beside the toothpick is a note. An address scribbled on the corner of a scrap piece of paper torn from a stack of important work documents.

She pulls out the toothpick and the note and reveals a second sheet of paper, this one whole, folded in quarters with fragmented sentences and paragraphs scrawled on all sides. "Everything I want, everything I need, and everything that, until I met you, I never thought would be possible to find in a person," one side reads. She unfolds it again and reads another sentence. "I promise to love you. For the rest of our lives, I promise to love you." There's a line drawn through the center of the words "our lives" with another word printed below them; a replacement.

"For the rest of *forever*, I promise to love you."

She sets the written vows aside to keep the words from bleeding, stabbed through the chest by cascading drops of overwhelmed emotion. She sifts through the rest of the box's contents one by one. A hospital wristband from the day their daughter was born, a brass key sticking out from the bottom of a familiar padlock, thirty-five pesos in exact change, and a dozen other fragments of a love story that was never supposed to end. A love story that was meant to be perfect.

She removes all but one of them, spreading them out across the floor around her. At the bottom of the box, rolled tightly and bound with a rubber band, lay the largest object of all of them. The one she's been avoiding because she knew it would push her over the edge because it so perfectly represented everything her husband had been. Stubborn. One-track minded. Simple. Humble. Oblivious. Wonderful.

She picks up the old brown leather belt, removes the band around it, and watches it unfurl itself in her lap, like a snake stretching its muscles after an afternoon nap.

Time slows as she watches it roll out onto the floor. That's when she sees him. She sees him standing outside the airport, asking if his tie is too short. Sees him on Christmas Eve, a week before he asked her to marry him, opening the only gift she could think of to get him. She sees him jogging down the street towards the bodega, towards her, and sees him stop a few paces short to straighten his tie and catch his breath before asking if she needed any help packing things away for the night. She remembers the nervousness in his voice and the certainty in his eyes as he held up her line of customers to ask her how much she charged for a cup of mango. She sees his smile. Hears his laugh. Feels his fingers wrapping themselves like a glove around her own.

A smile comes to her lips, and she hates herself for it. Hates herself for loving him so much that she can't stop even after he's gone. She shoots the door a wishful look, pleading with it to open. For him to step inside and smile that smile that could simultaneously make her world turn and keep it from spinning out of control.

Any minute he'll be here, she thinks, *because he isn't dead. He can't be.*

Her grip on the belt tightens, and she pulls her eyes off the door and drags herself back to reality. A familiar fire begins to grow inside her, gaining size and momentum as it burns through fuel previously discarded and left to rot in the forgotten corridors of her memory. Why did he get on that plane? Why did he choose to leave her? Why had he chosen to help them instead of telling his boss to "Fuck off" when he called that morning? Better yet, why hadn't he ripped the phone line from the wall after the first ring and gone back to packing boxes into their car, making sure to leave plenty of space for all three of them to drive to their new home. Together. As a family.

Why didn't he quit his job sooner? How many times had she asked him, no, begged him to? How often had she told him that all she wanted was to be with him, to be together, and then stood there as he kissed her on the forehead and left for the office?

Each unanswered question brands itself across her brain, anger and resentment burning red inside her eyes until one final question pours itself over her like ice water, dousing the flames and taking her breath.

What if it's my fault?

If she hadn't demanded so much, if she had just been happy with the way their life was, then he never would have felt the need to leave his job in the first place. If he never quit, he would've solved his client's problems before they spiraled out of control, and he would never have had to go to Cali. If he wasn't needed in Cali, he wouldn't have been at the airport. Wouldn't have gotten on that flight. Wouldn't be...

"I'm so sorry," she whispers, her head falling into her hands. She pulls it back up and looks at the door. "If you just come back, things will be different. Come back and, and..."

The words she wants to say catch in her lungs, and her

breathing becomes shallow. She closes her eyes, and when she does, all she sees is black.

She looks up to the ceiling and sees an exposed steel pipe running the length of the house above her. She squeezes the belt in her hands and bites her lip. Her eyes fall to the kitchen table and the four chairs surrounding it that will never be filled. Her fingers tighten around the belt.

Her head crashes against her chest and she takes a deep, stuttering breath. It would be so easy. One chair, one belt, one pipe. All it would take to end the pain. To slip away into the darkness.

She wipes a tear from her eye and notices something she hadn't before. A neatly folded scrap of paper at the bottom of the box. One that must have been hidden beneath the belt. She picks it up and opens it. On it are written six simple words.

We won't let the darkness win.

Santi isn't coming back to her, but she can't go to him either.

She falls asleep that night tucked into a ball on the floor. In the morning, she picks herself up and drives a car she hates to drive alone to a home she doesn't recognize to be with the only person left on earth who can save her.

Sometimes, it's the tiniest arms that we ask to be the strongest. To catch us when we fall the hardest.

CHAPTER 34

NOVEMBER 1989

JAVIER SPENT every waking minute of five years at Luz's side, never leaving for long enough to buy her a proper gift. Except for once.

"Tell me something beautiful," she says, slipping the same yellow dress she wore on the day they met over her shoulders.

"Not today, mi amor," he responds, rolling over with his palm pressed against his temple. "I'm not feeling well. Migraine."

She sits on the edge of the bed with her back to him and drops her thin string of pearls beside his pillow, pulling her hair out of the way for him to clasp them around her neck. "We'll stop by the market first then and get you some juice," she says. "That always seems to help with a headache. Then we can go to the park and sit for a while. Feed the birds, get to know the people. That's the best way to start the day in a town like this anyway." She stands up and takes his hand. "Vamos."

Javier responds by crashing back onto his pillow and closing his eyes. "You'll have to visit the park without me this morning, I'm afraid," he says, "but come back here for lunch, and I'm sure I'll be feeling better."

She puts a hand on his cheek, the dips, swirls, and patterns hidden in her fingerprints inscribing themselves into his skin.

"Okay," she smiles. "I'll be back in a few hours, but don't for one second think something so stupid as a head-splitting migraine can get you out of an afternoon of aimless roaming and hand-holding."

"I wouldn't dare," he replies.

She smiles wider and kisses his forehead, then walks out the door, leaving him alone. He rolls onto his back, counting the seconds since she left as he memorizes every last bump and crack in the ceiling above.

"One hundred eighteen, one hundred nineteen, one hundred twenty," he counts, swinging his legs over the edge of the bed, and pops to his feet. He pulls on his nicest shirt and least wrinkly pair of slacks and slips his left foot into his shoe. Before he slides on the right one, he pulls a thin stack of cash from under the sole and puts it in his breast pocket, giving it a pair of gentle pats as if telling the bills to be good in there and to play nicely with one another. He puts on his shoe and leaves to go to the only store in town that sells jewelry to buy his love a ring. The simplest of gold bands with the tiniest of emeralds. The perfect ring for the perfect woman.

He shakes the salesman's hand and kisses the ring before dropping it in his pocket, then walks off towards the town center. He knows Luz well enough to know that's where she'll be. Sitting on the centermost bench in the middle of the park at the heart of the city.

"To know a person, you have to first spend time here," she would always say, pointing a finger at his chest. "To know a place is no different."

He rounds a corner, and the park comes into view, an open square, patterned with trees and benches and surrounded by bakeries and cafes, all under the shadow of a Catholic church with tall stained-glass windows framing the door. At the center of it all, he sees a small crowd gathered in a circle and sets off toward it with a skip in his step.

"That'll be her," he says to himself. "Telling stories and making friends out of strangers."

He pushes his way through the surrounding crowd until he sees her. Only, instead of finding her sitting on a bench, she is lying on the ground, her head encompassed in scattered white pearls, a deep red circle growing steadily at the base of her ribs. Javier's heart falls from his chest, and he throws himself to the ground beside her, lifting her head onto his lap and adding his hands to hers, already applying pressure to her abdomen.

She blinks once and smiles when she sees it's him. "I'm sorry, amor," she says quietly. "I'm so sorry."

"Sorry? You have nothing to be sorry about," he says. Tears drip from his cheeks as he speaks and he presses harder against the wound in her stomach. "Who did this to you?"

Luz blinks slowly. "It happened so fast. He asked my name, so I offered him a seat. So stupid of me," she breathes. "He told me to give him my pearls. I refused. Then he ripped them off my neck and ran. I didn't even feel the knife until I got up to follow him. I'm so sorry."

"Stop apologizing, please, it isn't your fault, amor, it isn't," he begs. "Save your strength, dear, please, save your strength. Help is coming, I'm sure of it, help is coming."

Tears drip from his cheeks as he speaks, confirming to both of them that what he's saying may be true, but it's also irrelevant. Help might be coming, but by the time it arrives, it will be too late. Luz will be gone, and Javier will be broken.

She smiles and cups his cheek in her hand. "Javier," she says, "It's going to be okay. I'm going to be okay."

He nods and presses harder on her abdomen, looking around frantically for someone, anyone, who can help her.

"Javier," she says, pulling his eyes back to hers with the same undeniable force that she has pulled him with since the day he met her.

"Yes, love. I'm here. I'm right here."

"Tell me something beautiful."

He smiles at her through trails of tears and pushes a fallen strand of hair behind her ear. "You," he says. "You are my something beautiful."

She lets her eyelids fall shut, a smile on her lips.

The crowd around them has grown, but he doesn't care. Right now, they are the only two people on earth. One losing a life, the other their reason to live. One heart racing, the other coasting to a stop.

His chin crashes against his chest, and his shoulders shake out of control as tears pour out in buckets. What happens next is all a blur. Two men in white uniforms pull him off of her and lift her onto a stretcher. They carry her away from the park to a small ambulance parked nearby, and he follows close behind, watching the subtle rise and fall of her chest the whole way, each breath like an ocean wave crashing against the shore. Second after second after second.

The paramedics close the doors and drive away without telling him where they are taking her. Javier doesn't know what to do, so he does the only thing he can think of. He takes off running.

———

Javier hangs the chalkboard on the wall and grabs the broom as the scene from Luz's accident closes in his head. In a way, he lost a best friend that morning. Today, he lost another one.

He looks at the words written on the board, and pain draws itself across his face.

"You may not see them now, but family is forever."

———

Abuela stares at the clock on her bedside table until it flips to 6:25 A.M. She doesn't know exactly how long she's been awake, but it feels like all night. Maybe it was. Keeping track of time seems pointless now she has seemingly nothing and no one to look forward to.

By muscle memory alone, she pulls herself out of bed, gets dressed, opens her door, and trudges down the hall. She stops at the boys' bedroom and pulls back the curtain. The silence behind it greets her like a tsunami, and the beds inside pull her in. She steps into the room and sits down, her back against the dresser drawers, and begins to sob.

Through a fog of tears, she gazes at Santi's mattress on the floor, the bedsheets on top still without a wrinkle, same as the day he left.

The day he moved, she corrects herself, wishing so strongly she could still call that day the day he left, but no. That belongs to another day now.

Another wave of grief curls and crashes over her shoulders, dragging them down.

When she lost María, it was the first time anyone close to her had ever died. She had no idea what came next. What to expect. So she did what she thought anyone in her situation would do. She tried to forget.

She boxed up her clothes and put away her photographs and buried the rest of her things in her closet. She even stopped saying her name. Until something horrible happened. It worked. She forgot.

One day, she woke up, made her coffee, listened to the news, bought her groceries, came upstairs, sat on the couch, picked up the newspaper, and looked at the date. March 18th. The day after María's birthday. It hadn't even been two years since she'd passed and already she had forgotten her birthday.

It was then she understood the cruelest of all of grief's tricks, which is to convince you that the only way to erase the pain is to forget, and so you try and you try and you try to forget only to discover that forgetting doesn't erase the pain. Nothing erases the pain. You just learn to live with it. By the time Rosa realized that with María, it was too late. She had buried the memories of her so deep that many of them became unreachable, and the ones she could reach were like smoke, easy to see but impossible to hold.

"I won't make that mistake this time, mijo," she whispers in the direction of Santi's mattress. "I promise."

Slowly, she turns her eyes to the other half of the room. The side she's been avoiding. Coco's bed is buried beneath a pile of junk that's sat untouched since the day she threw him out the first time.

"The first time," she snorts, disgusted with herself.

Why couldn't she learn? Why hadn't she changed? Why was it so impossible for her to realize that he was just a kid trying his best? More than that, he was *her* kid trying his best. And why had it been so hard for her to understand that sometimes trying your best and falling short deserves a bit of slack, and other times it deserves all the slack you have?

The questions are loud inside her head, but the answers are silent.

She looks again at his mattress tucked up to the corner of the room. The same corner María's bed was in for two decades. They are so much alike, María and Coco. Independent. Brave. Misguided at times, but confident. Caring. Strong.

They were both so strong. They had to be to put up with her bullshit their whole lives. What would María say to her today if she saw what became of her boys?

She'd have my head, she thinks, but immediately shakes her head. *No. She wouldn't.*

She only hopes that with all the gifts Coco got from his mother, he got that one too. The strength to forgive.

The strength to come home.

CHAPTER 35

NOVEMBER 1989

NOTHING.

For some, it's the only word to adequately describe the feeling of losing someone. Nothing. You feel nothing. As if your brain and your body suddenly forgot everything they'd ever experienced. Every sound, every taste, every smell, every word, every feeling, every emotion. Everything. All gone.

It doesn't help that the only words of hope anyone else ever seems to offer is that even after our darkest nights, the sun rises. They think that's helpful. It isn't. Because the piece they leave out is that the sun that rises isn't the same sun as before. For those in the deepest trenches of mourning, the sun doesn't signify hope and happiness but truth. A poignant daily reminder that what's past has passed and that time has already moved on.

Coco sits on a bench on the edge of an empty park a mile above downtown. The sun has only just begun to make its mark on the sky above him and he longs for the warmth of a past life. He pulls back the slide of the gun in his hand and stares at the single bullet left in the chamber, then lets it go and watches it snap back into place.

Only takes one, he thinks.

He pulls the slide back again. He isn't scared of dying. Not like this, anyway. At least by pulling the trigger himself he gets to be in charge of how and when he goes out, instead of sprinting into the void with his head over his shoulder, wondering how long he has left until Andrés catches up, a folded photograph of him in his pocket with a dollar amount stamped over his face. This is better than that.

So why can't he just do it then? He has every reason to. He has no family left who loves him; no friends left to fall back on. That's not to mention the billionaire drug lord who in all likelihood, has made putting a bullet through his skull his top priority. He could make it easier on everyone if he just raised the gun and pulled the trigger. Closed the book after chapter upon chapter of anticlimactic disappointment.

But he can't. Not because he doesn't want to but because something is holding him back. A promise made a thousand times between two brothers too stubborn to say the three words they really meant.

He stands up and pulls back the slide one last time. He tips the gun over, and the bullet drops out onto the ground. He watches it bounce on the sidewalk, then throws the gun into the bushes.

"Pase lo que pase, hermanito," he says. "Pase lo que pase."

He turns to leave, and as he does, he feels the warmth of the sun on his face. He bites his lip and shoves his hands in his pockets, and walks away. Where to? He isn't sure.

Onward.

———

Sofia raps her fist on the metal door and hears the patter of a pair of feet dancing towards her on the other side, carrying with them a song of familiar squeals and giggles. When her mother and daughter open the door, both are smiling wider than Sofia has ever seen them. She attempts at first to mirror their joy, but the corners of her lips quiver and fold like the arms of an exhausted weightlifter raising a bar that is just too heavy. When they do, she crumbles. Not piece by piece but all at once, her neck, shoulders, back, and legs imploding in one dust-clouded heap and collapsing into two pairs of arms, neither of which should be strong enough to catch her. But they do.

"Can I stay with you for a while?" she asks her mom.

"Darling," she responds, taking her by the hand and bringing her inside, "you can stay with me forever."

CHAPTER 36

NOVEMBER 1989

THE MEDELLÍN CARTEL is an organization which means that, like any organization, its success is dependent on the level of trust given to and returned by its members. Unlike many organizations, the trust given to its members comes with conditions. These conditions are unwritten but well understood, and, when it comes down to it, they boil down to one very simple choice: say yes and live, or so say no and die.

"Something happened with Coco," Pablo says, tossing a clipboard onto the desk in front of him, the joints to the chair he is sitting on creaking beneath him as he leans back and clasps his hands in front of him. "What was it?"

Andrés steps towards the desk and takes a seat in one of two empty chairs. "His brother was on the Avianca flight. He didn't know until after it happened, and the shock hit him pretty hard."

"Do you think he'll go to the press?"

"No. The way he looked when I saw him, I think his only thought right now is to get away from it all."

"You saw him?"

He nods. "He stopped at our house a day or two ago. Filled a bag with cash and took off."

"Any idea where to?"

"Not exactly," he answers, "but I'm sure I could track him down."

Pablo scratches his chest. "Find him and bring him in," he says. "I'd like to talk to him myself before we do anything drastic. Who knows, he's kept his mouth shut this long. Maybe there is still some loyalty there I can squeeze out of him. It would hurt me to lose someone as valuable as he's proven to be."

Andrés winces at Pablo's words and he takes a deep breath before responding. "All due respect, Patrón," he says, "I've known Coco for a long time. He and his brother were close. This doesn't feel like the type of thing he'll ever come back from."

"What are you suggesting?"

"Let me take care of him. Eliminate the risk of him opening his mouth before he catches wind of any reporters out there sniffing around for leads."

Pablo's chair bobs backward and forward, "You two are close, is that right?"

"Coco and I?"

"Sí."

"We've known each other for years, as I said."

"Why do you want to kill him then?"

Andrés reaches up and presses his thumb against a small, round bruise on the underside of his chin. "Because who needs friends when you have an empire?"

Pablo takes his time digesting the answer, swishing it around in his mouth until he's satisfied with the quality. "Adelante, pues," he nods. "Take Guzano with you. It never hurts to have backup, even if that backup is notoriously hot headed."

"Of course."

"And come see me when it's done, and I'll make sure you're both compensated fairly for it," he says.

Andrés smiles. "Gracias, Patrón."

He stands up and walks out of the office where Guzano is waiting for him, sitting on a windowsill and smoking a joint. He stubs it out on the wall when he sees him and flicks it into the grass on the other side.

"So," he says, "what'd he say?"

Andrés pulls his pistol out of his back waistband and cocks it, stopping to look at the bullet that drops into the chamber before allowing the slide to snap back into place. "He said exactly what I told you he'd say," he answers.

"How much?"

"Didn't give me a number," he shrugs, "but it'll be worth the time. I'm sure of that."

"That depends on how long it takes us to find him," Guz responds, scratching the back of his neck and making his way to the car.

"Finding him won't be a problem," says Andrés, following him.

"What makes you say that?"

"Because I know exactly where he'll be."

He returns the gun to his back and climbs into the car. Guzano takes his place in the passenger seat, and Andrés turns the key in the ignition, his eyes equal parts black and red. Guzano looks at him and smiles when he sees the fire in his friend's face, any doubt he had over whether or not he would have the stomach to pull the trigger the next time they see Coco evaporating and drifting out the open window.

"Let's go get that hijueputa," Andrés says and drives away with determination flooding his entire body. He's killed before, but this one is different. This time when he pulls the trigger, he won't leave just one body behind; he'll be ending a friendship, a brotherhood, and a life, all with a single bullet.

———

Coco's lips hang on the end of the cigarette as if it were the only thing keeping him from slipping over the edge of a cliff and into the void below. His feet ache, and the shadows under his eyes are several shades darker than usual.

He drags a toe over the three sets of initials on the ground while a voice inside his head tells him he shouldn't be here. He ignores it. It's been six years since he, Cristian, and Andrés last smoked here together, and feels like at least twice as long, but still, he knows this will be the first place Andrés will come looking for him. So here he is. Ready.

When he woke up this morning, he thought again about running. All the talk of Pablo being able to find anyone anywhere, how true could that be? Unfortunately, Coco knows all too well how true it is. The very first meeting he attended in the inner circle, Pablo put a private bounty on the head of a man he called "Tiburón" who had apparently gotten drunk and slept with a reporter. It was just sex, he insisted, he hadn't let any sensitive information slip. Still, Pablo felt it would be best if he were dealt with, even if just to send a message to the others at the table.

Not even twelve hours later, Tiburón's body was found strung up from a lightpost. Half of it, anyway.

None of that matters, though, because even disregarding all that, Coco knows that running isn't an option. The second he disappeared, Andrés would walk straight to Abuela's house and knock on her door looking for answers she wouldn't have, and the thought of her blood on his hands scares him a hell of a lot more than a bullet to his chest.

He pulls the cigarette from his lips and exhales, watching the smoke float away an inch at a time. On the street to his right, a taxi pulls to a stop, and he watches Cristian climb out of the driver seat and shuffle toward him, his eyes pointed steadily at the ground. He pulls a cigarette from his pocket as he walks, and his strides shorten while he lights it and places it gingerly between his lips. The wrinkles on his forehead are deeper even than when he last saw him a few days ago, and the way he carries himself as if each step were the step immediately after crossing the finish line in a marathon, is proof alone that he isn't the only one here fighting a losing battle.

"You're late," he says once Cristian is close enough to hear without him having to shout.

He stops, and his eyes smile when they meet Coco's. "Hard to be late when no one is expecting you," he replies.

For a while, they smoke without speaking, the only noise being the rhythmic alternation of their breaths as they pull whatever pain relief they can from the flaming sticks they've long called medicine, until finally, Coco breaks the silence.

"Santi was on that plane," he says, causing Cristian to freeze mid-breath. "The Avianca flight, the one that exploded."

Cristian pulls the cigarette from his lips and stares at him, his mouth agape.

"I knew the bomb would be on that flight because I planned the whole thing," he continues, his eyes glazed over, pointed at the horizon.

Cristian drops his cigarette and stomps it out.

"When Abuela found out what I'd done, she told me she didn't want anything to do with me. She thinks it's my fault he's dead," he says. "Part of me agrees with her." He exhales another trail of smoke.

Cristian looks at the ground between his feet at his faded initials.

"Now," Coco says, his eyes filled with smoke, "my life's over too."

Cristian's head snaps back up to look at him. "You've got plenty left to live for, Coco," he replies.

"I'm not talking metaphorically," he laughs. "I mean it's really over. I'm dead. I walked out on Pablo as soon as I knew about Santi. When Andrés saw me, he threatened to come after me if I didn't come back, which isn't happening. I'm sure Pablo put a price tag on my head when Andrés told him what happened."

Coco's words begin clicking together inside of Cristian's head, and his eyebrows jump on his forehead. "If Andrés is looking for you, don't you think this will be the first place he checks?"

"I do."

"What the hell are we doing then? We need to get out of here," he says, taking him by the arm and attempting to pull him towards his taxi on the street.

Coco doesn't move.

Cristian's cheeks redden, and his eyebrows fall. "So that's it then?" he asks, his hands balling into fists. "You're just going to sit here and wait for him to find you?"

"What choice do I have?" Coco asks. "If I run, he'll catch up."

"You don't know that," he responds, raising his voice. "You don't know that."

"Maybe not, but I know what would happen if he didn't. He would come after you instead. And Abuela and Javier and Sofia. I can't let that happen."

"That doesn't mean you give up," Cristian says, the anger in his voice giving way to exasperation. "It doesn't mean you just stand here waiting to d–"

"Cristian," Coco stops him. He tosses his cigarette to the ground and turns so they are facing each other. "You aren't listening to me. My life is over. I have nothing..." His voice cracks, and he takes a deep breath. "I have no one left."

The red in Cristian's olive eyes fades away in an instant, replaced by a subtle hint of blue. "You have me," he says.

Coco puts a hand on his shoulder. "I know," he says.

Cristian nods, silently waving a nonexistent white flag. He pulls a fresh cigarette from his pocket and lights it, then offers it to Coco, who takes it from him and presses it to his mouth.

"Hey," he says, "do you remember that time we were playing cops and robbers at your house, and Santi kept begging to play with us, so we finally told him he could, but he had to be the stolen money?"

"And we put him inside a duffel bag and were about to roll him down the stairs when Abuela came home and smacked the hell out of both of us," Coco laughs. "How could I forget? I might still have a bruise back here somewhere," he says, turning his head and looking down his back.

"She said it was her turn to be the cop and that justice had to be served," Cristian says, a boyish smile spreading between his rosy cheeks.

"How about the time we stole all those fireworks on New Year's Eve and came up here to light them," he says, "but your hands were shaking so much you lit the wrong end of the wick and almost blew my whole damn hand off?"

"Your finger looked like morcilla for three weeks after that," Cristian responds, his shoulder trembling with laughter.

"At least that long," he smiles. "All I remember is you running around for a full five minutes after it happened, screaming, 'I'm deaf! I'm deaf!'"

Cristian keels over in laughter and waves a hand above his head at him to stop talking.

"And then we went back to your house and your aunt gave us some long lecture about how dangerous fireworks can be and you watched until she finished talking and then all you said was, 'WHAT?'"

"I couldn't hear a word she was saying!" Cristian wheezes, straightening up momentarily before folding in half again.

Coco drapes an arm over his back and joins him in uncontrollable laughter. The happiness of simpler times begins to wrap itself around him like a familiar blanket until it's ripped away by two words and two pairs of footsteps.

"Q'hubo maricas."

Coco and Cristian stop laughing and stand up straight. The cigarette between Coco's fingers slips and tumbles to the sidewalk, extinguishing itself in a perfect, black circle of ash at his feet. Andrés approaches them from the street, flanked on his right by Guzano. His face is caught between a smile and a snarl like an attack dog pitted against a cornered housecat, and he quickly closes the gap between them. Guzano bounces happily beside him, his oversized white t-shirt jumping off his shoulders at every step.

"Sorry to interrupt what looks to be a very intimate lovefest," Andrés says. "If you want, we can turn around until you've both finished."

"Shut up, Andrés," Cristian says.

Coco takes a step forward. "Took you long enough," he says. "You must be getting paid by the hour now."

Andrés snorts.

"How much did he offer you to kill me?"

"Not enough," he answers.

Coco laughs. "Of course not," he says. "If you want, I can call up a journalist real fast and spill my guts; then you can go shoot them too. Fatten up your wallet a bit."

Andrés shakes his head. "You still don't get it, do you?" he asks. "This was never about me or the money or any of that shit. It was supposed to be about us. All three of us." He points to himself, then to Coco, then finally to Cristian, who scoffs and kicks his toe against the sidewalk, his hands in his pockets. "Our road to the top of the world instead of staying at the bottom our whole lives. If you wanted out, you should have told me. I could have helped you. Shit, even Cris had the stones to tell me no back when this all started."

"Fine," Coco shrugs. "I want out. How's that?"

He laughs. "It's too late for that now. You already know that, though. You're not stupid."

"Just do it already, Andrés. I'm getting hungry," Guzano says, throwing his head back in dramatized impatience.

"You heard your boyfriend,," Coco says. "Just do it already."

"Not before Cris leaves," Andrés replies.

"Cristian, get out of here," Coco calls over his shoulder.

"I'm not going anywhere."

"Cris," Guzano says, pointing his gun at him. "It is Cris, isn't it? It's a pleasure meeting you, truly, but if you aren't going to take off, would you mind if I shot you? That way, my friend can kill your friend, and we can go get something to eat?" He aims his gun at Cristian's broad chest, lowering it again when he catches Andrés's eye.

"I told you," Andrés says, pulling his pistol from behind his back, "this is my problem, not yours."

Guzano raises both hands above his head and takes a step backward.

"Cris..." he says.

"I'm not going anywhere," Cristian repeats.

"Just do it, Andrés," Coco says. "Just do it, it's okay." His cheeks are sunken, but his shoulders straighten as he speaks, his body doing what it can to go out with some semblance of pride. He takes another step forward. Rests his hands at his sides. "I'm ready."

Andrés looks at the gun in his hand, and the muscles in his jaw tighten visibly. Coco closes his eyes. Cristian lunges forward. Andrés spits at his feet and, in a single motion, raises his gun and pulls the trigger.

BANG!

CHAPTER 37

NOVEMBER 1989

ROSA GREW UP WITH PARENTS. Not good, not bad. Just parents.

Her friends, most of whom had bad parents, used to tell her how good she had it because she had a mom who made her breakfast in the morning and a dad who asked her how her day at school was when he got home from work at night. Anytime one of those friends said something like that to Rosa, she would shake her head and scoff.

"Those are things parents are supposed to do," she would say. "Since when does doing just what you're supposed to do make you a good anything?"

To which her friends would blink, shrug, and run off to play somewhere else.

Of course, if Rosa were the type to change her mind about things, she might look back now and realize that she really did have it good. She had a mother who cared and a father who worked. She never had to sleep without a roof over her head or walk outside without shoes under her feet. She never wanted for anything. Somehow all that did was make her want everything.

Specifically, she wanted to experience things. Adventure, love, even pain. Which explains why, as soon as she turned seventeen, she kissed her mother, shook her father's hand, and ran.

It was exhilarating, experiencing life on her own, and she made sure to make the most of it. Then one day, she met a boy, had what some would call too much fun, and wound up pregnant. The day she realized it, she left him alone without telling him.

Reality caught up to her that day. Or maybe it killed her. She didn't know then, and she's even less sure now. All she knew was that if she were going to bring a baby into the world, she needed to be a good mother, or at least a mother who did all the things she was supposed to do. She needed a fresh start.

She thought she found that in Medellín, then again in María, but for as much as she loved that girl, and she loved her as much as she had ever loved anything, there were two thoughts that, beginning on the day she was born, became impossible for her to shake.

The first was resentment. Her entire world now fit snugly in her arms, and while that was a beautiful thing, it didn't stop her from longing for the world she had left behind. The one she felt she had only just begun to discover.

The second feeling was desperation, because she knew that whether she wanted it or not, this girl was going to leave her one day.

Couple those feelings with the daily draw on her patience that comes with raising a child, and she quickly became more irritable than she'd ever been. That only snowballed as María grew until Rosa's biggest fear came true. María left.

Rosa felt it coming, and she pulled and pulled to keep her from going but it didn't matter. María had made up her mind about going off into the world on her own, and Rosa was the last person who could fault her for it.

With María gone, she thought she might get back to the old life she had chosen to leave behind when she got pregnant. But the days rolled into months that turned into years and she fell asleep and woke up in the exact same bed for every last one of them. She hadn't even felt her life slipping through her fingers, but she could see them now. Both of them. Broken on the floor. It would have stayed that way too, but something incredible happened that changed everything. María came home.

That day Rosa opened the door and saw her daughter, pregnant, standing outside her door and holding the hand of a near two-year-old boy was among the happiest days she'd ever lived. She felt like she had been given a second chance at this second life of hers, and she was going to hold onto it with everything she had.

Then María died.

Her life was once again in pieces. Not by some grand explosion, but a silent, instantaneous implosion of the soul. She lost the ability to hold onto anything. She pushed without meaning to, without knowing it was even happening, until finally she'd pushed everyone around her hard enough and for long enough that they all left. For good.

All of them but one.

"Amor," calls a voice from down the hall, "breakfast is ready!"

She smiles and kisses her fingers, pressing them gently against the photo on her nightstand.

"Coming, Javier!"

———

The day after Luz was attacked, Javier woke up alone, unsure which side of the bed was colder.

The ambulance had taken her to the nearest hospital several kilometers away, and he had run after it the whole way. Didn't stop once.

When he got there, he demanded someone take him to her. They all refused, repeating the same useless bullshit.

She's in surgery. No, you can't see her. No, you can't sleep here. Come back tomorrow. If she makes it, you can see her then.

If she makes it.

He knew it was their job not to make promises, but couldn't they at least be optimistic?

If she makes it.

Come back tomorrow.

Finally, he accepted that he had no other choice and went home. He somehow managed an hour or two of sleep, and as soon as he woke up, he was back out the door running to the hospital. He grabbed the first nurse he saw and again demanded to see Luz.

"Have a seat," she tells him. "I'll go and get the doctor."

"Fine," Javier replies, not moving.

A moment later a doctor emerges from a closed-off hallway and attempts to shake his hand.

"Where is Luz?" Javier asks, his patience thin. "Is she okay?"

"She's weak and very tired, but she's going to be fine," the doctor answers. "She lost a lot of blood, so it's imperative that she take it easy for a while, especially with the pregnancy."

Javier's heart drops into his shoes.

"Pregnancy?" he asks.

The doctor blushes. "Perhaps it's better if you go in and speak with her. I'll take you to her."

Javier agrees and follows the doctor to a room at the end of a dimly-lit hallway. The doctor gives him a nod and excuses himself. Javier knocks once on the door and lets himself in.

Luz grins from ear to ear when she sees him and pushes herself upright. He crosses the bed and gives her a kiss on the top of her head before sitting beside her.

"Thank God you're okay," he says.

"Javier," she replies, squeezing his hand, "there's something I need to tell you."

He smiles at her and places both of their hands on her stomach. "The doctor already told me, amor," he says.

"Of course he did," she says, shooting an angry glance at the door. "Idiot."

He laughs. "Did you know?" he asks.

"I had a hunch, was just waiting for the right time to tell you."

"I guess this is it."

"I guess it is."

He laughs again and kisses her hand. At the same time, his foot taps an erratic beat on the polished concrete floor.

He's going to be a dad. Him. A dad. It's a beautiful thought, but equally as paralyzing. What qualifies a man to become a dad? He doesn't know, but he's pretty sure he doesn't have it. He and Luz hardly have a dollar to their name and haven't slept in the same bed longer than a week for five years and now he's expected to raise a baby? To provide for her? To protect her? How is he supposed to do that?

Suddenly, scenes from the day before flash in rapid succession behind his eyes. The throng of people circled in the park. The pearls from Luz's necklace scattered across the ground. The red circle growing from her abdomen. The disappearing lights of the ambulance leaving him behind.

How am I supposed to protect a baby when I couldn't even protect her?

"Javier?" she says, leaning into him. "Are you okay?"

"What? Oh, yeah, of course, of course, of course," he says. "I'm thrilled, really, I am. Just in shock, a bit still, I think."

She nods and he can see her biting her cheek.

"What is it, amor?"

She wipes her eyes before looking into his. "I think we need to stop running around and settle down," she says. "Find a place to call home. A place to raise a family."

He looks at her, confusion and relief flooding his brain. "This is unexpected coming from you," he says.

"I suppose getting stabbed and finding out you're pregnant in one afternoon is enough to make a person do unexpected things," she shrugs.

He grins. "Ok," he says. "If that's what you want."

"I can't say it's what I'll want forever, but for right now I think it's what's best."

"Well then consider it done."

"There is one other thing," she says.

"Díme."

She takes a deep breath. "I'd like to change my name."

He opens his mouth but she continues.

"I love my name, I do, but I always loved it most because it so perfectly embodied who I wanted to be. I wanted to be like the light. Light is beautiful. It goes everywhere, experiences everything, touches everyone." She pulls his hand back onto her stomach. "With all this that's happened the past twenty-four hours, it suddenly doesn't feel as fitting."

Javier's head bobs in silence, processing what she's saying. Then he asks, "Do you have a name in mind?"

She smiles. "My middle name I think fits quite perfectly. Equally beautiful, but the type of beauty that stays in one place. The type that needed Luz in order to get here, but now that she's grown can stand on her own."

"And you're sure?"

"I am."

"Okay, then," he nods. "Whatever you say."

She clears her throat and cocks her head at him.

"Sorry," he says. "Whatever you say, Rosa."

———

"Show me everything."

Those were the words that opened the first chapter of Rosa's and Javier's love story. A love story that was perfect. Until it wasn't.

Rosa's attack changed both of them. María's arrival changed them too. Both events together turned them into versions of themselves that were recognizable, but that had a shell around them made from previously nonexistent characteristics.

For her, that was irritability.

For him, it was paranoia.

It was her idea to move to Medellín. He resisted, favoring a small town where life would be quieter, safer, but she persisted. He knew it was because she needed to be in a city where she always felt there was more to be explored, something she couldn't get in a small town. So, he gave in, with just one condition.

"We find a two-story building where I can convert the ground floor to a convenience store," he said. "That way, I can work without ever having to leave you and María alone."

"Fine," she agreed.

She quickly regretted it.

As time passed, his paranoia only grew, which meant so too did her irritability. That was fine, for the most part, as long as they had somewhere to direct it, which for them was María. But, María got older, as children do, and pushed them away, as children do, and despite both of their best efforts to keep her close, she left.

It took a couple of weeks for the reality of that to settle in, but once it did, everything changed. Rosa hinted often at wanting to go back to their old way of living. Javier wouldn't do it. At the same time, he insisted on accompanying her anytime she left the house to do anything. She couldn't stand it. Pretty soon, all the time they spent together was spent either arguing or in complete silence. Neither of them wanted things to be that way, sometimes that's just what happens when two people who love each other dearly have such opposite ideas of how that love is best lived out.

Things improved when María moved back in and once again gave them a direction to point their emotions that wasn't each other. When she died, that improvement proved to be built of kindling and kerosene.

Losing María cemented in each of them the feelings they'd been feeding since the day Rosa was attacked.

She was no longer irritable, she was hopeless.

He was no longer paranoid, he was right.

Within six months, their love was up in flames. The spark that did it came one afternoon in the studio apartment behind the tienda. By that time, he was spending more time downstairs than he was upstairs, and had decided he needed a place to sit down when things were slow. So, he went downtown and bought himself a table and four chairs.

"It just makes sense since I'm down here all day to have somewhere to sit and read a book or have a snack," he told her when she saw it.

"A chair, fine," she replied, "but FOUR chairs?! What on earth do you need four chairs for? Who are you planning on having over? Because it won't be me."

It didn't take long after that for the table and four chairs to become a fridge, then a couch, then a bed. Just like that, it was like those first five years had never even happened. Now, they were just neighbors, and their love story was no longer perfect.

It was over.

———

Losing a child can tear two parents apart. It did that to Rosa and Javier. Losing a child can also bring two parents together. It did that to Rosa and Javier, too.

He rolls out of bed at the same time he has every morning for forty years. He leans down and kisses her one time on the forehead, then gets dressed and walks down the hall. He stops at the second bedroom, where he pulls back the curtain to look at the two mattresses on the floor. The silence of that room pounds against his chest like the ocean crashing onto the shore. Wave after wave, second after second.

He closes the curtain and heads for the door, pulling his coat off the hook and putting it on before going downstairs. He opens the tienda, writes a new phrase on the chalkboard outside, and grabs his broom. Then, he sweeps.

Swish, swish, swish.

Customers filter in and out as he remains outside, and he nods and smiles at each of them. Once he's sure he's made enough money to keep the lights on another day, he stores his broom inside and closes his doors. He goes through to the studio apartment in the back where he unplugs the radio, empties the fridge, and folds his bedsheets. He picks up each of the four chairs and stacks them neatly in the corner. Then he turns off the lights, locks the door and goes upstairs. Goes home.

Theirs will never be a perfect love story. They each made far too many mistakes for that. Fortunately for them both, a love story doesn't need to be perfect to be worth it.

Everybody knows that.

CHAPTER 38

DECEMBER 1989

Coco opens his eyes and clutches his chest with both hands, frantically fighting for air. The pain reverberates throughout his body, and he silently wishes for death to take him quickly. To spare him from suffering.

When he finally manages a breath, oxygen floods his lungs like a river bursting a dam. He pulls his hands away from his chest and looks at them. It isn't until he sees his fingers and notices the absence of blood on them that he realizes that the pain in his chest wasn't caused by a gunshot, but by the anxiety of expecting a shot that never came.

He looks at Andrés with inquisitive eyebrows, but before he gets answers, he hears a gurgling noise next to him, and he turns and sees Cristian with his hands on his stomach, his face colorless.

"Cristian," he gasps, reaching for him.

Cristian stumbles sideways a step and folds over the block wall to his right. He struggles to hold himself up as he vomits once, twice, three times onto the ground on the other side. Coco grabs him by the back of his coat and attempts to pull him up, but the dead weight of his body is too much for him alone. He pulls again, and this time a second pair of hands join his on Cristian's back, and together he and Andrés manage to get him back on his feet.

"Are you alright, Cris?" Andrés asks, slapping him twice on the back before taking a step away from both he and Coco.

Cristian doesn't answer, too busy wiping tears from his eyes and vomit from the corners of his mouth. Andrés turns on his heel, walking a few yards down the sidewalk before squatting to the ground. He unfurls Guzano's lifeless fingers and frees the pistol clenched in his hand, careful to avoid touching the spattering of blood on his chest and the increasingly larger pool spreading beneath his back.

When he stands up, he shoves Guz's body with his boot, rolling him onto his side with his face pointed away from Coco and Cristian. Then he turns and walks back to his friends, now sitting on the waist-high wall, Coco with one hand on Cristian's shoulder and Cristian with both hands behind his neck, his head between his knees.

"You okay, marica?" Andrés repeats.

Coco pulls his hand from Cristian's shoulder and holds it out towards Andrés, stopping him in his tracks.

"In my defense," Andrés says, his hands raised, a pistol in each one, "I did tell you to get out of here, Cris. I didn't want you to have to see that. It's pretty..." he looks at Guz's dead body. "I puked too, actually, the first time I saw someone...you know, the first time I saw something like this."

Cristian spits on the ground and wipes his mouth, then pulls himself up and turns to sit on the wall. "What the hell is going on?" he asks, looking back and forth from Andrés to Coco as if expecting them to both start laughing and tell him that everything that had happened over the last three years had been some violent, elaborate practical joke. He waits for them to respond, and while he's waiting, his eyes drift past Andrés and lock onto Guz's body surrounded in blood, and he spins back around over the wall to vomit again.

"Seriously, Andrés, what the hell is happening?" Coco says.

"If you two would give me a minute to explain instead of shooting me dirty looks or hurling every five seconds, I could tell you," Andrés says back. "Pablo wants me to bring you in, which you and I both know means he wants you dead. I wasn't too fond of that idea, so I came up with a plan of my own."

Cristian gives a thumbs up over his shoulder, his head still out of sight behind the wall, but Coco shakes his head.

"No," he starts. "No plans. No games." He shakes his head some more. "You were supposed to shoot me. This is supposed to be over."

"Are you telling me you'd rather be dead?" Andrés asks, irritated.

"Of course not," he says. "But I have to be. You said yourself, if I run, Pablo will find me, and he'll find Abuela and Sofia and Javier. I can't take that risk."

"What I *actually* said was if you run, *I'll* find you," he corrects. "Which I did. Which is why you're still alive right now. As for the others, don't worry about them, they'll be fine. Pablo's never going to find them."

"How do you know?"

"I know because I took care of it."

"I have to be honest, Andrés, you saying that is more nerve-wracking than it is comforting," Coco says.

"He's right," Cristian mumbles, still out of view.

"You wouldn't be saying that if you knew what I meant. This plan's sure as shit after mondongo, I promise."

"Let's hear it then," says Coco.

He rubs his palms together, then flashes them at Coco like a magician setting up for his first trick. "What does everyone in the world, including Pablo, call you?" he asks.

"What do you mean?"

"I mean your name, dumbass. What do they think your name is?"

"Coco?"

"Exactly. Which is great because Coco isn't your real name,

and it's pretty hard to track down a guy or his family when all you've got to go on is a nickname."

"I guess," he says, following along. "You don't think Pablo could find a way to figure out my real name?"

"Oh no, I do, I definitely do," Andrés shakes his head. "That's why I already told him what it was."

"You lost me," Coco says.

"Me too," Cristian echoes, finally shaking off enough nausea to sit up straight and face them.

"Instead of letting him do his digging until he found out your real name, I gave him a fake one," he says. "Diego Luís Rincón Bedoya."

"You gave Pablo a fake name?"

"Technically, it's a real name. The guy lives in Medellín, downtown somewhere. I did my homework," he winks at Cristian.

Coco looks down at the ground, his eyes darting back and forth. "So, how long do we have before he realizes that this Diego guy isn't me?"

"A few hours, maybe a day tops," Andrés shrugs, "but by then, you'll be gone."

"What about you?"

He smiles. "I'll be gone too," he says.

Coco says nothing. Could this work? Could he get away from all of this without putting anyone else in harm's way? The wheels in his brain spin faster and faster until pillars of invisible smoke start to billow from his ears. Then they stop. "Okay," he says. "What do we do next?"

Andrés reaches into the back pocket of his jeans. He pulls out a wad of cash and a few small pieces of paper. "Here's what you need to do," he says, handing him everything. "Leave here and go straight to the bus station. There are two tickets there," he points at the papers he just gave him. "One to Pereira, the other to Bogotá. Get on the bus to Pereira right away and sit in the first seat behind the driver. As far as we know, I'm still the only person

Pablo has looking for you, so you shouldn't have any trouble, but still, keep an eye out for anyone who looks at you twice or who avoids you altogether. If someone stands out, get off. Otherwise, wait until the bus pulls out of the station, then immediately stand up and tell the driver to let you off. If he refuses, pay him until he changes his mind."

"Got it," Coco says, pulling the ticket marked "Pereira" from the bottom of the stack in his hand and placing it on top.

"When you get off," Andrés goes on, "flag the first cab you see and tell the taxista to drive anywhere for half an hour and drop you back off at the terminal. Make sure he sticks to the highways and avoids downtown, and keep your head low and on a swivel, especially in traffic." He mimes ducking down and twisting his head from side to side. "Like this," he says.

"I know what a swivel is, but I appreciate the visual," Coco says.

"What's the longest you've ever gone without being a smart-ass, just out of curiosity?" Andrés asks.

Cristian smiles.

"Anyway," he goes on, "when you get back to the station, find the bus to Bogotá but don't board until just before it pulls off the curb. Slip the driver some cash when you get on and tell him not to open the door for anyone and to keep his gas stops short. Then, once you're in Bogotá, find the next connecting bus out of the country, buy a ticket, and you're home free."

"Home free in another country," Coco mutters.

"*Alive* in another country," Cristian corrects.

Andrés points at him and nods.

"You think this is going to work?" asks Coco.

"Of course," he says, smacking him on the shoulder. "I planned it all myself." He pulls the gun he took from Guzano from his waistband and hands it to him. "Probably ought to take this, though," he says, "just in case."

Coco hesitates but takes the gun from him and puts it on his back.

"Oh, and Cris," Andrés says, "you might want to skip town for a little while too. Especially if you're going to drive him to the station."

"Oh," Cristian nods, "Right, okay, yeah."

Andrés bites his lip, and all three of them go quiet and simultaneously drag a toe across the ground.

"Alright," says Andrés, rubbing the back of his neck, "enough small talk." He grabs Cristian by the arm and yanks him to his feet, then does the same to Coco. "Get out of here. Both of you. I'll see you when all this is over."

Coco squints his eyes at him. "What are you gonna do?" he asks.

"The less you know about that, the better," he answers.

Coco opens his mouth but decides not to press. "See you soon then, I guess."

"Yeah," he nods. "See you soon."

Coco nods at Cristian, and together they walk towards Cristian's taxi parked on the street. Cristian opens the driver's door and climbs in, but Coco doesn't follow right away. Instead, he turns and walks back to Andrés and asks, "Why did you do this? You had everything you ever wanted, and you're giving it all away. Why?"

Andrés slides both hands in his pockets and shrugs. "Because family comes first," he says, "and you're the only family I've got."

Coco bites down hard on the inside of his cheek and holds out a hand. Andrés slaps it and pulls him into an embrace. Neither of them says the words they're thinking. They don't have to.

When they separate, Andrés nods, and Coco nods back. Then he walks to the taxi, opens his door, and gets in.

Andrés watches them leave before bending down and picking up a half-smoked cigarette from the sidewalk. He pauses to check out the three sets of faded initials carved on the ground. When he stands up, he leans against the wall behind him and pulls a lighter from his pocket. He inhales as the charred tip of the cigarette gains new life and holds the smoke in his chest while he takes in the view one more time.

Medellín, Colombia. It's just a city, but as far as he is concerned, he can see the entire world from right here. He smokes until there's nothing left, flicking the butt at the ground when he's finished and walking to the street. He passes Guz's body but avoids looking at him; his chin held high. Then he climbs onto his motorcycle and rides away.

He has a phone call to make.

————

Cristian pulls over to the curb opposite a long row of buses, each with the name of a different city stuck to the inside of the front windshield, and watches the people in and around the station all move in different directions at different speeds.

"There it is," he points to a yellow bus with faded red and blue stripes parked two-thirds of the way down the row.

Coco's eyes follow his finger, and he sees the white sign with the word "Pereira" printed on it hanging in the window. "Right," he swallows. "That must be it."

"Are you nervous?"

"You're remembering that Andrés planned this whole thing himself, aren't you?" he says with a quiet laugh. "Of course, I'm nervous." He takes a deep breath and exhales slowly. "But an hour ago, I thought I would be dead right now, so I guess I'll take nervous."

"Well, relax," Cristian reassures him, "everything will be fine."

"Fine's not good," Coco points out.

"Fine, everything will be *good* then. How about that?"

"Good's not great," he clarifies with raised eyebrows as he looks out the window.

"Really?" Cristian asks, looking at him as though he would like nothing more at that moment than to treat the back of

Coco's head like the bottom of a ketchup bottle. "Of all the times to be a smart-ass?"

"Sorry," he says, "that's the nerves talking."

"You must be nervous a lot," Cristian says, putting a smile on Coco's face. "Just keep your head down and stick to the plan. Everything will work out."

"I know it will," he agrees. Then he shakes his head. "You know, for all the times I've imagined how my life would turn out, I never saw it going this way."

"Hold on," Cristian cuts him off. "You're telling me that not *once* did you expect to narrowly avoid being murdered by one of your best friends before being forced out of the country to escape a deranged drug dealer?"

"Crazy, right?" Coco laughs. "Don't get me wrong, I know I've always been something of a screw-up, but I guess I always thought that at some point I would get my shit straight. Get life figured out." He turns away from the window and looks at Cristian. "I never pictured anything like this."

Cristian sees a glint of emotion in his eyes, and he puts his hand on his shoulder. "Life's not over yet," he says. "You've still got plenty of years left to get your shit straight. Or not," he shrugs.

An unintentional breath of laughter escapes Coco's lips. He turns back to the window and sees the first passengers start to board the bus that will soon take him away from all of this. "Hey," he says, "why don't you come with me?"

"What?"

"Come with me," he says again. "Go buy a bus ticket right now and we'll go together. A fresh start for both of us."

"I don't know..." Cristian starts, rubbing the back of his head and eyeing the row of buses.

"Come on," he insists, shaking his friend by the arm. "I'm sure we can find a nice, quiet place with a great view for you to smoke at every day if that's what you're worried about."

Cristian laughs and shakes his head. "No, that's not it, it's..."

"Well, what is it then? It can't be work. You hate driving this stupid taxi around all day. What else could be holding you back?"

Cristian pauses, twisting his hands on the steering wheel. "I just think it would be better if I didn't," he says after a minute.

Coco's chest deflates. "Oh," he says.

"It's not personal, obviously. I mean, you're my best friend, always will be, but this, to me, feels like the moment where we're supposed to go our separate ways," he explains. He looks over at Coco. "Like it's fate or destiny or whatever. You know?"

"What? Oh, yeah, totally," Coco says. "So, what *are* you going to do?"

"Don't know," he answers, shrugging. "Drive, I guess. See where I end up. Someplace quiet, with any luck."

"Quiet," Coco nods. "Quiet would be nice."

"Right?" Cristian laughs.

"Well, hey," Coco says, checking his pockets to make sure he has everything he needs, "in case I don't..." he stops and bites his cheek until his voice steadies. "In case it's a while before we see each other, thanks for always being there for me. I'm sorry I was such a shitty friend sometimes."

"Most of the time," Cristian corrects.

"Sure," he grins. "Seriously though, parce, te quiero."

Cristian smiles. "Good luck," he says.

They slap hands and embrace as best they can in the front seat of the cramped taxi. Cristian watches him board and keeps watching him through the window until the bus backs away from the curb and pulls around the corner, out of sight.

A woman approaches his taxi and leans her head down.

"¿Estás libre?" she asks.

Cristian pulls his cigarette from his lips and exhales. "No," he answers. "Not really."

CHAPTER 39

NOVEMBER 1989

IT'S OFTEN SAID that the moment before you die, your entire life flashes before your eyes, and you see everything you've ever done replayed in a single, instantaneous shot. That may be true when death comes unexpectedly, but when you approach death knowingly, the opposite occurs. Time stops. Instead of seeing your life in a flash, you see it all in great detail, as if you'd been given the chance to live it all over again but without the ability to change anything.

Andrés sits on a cold, metal chair in the center of an otherwise empty room. Pablo Escobar stands a few feet in front of him, his arms folded. Behind him stand two men Andrés has never seen before. New recruits being given a chance to earn their place at the table.

"Do you know why I asked you to meet me here?" Pablo asks, uncrossing his arms and putting his hands in his pockets.

"I assume to talk about what happened with Coco," Andrés responds coolly.

He blinks, and when he does, a scene unfolds inside his eyes. He is a four-year-old treasure-hunting knight running down a narrow hallway being chased by a fearsome dragon dressed in a bright green button-up and slacks. When he emerges from the hall into the heart of the castle, he's swooped up by a beautiful heroine with flowering eyes and strong arms. She spins him around and drops him back on his feet, and together they attack the dragon with pokes and tickles until he kneels in surrender at their feet, at which point both the knight and the heroine lean down and kiss him on either cheek, wishing him better luck next time, and the dragon laughs.

Andrés's parents were the best kind of people. His dad worked every day from sunup to sundown, somehow managing to come home each night with enough energy leftover to wash the dishes and play a game of fútbol with him before he went to bed. As a boy, he never once heard his father complain or raise his voice, nor did he see him leave the house without kissing his wife and telling her that he loved her.

Andrés's mother was an angel. The world could say a million kind things about her, and all of them would be true, but still, they wouldn't be enough to convey just how wonderful she was as a mother, a wife, and a person.

His parents were the best kind of people. Until they weren't.

He opens his eyes and sees Pablo nodding his head.

"And what *did* happen with Coco?" he asks.

"He took off as soon as we found him," Andrés says. "Like I said on the phone, we tried to talk some sense into him, but he pulled his gun before we could get a word out, shot Guz, and bolted."

"I see."

He's five now, standing beside a hospital bed where his mom lay connected to a series of tubes and wires. Lying against her bare chest is the tiniest human being he has ever seen. He inches closer to the bed and lifts himself onto his tiptoes to get a closer look at his baby sister.

"Remember what we talked about, Andrés," his dad says, holding onto his shoulders. "Your sister is going to need lots of very special attention for a little while. From all of us. Especially you."

He looks up at his dad and nods in understanding.

"She might not be able to say it right now, but she loves you very much," his dad finishes.

Andrés looks at her and smiles. "I love her too," he says.

Pablo pulls his hands from his pockets and loops his thumbs in his belt as he paces back and forth in front of him. "So he shoots Guz," he says, "and runs. Is that right?"

"Sí, Patrón."

"And there was nothing you could do to stop him."

"No, Patrón."

It's beach week, Andrés's favorite week of the year. He's building a castle in the sand with his little sister while their mom rests her eyes on a chair a few yards away from them and their dad is off buying drinks from a cabana down the beach. He pats the top of his castle with his palm and looks around him for a leaf to serve as the flag for his new kingdom. Before he can find one, his dad approaches them with four colorful drinks balanced in one arm. Andrés stands up, wiping the sand from his hands on his shorts.

"Where's your sister?" his dad asks.

Only then does Andrés look behind him and realize he has been building his castle alone. His mother opens her eyes and sits up in her chair. Both of his parents look past him, and Andrés follows their eyes to the two tiny knee prints and pair of footprints tiptoeing toward the waves.

"No," his mom whispers, panic flooding her face as the drinks in his father's grip slip and crash to the sand.

Then they take off running, up and down the beach and in and out of the water shouting her name at the top of their lungs until their voices fail them. She never calls back, never giggles, never pokes her smiling head out from under a chair or behind a table the way she does at home when they play hide-and-seek.

Andrés sits in a puddle of disbelief, writing his sister's name with a trembling index finger in the thin layer of dust coating his legs. At the same time on opposite ends of the beach, his father collapses onto his back in the sand and his mother falls to her knees in the water. One of them screams and shakes their fists at the sky. The other sobs silently. Both feel pain so sharp and so deep that it breaks them into a million pieces, most of which are immediately pulled away by waves and lost to the sea.

The bus trip home is dark. Neither of his parents says a word for hours until the bus stops for gas and his dad gets off to use the restroom. That's when his mother turns in her seat and says to him, "It's not your fault, Andrés. If only your father hadn't gone to get drinks."

Hours later, the cab they take from the bus station pulls in front of their house, and Andrés's mom is the first to get out and go inside. His dad stops unloading their luggage and puts his hand on his shoulder.

"It isn't your fault, Andrés," he says. "If only your mother hadn't closed her eyes."

Pablo takes a deep breath, his patience fading. "Trust is important, Andrés," he says, "especially in our business."

He shifts his weight and locks his fingers together on his lap.

"Do you trust me, Andrés?"

"Of course, Patrón."

"Good," Pablo says. "Do you know who I trust?"

Andrés tilts his head. "No one?" he ventures.

Pablo nods once. "And do you know why I don't trust anyone?"

Andrés narrows his gaze and scratches his left kneecap without answering.

His parents are shouting again. It's been a year since they got back from the beach, and every day since has been the same argument with different words.

"How do you expect me to buy more beer for your drunk ass if you never go to work?" his mom yells, when what she means is, "It was your fault!"

"How about you try getting a job and I take a turn being

good-for-nothing?" his dad barks back, when what he wants to say is, "My fault? It was *your* fault!"

His mom doesn't respond, she doesn't even look at him. Her eyes are clouded over, her forever-present smile tucked down deep, somewhere unreachable. She opens the front door to leave but before she does she looks at Andrés and says, "I'll be back. I love you."

Then she walks out and slams the door behind her, leaving him to wonder for the rest of his life if her last words to him had been two lies or just one. Tears begin to fall from his eyes as he stares at the inside of the closed door. His dad looks at him and picks an empty bottle up off the floor and breaks it across Andrés's cheek.

"There," he says, "now you have something worth crying over."

Andrés follows his mom outside, pressing his hand hard against his bleeding cheek, but he passes out on the curb before he can find her. The owner of the convenience store across the street, an older gentleman, sees him and comes to his aid. He lifts him and carries him to the apartment upstairs, where his neighbor pulls a first aid kit from a cupboard and cleans and stitches the wound shut.

Andrés wakes up the next morning to the same woman shouting, "Don't touch him, he needs to rest!" at her two grandsons who are standing, hovering over him on the couch, the older one daring the younger to touch his face to see if he is still alive.

Pablo stops pacing. "Andrés?" he asks. "Do you know why I don't trust anyone?"

"Tell me."

"I don't trust anyone," he explains, "because the moment I trust someone, they stab me in the back. They try taking things that belong to me. Or worse, they try taking something that I want."

"Forgive me for saying this," Andrés says, "but it sounds like you need to find better friends."

A teenage Andrés sits on the sidewalk outside his house with his head in his hands, hoping to fall asleep before the ache in his stomach inevitably kills him. He hears a pair of footsteps approaching him from the other side of the street and looks up to see Javier walking toward him with a large bag full of food.

"On the house, Don Andrés," he says. "I insist, really, I insist." He drops the bag at his feet. "Anytime you need anything, you come to me. Okay?"

"Okay."

Pablo shakes his head. "I don't want friends, I want loyalty," he says. "Something I felt was missing when I sent you to find Coco." He pivots and walks forward, now standing just a few steps from Andrés's chair. He points at the two men behind him. "I sent these two to find Coco. Or, excuse me, to find Diego Luís Rincón Bedoya. That was his name, right?"

The two men nod in unison.

"City records told them he owned a clock and watch repair shop downtown, so they went and paid him a visit," Pablo continues.

"And?" Andrés asks.

"And they found him."

The match ends, and Andrés and his two best friends swing their legs over the wall skirting the court, laughing at a joke they won't remember ten minutes from now. He pulls the marijuana and papers he managed to steal from his dad's dresser drawer out of his pocket and rolls a joint for each of them, happy to finally be providing something of value to the group. The other two found their roles before Andrés even came into the picture. Coco was the funny one, Cristian the level-head. And Andrés? Before today, he always felt like the tagalong. The one they felt obligated to invite because he was decent at fútbol and had a shittier life than they did. Not anymore, though. Now he was the one who brought the weed.

"Hey," he says, "we should carve our names on the sidewalk right here, so everyone in the neighborhood knows this spot belongs to us." He pulls out a pocket knife and unfolds the blade. "What do you guys think?"

"Definitely," Coco says, smacking him on the back.

He takes the knife from him and passes it to Cristian, who accepts it and kneels to start scratching the letters of his name.

"Andrés, this knife sucks," he says. "It's going to take forever to carve our names with this thing."

"Just do your initials then," Coco suggests.

"Aren't you supposed to be the smart one?" Andrés supplies.

Coco laughs.

Cristian carves his initials and hands the knife off to Coco to do the same. He hands the knife back to Andrés once he's finished, and he kneels and eyeballs the distance between the letters on the ground. Then he starts on his own, putting them ever so slightly closer to Coco's than Cristian had.

"There," he says, standing up and pulling the joint from his mouth to exhale. "Now no one can take this place away from us."

Pablo nods back at one of the two men, and he steps forward and drops a red-speckled handkerchief onto Andrés's lap.

"He said to give you this," Pablo says as Andrés picks up the cloth and begins unraveling whatever is inside.

"And this is?" he asks.

"His middle finger," Pablo explains.

Andrés's face remains expressionless as a severed finger falls from inside the kerchief and into his hand waiting below.

"These two thought that cutting it off might encourage Señor Diego to tell them where the real Coco was. By the time they realized he had no idea who they were asking about, it was, I'm afraid, too late."

He wraps the finger back up and drops it on the floor. "I'm guessing he wasn't too pleased about that," he says, looking back at the two men standing over him.

Andrés hops up and sits on top of the store counter while he waits for Javier to finish helping a customer.

"Hungry?" Javier asks after the woman leaves.

"Nah," he replies, "just here to hang out a while. My dad threw me out after he heard what happened today with me and Coco."

"I see," Javier nods. "If it's any consolation, I have always been of the opinion that school isn't for everybody. Some of us are better suited to learn life as we live it."

"Yeah, well, it might not be for everyone, but it beats sleeping on the sidewalk."

"Why not go upstairs?" Javier suggests. "I'm sure Doña Rosa would happily allow you to sleep on her couch before she let you spend a night outside."

"If she did, it would only be so she could smother me in my sleep," he laughs. "No way I'm going up there. Do you know how pissed she is at me for getting Coco thrown out of school?"

"Trust me," he says. "Go."

Andrés opens his mouth, but Javier shakes his head.

"Go," he repeats.

He slides off the counter and walks outside and up the stairs, and knocks on Abuela's door. She lowers her eyebrows when she opens it but lets him inside without asking any questions. Three weeks later, he watches as she puts on her coat, marches across the street, and bangs on his dad's door. When she comes back, she looks at him and says, "You can go home now," and walks back to her bedroom to take a nap.

Pablo takes a deep breath instead of responding immediately. "Luís here called me from the man's shop and told me it was a dead end. Coincidentally, you called me just minutes later to tell me you had found Coco but that he got away from you," he says, "That's when it all clicked." He snaps his fingers, then says, with a shrug, "You let him get away."

"Now, why would I do that?" Andrés asks, leaning forward.

Another car pulls to a stop, and Andrés leans down to tell the woman in the driver's seat to step outside. She obeys, handing over the keys and answering his questions without looking him in the face. Guz nudges his shoulder, but Andrés already knows the thought running through his mind. A woman traveling alone at this hour? They could easily take her off the side of the road, have some fun with her, and send her on her way. No harm, no foul. For a second, he considers it, but then he notices her glance out of the corner of her eye at the back window of the car, and he stoops down to see what's back there.

He sees a pair of infant legs bouncing from a baby seat, and the baby girl to whom they belong smiles over at him.

She might not be able to say it right now, a voice in his head says, *but she loves you very much.*

He steps back and whistles at his men to remove the barricade barring the road. "Have a safe trip," he says to the woman and hands her back her keys.

Pablo frowns. "Maybe you did it because you have a death wish you've been hanging onto," he says. "I don't think so, though. I think you did it because you're a coward."

"Let's go with that one," Andrés smiles.

"I assume that means you won't be telling me where Coco is?" he asks.

Andrés laughs.

Pablo's face twists at the sound. "That's a shame," he says. "You know, had you made smarter choices, you could have had everything you ever wanted. Instead, you chose this." He signals to the two men. "Put the body somewhere people will see it," he instructs, then turns and walks away.

Andrés clenches his jaw and shuts his eyes. He takes a deep breath and holds it before opening them again. When he does, he smiles.

"Have at it, boys," he says.

Then everything goes black.

CHAPTER 40

NOVEMBER 1989

JAVIER BLINKS the sleep from his eyes and carefully lifts Rosa's arm off of his chest and places it back down on the mattress, not wanting to wake her. He rolls from his back to his side, then stands up and slips his feet into the pair of slippers at the foot of the bed.

He walks into the kitchen where he ignores the empty coffee mug on the counter. He hasn't had the appetite for it since he found out about Santi. He's been so worried about Coco and Sofia that his stomach is in more knots than a sailing rope. He's also nervous for Andrés. If Coco was involved with that bomb, he will have been too.

Every news, radio, and TV report about the bomb calls it the same thing. "A failed assassination attempt." They say it like it's a good thing, but Javier knows better. He knows that if the plan failed that means that Coco and Andrés failed too. He can't imagine the people who put them up to it are very pleased with that outcome.

He opens the front door and walks down the stairs. He takes a deep breath before opening the door to the street. He unlocks the tienda, then bends down to pick up the stack of newspapers that was delivered earlier this morning. That's when he stops.

"Man Left Hanging from Bridge." The words shout at him in dark, capital letters from the top of the page. That isn't what makes him pause, though. That would be the picture underneath. It's dark, and heavily pixelated, but he recognizes the boy hanging from the bridge immediately. He could recognize that scar anywhere.

A single stripe of darkened skin stretching from the tip of his left eyebrow down to the corner of his lip.

His hands tremble as he picks up the stack of papers and walks them inside where he slides them on the floor behind the counter, out of sight. Then he walks back to the sidewalk, takes the chalkboard off the wall, and turns to face the house across the street. He wipes yesterday's message clean and pulls a broken piece of chalk from his breast pocket. Then he writes a message. A different kind of message than usual. This one isn't for his customers or his neighbors or anyone else who happens down his street. It isn't for Rosa. It's for his boy. For Andrés.

He smiles at the words he's written and replaces the board to the wall. Then he locks the door to the tienda and goes upstairs. He walks down the hall and slides off his shoes at the foot of the bed, crawls into bed and rolls to his back. Lifts Rosa's hand off the mattress and places it on his chest. Then he closes his eyes.

"What's wrong?" she asks quietly.

"Nothing, amor, nothing at all," he replies.

"I don't believe you," she says.

"And why is that?"

"Because your heart is beating twice as fast now as it was when you left."

He pauses, holding his breath.

"What do you say we sleep in this morning? Pretend reality doesn't exist and spend all day in bed?" he exhales.

His eyes are still closed, but he feels her smile.

"I say that's a wonderful idea."

———

Sofia looks twice over each shoulder before locking the door and scurrying to the car. She opens the back door and lays her baby girl in a bassinet on the floor between the seats, then climbs into the driver seat. She takes a deep breath.

"Whew," she exhales. She wipes her brow and puts the key in the ignition, then stops.

I'll do whatever I can to keep them from coming after you, but still, you need to get out of here.

What had Coco meant by that? And how seriously had he meant it? She looks down at the key in her hand, then shakes off the thought that comes next.

"Stupid," she whispers, and turns the key.

The car roars to life and she breathes a silent sigh of relief and puts it in drive, then pulls away from the curb. She drives slowly, consulting the map on the dash where she's drawn a star over her destination. She rounds the corner at a particularly busy intersection and glances up at her rearview mirror. That's when she sees the man on the motorcycle.

He's wearing a black jacket and a white helmet and wouldn't for a second have made her pause at all, had she not seen the same man on the same motorcycle earlier that morning just two houses down. Sofia takes an immediate left turn and checks her mirror again. The motorcycle rounds the corner seconds later. She turns again and again, and each time the motorcycle is no more than a few seconds behind. Finally, she presses the accelerator to the floor and speeds around a corner, then another, then another, then nearly runs head on into a wooden cart of avocados being pushed across the street by a teenage boy. She slams on the brakes to avoid hitting him, and by the time she's composed herself, the man on the motorcycle has pulled up directly beside her. He taps on the glass and motions for her to roll it down.

"Who are you?" she asks, opening the window a crack.

He reaches his hand inside his jacket and she digs her fingernails into her palms.

"This is for you," the man says. He pulls his hand from his

jacket and with it an envelope, and slips it through the cracked window. Then he rides away.

The envelope falls onto her lap and she picks it up. Her hands shake as she turns it over and finds her name scribbled on the front. She pulls the flap open and slides a folded sheet of paper out of it. She unfolds it, and reads,

Sofia,

Writing has never been a strong suit of mine. Pretty much the opposite, actually. But there are things I need to say, to you and to others, and saying them in person is not an option, so... here we are.

First, I need to tell you that I'm sorry about what happened to Santi. I never met a kid better than him, honestly, and I'm terribly sorry he's gone. I'm assuming you think it's my fault it happened. You're not wrong about that. I've made plenty of mistakes in my life, but none like this. I just hope that one day, a long time from now, you can pick up this letter and feel just how sorry I am, and that you can forgive me.

I want you to tell Abuela how sorry I am too, if you see her. Which you should. She's going to need you.

Please pass on the message that as far as I know, Coco is safe and out of the country. It was the only way for him to stay clear of this shit. He also likely won't be able to come back, at least not until Pablo is dead and gone. And I wouldn't bet on that happening anytime soon.

Oh, and please tell the old man that I love him. Except maybe don't use those exact words. I wish my life had turned out differently. I'm sure in the next few days, Javier will have that same thought. You can let him know that, while my life was almost exclusively a shit-show from start to finish, the last good thing I did, I did because of him. Because it's what he would have done.

I wish you nothing but the best, Sofia. I really do.

Siempre,
Andrés M.

Sofia finishes reading and folds the sheet of paper back up and replaces it to its envelope. She wipes her eyes, then picks up the map and searches until she finds what she's looking for. She pulls a pencil from her pocket and draws a large circle around her new destination. Behind her, her baby girl begins to whine.

"Change of plans, mijita," she says to her. "We're going to see your Abuela."

———

Javier and Rosa are still in bed when they hear the knock at the door.

"Are you expecting anyone?" he asks.

She shakes her head just as a second knock follows the first. He slides out of bed and into his shoes, holding a hand out towards Rosa telling her not to move. He steps quietly down the hall and through the family room to the door, opening it just wide enough to see who is on the other side.

"Hola," says a quiet voice. "Is Abuela home?"

He turns his head back to the hall where Rosa is standing, waiting to see who it is.

"Of course," he answers and swings the door open.

Sofia takes a hesitant step inside while the baby girl on her hip flaps her arms dizzyingly like a hatchling desperate to flee its nest. When Abuela sees them, she rushes across the room with a bounce in her step Javier never expected to see again after the accident. Tragedy has a way of doing that. Making everything around it seem permanent.

"Sofia, dear," she says, taking her face in both hands and kissing her once on each cheek as he shuts the door and escapes back to the kitchen to give them their privacy. "How are you? Actually, that's a stupid question, don't answer that." She shakes her head, embarrassed, then smiles. "I'm so happy to see you. I wasn't sure I would."

"You almost didn't," she replies. "I almost didn't come." She looks at her daughter, her eyes two diamonds of pain, and her daughter looks back at her with an expression of innocent wonderment. "But I knew the two of you needed to meet each other. To love each other. It's what he would have wanted."

Abuela smiles with quaking lips at the baby girl in her arms.

"Amor," Sofia says to her daughter, "this is your Abuelita. Abuela, this is Luz-María."

Abuela's eyes widen, and behind her, Javier drops a bag of rice onto the floor.

"Did I say something wrong," Sofia asks, noticing the looks on their faces.

"No, dear, of course not," Abuela assures her. "Her name, it's... I had no idea her name was... I can't believe he never told me... It's a beautiful name," she says.

"The most beautiful name I've ever heard," Javier echoes from the kitchen.

"It wasn't my first choice," Sofia admits, "but Santi insisted."

Abuela runs a finger along Luz-María's arm, and she reaches for her with both hands.

"I have a gift for you," she says, taking her from Sofia. "Would you like to see it?"

Luz-María giggles and buries her head between Abuela's shoulder and neck.

"Well then," Abuela says as a smile spreads across her face, "we better go and find it." Together they walk into the hallway and duck behind the curtain to the first bedroom, emerging after a few seconds with Luz-María clutching the stuffed, purple tiger. "This is a very special gift," she says, sitting on the couch. She moves her to her lap so they are facing one another. "Not only is she beautiful, she is also fierce. Just like you," she bops her on the nose and looks over at Sofia. "Life may break our hearts, but if we fight back, if we are fierce, we'll find there is immeasurable strength in the pieces."

PART NINE

RESOLUTIONS

CHAPTER 41

CHRISTMAS EVE 1993

COCO TAKES a step towards the door only to take two steps back. He stares again at the message written on the chalkboard and shakes his head.

"Wherever you go, home will be here when you get back."

Home. He reads the word again and again, tumbling it around his brain like the first sip of fine wine. What is home, really? Is it a place? A person? A feeling? Maybe. Whatever it is, Coco hasn't had one for three years. Then three days ago, he stepped inside a bar in Buenos Aires, Argentina, the same one he'd frequented for months, and called for a bottle. His eyes drifted to the television hanging over the bartender's head, where a local fútbol match was being interrupted by a breaking news broadcast.

"Sources confirmed earlier today that Pablo Escobar, the infamous criminal leader of the Medellín Cartel, was shot dead today on a rooftop in central Colombia," the reporter states. "It is yet to be seen how his death will impact others involved with the Cartel, as well as the city of Medellín and the whole of the country of Colombia."

Before his drink got delivered, Coco was on his way to the bus station. He boarded one, then another, then another, and found himself stepping onto the same curb outside the Medellín terminal he had left three years prior, seemingly in the blink of an eye.

He reads the words on the sign again and exhales sharply. He puts his head down, pulls open the door that leads upstairs, and takes the steps two at a time, reaching the landing outside the door before his brain has time to communicate to his feet to run away. He raises a fist, but instead of knocking, he leans his ear to the door and listens. That's when he hears it. Laughter. Not just from one person but everyone inside. They're happy. He can't take that away from them, not again.

His hand falls to his side, dragging his head down with it, and he turns and trudges back downstairs. Outside, he pulls a cigarette from his pocket and lights it, and walks up the hill to find a better place to smoke. Somewhere he can be alone. Somewhere that will always feel like home.

———

Abuela casts a hopeful glance towards the door but quickly turns her attention back to the vat of oil in front of her. She dips the metal scoop down and pulls out two buñuelos, letting the excess oil drip off before transferring them to a plate to cool.

"How is the natilla looking?" she asks.

"Almost there," Sofia's mother responds. "Should be ready to serve when you are."

"Only a few more, and I'll be finished too," she says.

She drops the last of the dough into the oil and watches it dance. In the family room, the radio sings joyful holiday tunes, and she smiles at it, her eyes drifting again towards the door before snapping back to the task at hand. She scoops the buñuelos out and places them next to the others, then wipes her hands clean with a damp rag hanging over the faucet. She dries them on her apron before pulling it over her head and draping it over itself on the counter. Then she reaches into her breast pocket and digs out a ring. The simplest of gold bands with the tiniest of emeralds. She smiles and slips it around her fourth finger.

"Has anyone seen Luz-María?" Javier asks, entering the living room from the hall. "I can't seem to find her anywhere." He taps his chin with his forefinger and turns, so his back faces the kitchen, revealing to the rest of the room a giggling three-year-old girl with her arms wrapped around his neck.

"She isn't in the kitchen," Abuela answers.

"Not under the table either," Sofia's mother says, lifting the tablecloth and taking a peek underneath.

"Maybe resting a minute will jog your memory," Sofia suggests and pats the spot on the couch next to where she is already seated.

"Good idea," he says. He sits down beside her and leans back. "Wait a minute," he says, turning around. "What's this on my back? What is this? Ahhhhh!" He peels Luz-María from his back and pins her to the sofa with tantalizing tickles. She reaches for her mother to save her, but her mother joins in the fun, attacking Luz's armpits until her cheeks are rosy with joy and the rest of the family is warm with laughter.

"Alright, alright, enough tickle torture," Abuela instructs as she carries the plate of buñuelos from the kitchen to the table and places them next to the dish of natilla. "Come and eat."

She waits until the rest are seated before pulling out her chair. She looks at the door after she sits, then turns her attention to her family and smiles. They smile back, apologizing with their eyes that the thing she had been wishing for seemed not to be coming to fruition.

"Well," she says, staying true to character, "what are you all looking at me for? Let's eat."

———

Cristian breathes out a pile of smoke and drags a toe across the smoothened spot of concrete in front of him. His initials are gone, as are the others. Pages ripped from the history books. He hears the sound of shuffling feet to his right, and he turns to see a man walking toward him with his chin on his chest, a thin trickle of smoke slipping upward from his cheek and encircling his head in a hazy halo.

"You're late," he says to him.

Coco lifts his head when he hears the words, like a dog who's just heard his owner whistle. "Hard to be late when the world revolves around you," he grins.

His face looks like it's aged a decade since Cristian last saw him three years ago, highlighted by the thick black stubble poking through the rough skin covering his jawline like charred tree stumps after a wildfire. The rest of him is familiar. The unintentional bounce in his walk as he bounds over to hug Cristian, the hardly noticeable crookedness to his smile that suggests he's up to more than he's letting on, and the perfect balance between color and blackness in his eyes, a never-ending tug of war between wild and lonely.

"You're back," he says when Coco releases him. He takes a step back and returns his cigarette to the corner of his lips. "I never thought I would see you again."

"Sorry to disappoint," Coco replies. "I didn't expect to find you here either. I figured you would be long gone by now, off someplace quiet and open and free, like you used to tell me about when we were kids."

"I left for a while," he says, turning towards the city below where lights are beginning to dot the darkening landscape like fireflies illuminating a midnight canvas, "but I didn't last long. This is home, you know? Hard to escape it forever."

Coco nods in agreement and drags slowly on his cigarette. "You haven't heard anything from Andrés, have you?" he exhales. The crack in his voice when he says his name implies he already knows the answer.

Cristian clears his throat and coughs once into his shoulder. "I'm sorry," he answers. "They killed him the same day you left. I saw it on the news the next morning; his body strung up from a bridge over on the north end."

Coco swallows, neither of them saying anything for several minutes as he digests Cristian's words.

"What are you doing here?" Cristian asks suddenly.

He shakes his head in response. "I don't know," he answers. "I saw they took out Pablo and I guess in my head that meant it would be safe for me to come back, so I did."

"Nah, that isn't what I meant," Cristian refutes. "I mean why are you here?" He signals with his hands at the sidewalk they're standing on. "It's Christmas Eve. You haven't seen your family in three years. Go home."

"I'm the last person they want to see."

"You don't know that."

"I do, though," he says. "I was just over there, at Abuela's. Right before I came up here."

"You saw her?"

He shakes his head again. "I didn't need to," he says. "I could hear them. Laughing. They were happy. If they saw me, it would only remind them why they shouldn't be."

"Or it might remind them of how much they still have to be grateful for," Cristian says.

Coco laughs. "That sounds nice and philosophical and all, Cristian, but I know how they feel. Abuela made it pretty damn clear."

"Three years is a long time."

"Not long enough." He looks around as if hoping that if he strains his eyes hard enough, he might find something strong to drink hidden nearby. "Besides, if I go back now, that leaves you here alone, and you're just as much my family as they are. More, maybe." He puts an arm around Cristian's shoulder, but he ducks away from it.

"I've been on my own a long time," he says. "Don't worry about me. Go home."

Coco stubs his cigarette out on the wall behind him and

tosses it to the other side. "Okay," he says, "I'll go home, but only to prove to you that I'm right. When they throw me out, I'm coming right back here, and we're getting so high we'll be lost 'til New Year, so don't go anywhere."

"Do I ever go anywhere?" Cristian asks, smiling and throwing his arms in the air.

"Good point," he laughs. "I'll be back."

"Sure."

"And Cristian," he adds.

"Díme."

"It's good to see you."

Cristian nods. "Go," he replies.

Coco slaps his arm and grins and walks away, the bounce in his step carrying him quickly to the street and down the hill out of sight, leaving Cristian alone, smoking the end of a burned-down cigarette and rubbing away any final traces of his existence with his sneaker.

If Cristian's were a perfect love story, he would have asked Coco to stay, not tell him to leave. Then again, how do you ask someone to stay with you, knowing they have no idea what you really mean?

How do you tell the person you love that every time they walk away, you stay right here, in the same spot, because you know that if they ever come back, this is the only place they might come looking for you?

How do you do that? Sometimes you don't. Because perfect love stories don't exist.

Everybody knows that.

Cristian looks one last time at the spot where Coco's just disappeared from view, and pulls all the smoke he can from the cigarette in his mouth. He tosses the butt to the sidewalk and exhales, then he turns and walks away in the opposite direction.

———

Coco shakes his arms and tilts his head a little to the left, then a little to the right like a sprinter loosening up for what they know will be the most important race of their life. He raises his fist and knocks on the door, and at the same time, a bead of sweat pokes its nose out from his hairline to get a better view. He wipes it away with his finger and takes a deep breath.

Inside, he hears the pitter-patter of a pair of tiny feet approaching the door, and he straightens up before they arrive. A little girl opens it just wide enough for her to slip her head between it and the frame, and she looks up at him with a beaming smile, illuminating the entire stairwell.

"Hola," she says. "What's your name?"

He looks at her and can't help but smile back. He kneels on the rough concrete landing, bringing himself face to face with her, and sees the eyes of three people staring back at him.

"Hola," he replies softly. "I'm Coco. Is your Abuelita inside?"

"I have *two* abuelitas," she responds, sticking her hand out the door and proudly holding up three fingers, "*and* I have an abuelito, *and* I'm almost four years old."

He laughs. "Sounds like you are a very lucky, grown-up little girl," he says to her.

"Luz-María, who is it, sweetheart?" a voice calls from behind her.

The door swings open, and Sofia glances down at her daughter before recognizing Coco and nearly losing her balance.

"Coco," she whispers.

He stands up, and his smile disappears. "Hola, Sofia," he replies.

Behind her, silverware clatters onto plates, and he sees Abuela stand up slowly until she's able to make eye contact with her boy over Sofia's shoulder. Javier stands up too, resting one hand on her elbow and the other on the small of her back. A third woman Coco doesn't recognize looks back and forth from him to Abuela to Sofia in obvious pursuit of clarity.

"I'm sorry to show up like this, unannounced," he says. "I

should have called, or left a note, or not come back at all, but I... I was hoping that, that maybe..." His eyes bounce from Abuela to Sofia and back again. "I'm sorry. I should leave."

He turns his head as if to go but his feet refuse to move, having already glued themselves to the floor.

"Coco," Sofia says, louder this time as she takes her daughter by the shoulder and gently nudges her out of the way. She takes a step forward, then raises her hand to him. "Pase lo que pase," she says.

He stares at her. "Pase lo que pase," he finally replies, and slaps her outstretched hand and pulls her into a familiar embrace.

By the time they separate, Abuela has moved from the table to the entryway, and Sofia steps aside so the two of them can be face to face. Abuela puts a hand on his cheek and wipes away a falling tear with her thumb.

"Mijito," she says, "you're alive. And you're home." She embraces him until she knows he's low on oxygen, then pushes him away, holding him by the shoulders at arm's length. "You're too skinny," she says. "Come and eat. What have you been doing, starving yourself?" She drops his shoulders and shoves him in the back towards the table.

"No," he answers with a crooked smile, "but if you cooked tonight, I might have to start."

Before he has time to protect himself, she has already slipped off her left chancla, and he finds himself unsuccessfully attempting to block the ensuing blows to his shoulder and head.

"Came back the same level of smart-ass, I see," she says, dropping the sandal to the floor and sliding her foot in.

"Would you rather I hadn't?"

She grins at him. "Now, where's the fun in that?"

She follows him to the table, and they each take a seat, followed by Sofia and Javier. Luz-María runs a lap around the kitchen before hopping up onto Javier's lap and happily begins eating the leftover food off his plate, her own having already been licked clean.

"Abuelito," she says, looking back at him with a mouthful of natilla, "tell me something beautiful."

Javier smiles and kisses the top of her head. "You, my dear," he tells her, "you are my something beautiful."

"Ahem," says Abuela with raised eyebrows.

"You too, of course," he apologizes.

"Not me?" Coco asks.

"And what about us?" Sofia says, pointing to herself and her mother.

"All of you," Javier corrects himself. "This," he says, raising his hands and signaling to all of them, "this is my something beautiful."

"That it is," Abuela nods. "That it is."

Afterword

There is a line from this book that perfectly epitomizes my experience in writing it: "The steeper the hills, the better the view."

There is a lot I could say about the process of getting this story out of my head and onto the page, but the short version is that it was hard. Quite a bit harder than anticipated, in fact. And because it was hard, it is that much more fulfilling to see it come to life.

The steeper the hills, the better the view.

———

Several readers have asked me who the characters in this story are based on. While some of them have traits or habits inspired by others, the truth is that every character in this book is in one way or another based on me. Some part of me, at least.

So I guess in some overly-poetic way, this is really a story of me learning to live with myself. I didn't intend it to be that way, but I will say that reading and re-reading it has given me insight into becoming a better husband, father, son, brother, and friend.

I hope to some extent it can help you too. In addition, of course, to being entertaining.

There are a dozen or so "Easter-eggs" in the text that most won't pick up on. Some that are more obvious than others, some that really only make sense to me. If you're curious what they are, send me an email and I'll point them out to you.

After all, keeping secrets is much less fun than sharing them.

Enjoy.
-JLA

ABOUT THE AUTHOR

Jason L Allen is an emerging author from Mesa, Arizona. After graduating high school, he spent two years as a volunteer missionary in and around Medellín, Colombia, which is where the idea for this novel came to life.

Currently, he lives in Mesa, Arizona with his wife and two children, with a third on the way.